The
CURSE

HAROLD ROBBINS'

The
CURSE

JUNIUS PODRUG

A TOM DOHERTY ASSOCIATES BOOK
NEW YORK

This is a work of fiction. All of the characters, organizations, and events portrayed in this novel are either products of the author's imagination or are used fictitiously.

THE CURSE

A Forge Book
Published by Tom Doherty Associates, LLC
175 Fifth Avenue
New York, NY 10010

www.tor-forge.com

Forge® is a registered trademark of Tom Doherty Associates, LLC.

Library of Congress Cataloging-in-Publication Data

Robbins, Harold, 1916–1997.
    The curse / Harold Robbins and Junius Podrug.—1st ed.
      p. cm.
    "A Tom Doherty Associates book."
    ISBN 978-0-7653-2714-7
    1. Women archaeologists—Fiction. 2. Antiquities—Fiction. I. Podrug, Junius.
II. Title.
  PS3568.O224C87 2011
  813'.54—dc22

                                                                    2011021623

First Edition: December 2011

Printed in the United States of America

0 9 8 7 6 5 4 3 2 1

For
Eugene Winick,
who has been
there for all
of us

❖

Acknowledgments

Books get published only because many people work to make it happen. This book made it into print with the help of Forge editors, Katharine Critchlow, Eric Raab, and Bob Gleason. I also want to thank the copy editor, Sabrina Roberts, who worked silently in the background to correct my rocky grammar and bad spelling.

❖

Harold Robbins

*left behind a rich heritage of novel ideas
and works in progress when he passed away in 1997.
Harold Robbins' estate and his editor worked with
a carefully selected writer to organize and complete
Harold Robbins' ideas to create this novel,
inspired by his storytelling brilliance,
in a manner faithful to
the Robbins style.*

❖

TOMB OF TUTANKHAMEN
Valley of the Kings
November 26, 1922

Howard Carter made a "tiny breach in the top left-hand corner" of the tomb's doorway.

As he peered through the opening with the light of a candle, Lord Carnarvon, behind him, asked, "Do you see anything?"

"Yes," Carter said, "I see wonderful things."

The CURSE

1

❖

New York

I was lying naked on a warm sandy beach, the soles of my feet teased by the gentle Caribbean waves, while a hunk with a golden tan and sculptured pecs whispered in my ear, his teasing fingers turning my sensitive pink spot blazing red, when a harsh call of my name sent me crashing out of bed.

I felt myself free-falling and then hit the floor hard.

What the hell?

I heard the irritating, raucous voice again.

"Madison Dupre!"

That's my name, all right. But it wasn't a friend summoning me because they would've called me Maddy. And I'm sure it wasn't God calling me out of a wet dream—the way things have been going in my life it was more likely to be the devil and she was welcome to come on down, or up I guess would be more like it, and make a deal with me.

I was an art investigator with a specialty in antiques, but business stunk ever since the economy turned bad.

❖

A deal with the devil couldn't be any worse than letting my landlord take it out in trade because my rent was late.

I was so down-and-out and broke that I was considering making a type of oral contract with my landlord that was found in law books in the section for unnatural acts.

Any intimate contact with my landlord beyond a handshake would be considered bestiality. The guy gave new meaning to the expression "hairy ape."

Morty, my cat, had been sleeping next to my feet, at the bottom of the bed. He lifted his head and glared at me with half-shut eyes as if I were to blame for disturbing his sleep.

I got up to go to the front door, thinking someone was yelling my name on the other side of it when the call came again . . . from the street.

"I know you're up there!" the jarring voice outside yelled.

Who the hell was calling my name at this time in the morning?

I reversed direction and staggered toward the window, glancing at the clock by my bed as I did. Eight A.M. Early for me now that I had gotten into the habit of waking up in the middle of the night with money worries playing in my head like a bad movie on automatic replay, but early anytime for having my name shouted from the street below. My apartment was a third-floor walk-up studio.

I had the window open a few inches for air. I raised it higher and stuck my head out as the voice boomed again: *"Madison Dupre!"*

A man was standing just off the curb below with a bullhorn, a skinny runt with big black frame glasses and acne on his face. The bullhorn didn't fit. Guys with bullhorns were hostage negotiators who tried to talk wackos with guns and hostages out of buildings. He looked more like a computer nerd.

"You are a deadbeat, Dupre!" he said when he saw me.

I recognized him and flinched back, hunching my shoulders, and cringing in pure horror and shame.

Oh, shit.

He was the geek from the computer place where I had bought my netbook. I'd seen the company's ad in the paper advertising used and reconditioned computers for sale at very low prices. It sounded good at the time since I didn't have the money to buy a new one.

The computer I bought was refurbished and was supposed to run like a charm, but it turned out to be a lemon. It froze up half of the time and didn't boot up the other half.

My mentality definitely was BC when it came to computers, smartphones, and anything that came along after I finished high school. I was lucky to find the power button on some of the stuff kids found so easy to use. Worse, I didn't have patience for the damn things.

Whether I was being heavy-handed on the keyboard, pressing too many keys or the wrong keys or whatever, me and computers just didn't work well together. I'm sure the nerdy little bastard slandering me on the street probably stroked his own computer more than he did a woman.

Anyway, my old computer crashed and burned, so when I saw the ad for reconditioned computers and a low-financing rate, I jumped on it.

Unfortunately, I hadn't bothered to read the fine print. Who reads that stuff anyway? The warranty lasted only as far as the store's front door and the free interest rates hadn't lasted much longer. And neither did the computer.

Now it was judgment day for another mistake I'd made in my life. To get to the third floor and my bed, the sound had to carry a long ways, making me a deadbeat from SoHo to Little Italy and down to Chinatown.

"It's a piece of junk," I yelled down.

"Give it back—no pay, no play, Dupre, no pay, no play, Dupre . . ."

He kept singing it, doing a little jig.

Violent reds, purples, and blacks erupted in my head like thermonuclear explosions. I now knew why people went on a rampage and killed other people in a heat of mindless anger.

I grabbed the little netbook off the side table by my couch and threw it at the window opening.

Oh, hell.

The computer slipped out of my hand and went *through the window,* blowing a big hole in it, sending glass flying.

I ran to the window and stared out the shattered opening and down

❖

to the street below. The geek had backed into the street to avoid the computer and flying glass and I watched dumbstruck as a yellow cab came at him.

The cab swerved and nearly slammed head-on into an oncoming truck that careened to avoid a collision.

The geek didn't even appear to notice how close he had come to being turned into roadkill.

He stepped over to the computer and stared down at it and then knelt beside it. He touched it, gingerly caressing the casing for a moment before he looked up at me.

"You broke it."

He sounded like I had broken his heart.

"It was junk!" I screamed down. "You sold me a piece of junk."

"You broke it," he said again.

"Junk! Junk! Junk! It never worked. No work, no pay, no work, no pay!" I chanted, doing a little jig that he couldn't see from three stories below.

He bent down and picked up something and then looked back up at me. Grinning.

Oh my God! My sixteen-gigabit flash drive.

My entire life was on that little storage device that was not even longer than a cigarette. Because the damn computer was constantly crashing, I worked off the flash drive rather than the hard drive. On it was a list of contacts, art gallery owners, and museum curators who might throw business my way, along with every art collector I had dealt with or wished I could deal with.

The only backup for that information was the flash drive and the computer that lay shattered at the computer nerd's feet.

"That's mine!" I yelled down.

His grin grew wider.

He put the flash drive's metal end that plugs into the computer between his teeth and bit it off.

❖

Allah! Torment my enemies with a mighty curse!

—THE KORAN

2

❖

Fatima Sari watched the man with the bullhorn and the woman on the third floor yelling as she approached the outside steps to the apartment building.

She recognized the woman's name being shouted and wondered if there really was a man on the street booming out the name or if her mind was playing tricks on her.

She was confused as she approached the building. She always seemed to be bewildered lately; a feeling of being dazed and even remote from her own body, as if she had left her physical body and was observing herself moving through the world from someplace above.

Despite that feeling of separation, Fatima's whole body itched and nothing relieved the sensation. The itch had been there for days, ever since she had lost the artifact. Ever since her thinking no longer seemed clear.

Sometimes she imagined that bugs were crawling all over her and had to resist the urge to take off her clothes and shake them out.

Fatima finally decided that the cause of the impulse to scratch herself

❖

until she drew blood in a dozen places was part of her punishment, torment inflicted upon her.

Fear suddenly gripped her, and she turned looking back down the street to see if she was being followed.

She recognized no one behind her but still had a constant sense of being stalked, of being hunted like a wounded animal. But she kept on the move, driven by a sense of sacred duty that overrode her fears and her deep sense of morality.

She had come to New York to kill the woman whose name was being shouted by the man in the street.

Fatima knew the woman had to die, but she couldn't have given anyone an explanation as to why because she wasn't sure herself why the woman had to be killed.

What she did know was that something had been taken from her besides the artifact—a piece of her mind had been stolen.

That was how she thought of it, that part of her mental faculties had been taken. It made her thinking foggy, but she knew clearly who she was and that she had to kill the woman. But the reason for her actions was more akin to the instincts of a wounded animal than a rational human being.

Fatima's thinking had not always been twisted and shadowy. She was an educated woman with a worldly sophistication far beyond the vast majority of women of her country and religion. Her parents had both been educated teachers and saw to it that she received a university education.

Well traveled, with an advanced degree in Egyptology, she had left her native Egypt and taken a position as assistant curator to one of the great private collections of Egyptian antiquities.

She had embraced the Age of the Pharaohs with a passion bordering on political and religious fanaticism.

No other ancient civilization radiated as much mystery as Egypt of the mighty god-king pharaohs and the dark magic of its priests, who commanded their Nile gods to curse their enemies, and incurred the wrath of Jehovah who hurtled plagues at their Nile land.

The Old Testament recounted the struggles between the powers

❖

given the favorites of the god of the Israelites and the magicians of the pharaohs, while the Egyptian *Book of the Dead* recounted the incantations of the dark side.

Fatima had embraced the wondrous history and ancient mysteries of her land, and believed that while her body was in the modern world, her heart and soul belonged to the past.

She took the job in England because it permitted her to become the keeper of a sacred treasure.

She failed in that responsibility and now was cursed and damned for her failure.

But it wasn't just the dark magic from the time of the pharaohs that she believed cursed her, but her own faith. She felt as if someone had called down a curse of Allah upon her, punishing her for the failure to her profession and to her people.

The only way she could redeem her soul was to kill the woman.

❖

3

❖

The woman whose code name was Sphinx hung back as Fatima Sari stepped up to the front entrance of the apartment building and paused by the tenants' mailboxes.

It hadn't been that difficult to avoid being seen by Fatima. Fatima was in a mental haze. The hard part was keeping Fatima going in the right direction. Even that objective proved challenging as Fatima frequently stopped and looked behind her, paranoid that she was being followed and looking confused at the same time.

Sphinx couldn't suppress her excitement. She almost laughed out loud as the haggard woman studied the mailboxes. Even at a distance, Sphinx could see the struggle that the woman was going through as she tried to focus on the name she was looking for.

The name was Madison Dupre and it was on the mailbox for apartment 305. Sphinx had made sure of it before she maneuvered the Sari woman to the building.

Sphinx was about the same age as Fatima and was from the same country, but she had no sympathy for the bewildered woman. Like most modern political movements, the one Sphinx obeyed considered people who got harmed because they were used or got in the way as collateral damage.

She had helped warp Fatima's mind with drugs, fears, and superstition, making her easy to manipulate, so confused and subject to suggestion that she could be led to do something Fatima would have considered reprehensive had her thinking been clearer.

Overwhelmed by narcotics, Fatima would be easy to kill when the time came to dispose of her.

Sphinx's phone vibrated and she received a text message. The missive started with SX, for Sphinx, identifying it as genuine.

The message was from Fatima, waiting for her confirmation on where she was and what to do.

You know what you have to do, Sphinx messaged back. *There is no other way.*

Sphinx liked her code name.

Often portrayed as having the body of a lioness, the head of a woman, the wings of an eagle, and a tail tipped with a serpent's head, to her own people a sphinx was a frightening beast, with the Great Sphinx at Gaza capable of rising from its mound to kill the enemies of the pharaohs.

The ancient Egyptians venerated the lioness as one of their war gods. The word "sphinx" was not Egyptian, but a Greek word derived from the Egyptian word "strangler," as it was used to describe the way fierce lionesses attacked the animal they hunted.

Lionesses, the most savage hunters in a pride, killed their prey by strangulation—sinking their teeth into the throat and holding an animal down until it died.

The strangulation gave rise to the riddle of the Sphinx in which the goddess accosted strangers on the road to Thebes and asked them to answer a riddle, strangling them when they could not.

More than the preternatural violence of the sphinx, the woman who operated under the code name identified with the name's enigmatic nature, the inscrutable and mysterious qualities that people had imbued to it over the eons.

❖

Sphinx lived behind a mask. The world never saw her real features, never knew her capability for greatness.

Now she had an opportunity to act as she saw herself, to possess the most significant power a person can wield: the power of life or death over another human being.

As Fatima Sari disappeared into the apartment building, Sphinx resisted sending a text message to her controller explaining what she was doing.

She was out of bounds; off the reservation was how modern spy networks described an agent who was not following orders.

4

❖

The day wasn't going well. Actually, my life wasn't going well at the moment.

I had offended someone in a high place, probably a lot of someones, the whole crew of gods on Mount Olympus and maybe the people who manufacture good and bad karma, too.

I was unattached, worked as a self-employed art investigator, and right at the moment was short on money, clients, friends, and lovers.

My love life had more overdrafts than my bank account and the friends that had once hovered around me like bees to honey when I was in the chips treated me like I was on a terrorist watch list now that I had gone from a high-paying job to one step away from a homeless shelter.

I once prided myself on doing things in a big way. When I got out of college, nothing was going to stop me from climbing to the top in my profession.

What I didn't consider was that the higher you went, the greater the drop when you fell.

My fall took me from a penthouse on the Upper East Side to a studio

❖

walk-up on the cusp of Chinatown, Little Italy, and SoHo, a neighborhood of working people who bused tables in restaurants, cleaned offices at night, cooked pungent-smelling foods, and had lots of babies.

Fifteen-million-dollar converted factory lofts were within walking distance in SoHo, but none of the money drifted down to the cusp, unless it was in the form of restaurant tips or something for the undocumented maid at Christmas.

I actually liked the neighborhood I was in, enjoying the mix of people, food smells, loud music, and nice smiles. In some ways, I felt more comfortable here than I did on the Upper East Side where I hardly knew my neighbors and mail and deliveries went astray if the doorman wasn't pleased with his Christmas gift.

I just wished I could afford to keep the wolf from the door and Morty in good-quality cat food.

I was also tired of living like a hermit in seclusion, afraid of going out and facing the world.

My shower had been dripping for weeks and I hadn't gotten around to telling Arnie my landlord that it needed to be fixed, mostly because I hated going to him for anything. The guy was a jerk and I avoided him as much as I could, even dropping my rent check in his mail slot instead of hand delivering it.

I put up with him because the apartment was cheap, and now that I was a month behind in rent again, I tried to avoid running into him because he kept threatening me with eviction papers.

I hadn't had a single business call in weeks now, but the bill collectors still called. The really determined ones had long since stopped falling for the "deceased—return to sender" I scribbled on the envelopes before dumping them into a mailbox, though none had been as creative about collecting as the damn computer geek.

The bills were all debris from the days when I was flying high. Like a criminal who had to do the time because she did the crime, I was stuck with debts I accumulated when I had a steady income.

I'd whittled down the amount of money I owed creditors, agreeing to pay them whatever I could every month, but the last few months had been pretty lean. I was expecting a payment any day now from a client

❖

who owed me money but was avoiding my calls. I felt like a bill collector myself when I had to call people for money.

I realized it was a tough time for everyone.

The only people I really didn't feel too sorry for were for the well-off and that was the case of the woman who used my services to find a piece of art and then made it hard to collect. She was the worst type—the kind who didn't earn their money and the hardest to deal with because their sole contribution to what they had in the bank was spending only what was absolutely necessary. I guess I wasn't on the necessity list.

I try not to think about those times when I didn't have to worry about money, but that was impossible.

My life went to hell less than two years ago when I went from a six-figure job to a no-figure job, not realizing at the time that I had been spending way more money than I was earning and not saving anything.

When I became head curator at the Piedmont Museum on Fifth Avenue across from Central Park, I thought I had found my dream job. The museum was in the area known as the Museum Mile that included a dozen or so prominent museums, with the Metropolitan Museum of Art topping the list.

As curator, I managed the collection, making decisions on what to buy, sell, or trade to build the holdings of the Piedmont into a world-class museum.

My new job and salary allowed me to change from a tiny studio apartment on the Lower East Side to a penthouse in the Upper Eighties with a partial park view and a short walk to where I worked.

The man I worked for, Hiram Piedmont, lived in one of those exclusive buildings on the Upper East Side facing the park that had multi-floor units with a dozen rooms. He occupied the top two floors of one of them. Hiram had inherited more money than the gods and wanted a museum to glorify his name. He hired me to get it for him.

My expertise centered on Mediterranean antiquities—Egyptian, Greek, Roman, Mesopotamian—but I focused Hiram's museum on the Babylonian era and displayed the museum pieces in a way that brought out their magnificence as well as their cultural context.

I created an eminent museum that gave him bragging rights, but

❖

world-class art is a frantically competitive, cutthroat business in which no quarter is given. My world crashed and burned when I purchased a looted antiquity for the museum—$55 million dollars' worth—at an auction.

Of course, I hadn't realized it was a looted piece. There were some clues, but I had pressure from Hiram to buy the piece regardless of my doubts. Naturally, when things got nasty, I was the one thrown to the wolves.

Hiram was rich enough not to take the blame for anything. And it gave him a nice tax write-off as my career and comfortable life was thrown out the window of a very high building.

As a result I lost my job, my penthouse, my sports car, along with a covetous Manhattan parking space that cost more than the rent on my current studio on the cusp.

I even lost the black American Express card that had been my own measurement of having "made it."

The only things I kept were the debts that remained after the car and furniture were sold for less than what I owed on them.

During the first few months of scraping bottom I sold off my jewelry and expensive clothes for a fraction of what I paid for them because I needed the money for food and shelter.

I didn't go to upscale restaurants or shop at high-end stores and boutiques anymore. Now I bought clothes from sale racks in my neighborhood, and I ate cheap deli food or takeout from my favorite Thai and Italian restaurants, stretching out the pad thai noodles and spaghetti Bolognese for a couple of days.

I also lost something I didn't realize I had had—a desire to possess material things.

I no longer missed the penthouse and the expensive sports car. I wouldn't replace them if I won the lottery. But the great clothes and good restaurants were another thing. I did miss that.

All in all, I was really more at peace with life and myself. I just wished I had a few less debts from the old days and a little more money for the lean cycles I constantly went through.

Having my reputation back would help, too. Being involved in one

THE CURSE

of the great antiquities scandals and frauds in history naturally got me blackballed as a curator in the art world. Nobody wanted to be associated with me, even though I had been an innocent player in the whole thing.

Well, basically innocent. The art business operates with many shades of grays rather than blacks and whites. It was inevitable that pieces with shaky provenances sometimes found their way onto the auction block and you had to look the other way to make sure no one else grabbed the item before you did.

The "provenance" of an item in my business basically refers to its chain of ownership. It's like buying a house—you have to check to make sure the party you're buying from is the legal owner.

However, houses have ownership histories that are easy to examine, while it can be difficult and even impossible to trace the owner of art pieces thousands of years old that might have passed through many hands over the millenniums or had been dug out the ground yesterday.

Artifacts by the tens of thousands have made their way from antiquity sites in Europe, Africa, the Middle East, India, the Far East, and the Americas, be it legitimately, by conquest, or by just plain looting.

It wasn't that long ago that colonial empires were emptying archaeological sites around the world. Some regions have had one conqueror after another loot their historical treasures. Looting occurs all around the planet even today—there are thieves in Cambodia using electric saws to cut out pieces of irreplaceable Khmer art, peasants in Iraq looting Babylonian sites in order to feed their families, even construction workers in Italy who occasionally find rare artifacts when digging and sell them on the black market.

All in all, it wasn't that big a deal for me to have accidentally purchased at auction a piece that turned out to be looted—except for the fact that I paid more than fifty million for it and had to violate a few laws of man and nature to get it back to where it belonged.

Unfortunately, the international art trade was literally a cottage industry with all the major players knowing—and spying—on each other. It wasn't easy to keep a low profile when you had once run with the big dogs.

❖

Since nobody wanted to hire me I became self-employed as an art appraiser and investigator; that meant I got paid when clients wrote a check, which usually didn't always happen in a timely manner.

Morty eyed me as I came back to bed. He didn't seem to care that I had just lost my computer and my flash drive. He closed his eyes and went back to sleep.

He had the right idea.

I was about to crawl back under the covers and cover my head when I saw the white envelope that had been slipped under my door.

My first thought was that it was an eviction notice from my landlord, but I quickly rejected that notion. As bad as the geek bastard with the bullhorn, he would have served the notice by pounding on my door and yelling so the whole damn building could hear him, which is what he'll be doing when he finds my window broken.

A bill collector was also definitely high on my list, but there were other candidates. The lock on the entry door hadn't been working longer than my shower had been dripping, permitting entry by the army of restaurant menu distributors that littered the city, along with muggers, rapists, and anyone else who wanted to step inside where the hallways were dark because the landlord used refrigerator bulbs to light them.

As I bent to pick up the envelope, I heard a tiny, almost timid tap on the door.

I took a peek through the door peephole and saw a woman with cinnamon-colored skin, rather dark wild hair, and Middle Eastern features.

I couldn't see much through the little round opening but I could see that she looked nervous and stressed.

I opened the door a little, keeping my shoulder against it, and asked, "Can I help you?"

She stared at me as if she was puzzled, even dazed. The first thing that struck me was that she'd had a bad drug trip.

"Are you all right?" I asked.

She pulled a blade out of her pocket and lurched forward, jabbing it at me.

❖

I immediately shoved the door forward with my shoulder. The pointed end of what looked like a letter opener went into the wood.

She pushed against the door and I pushed back in panic as hard as I could. The door finally closed and the latch caught. She kicked at the door as I ran for my phone.

As I frantically pressed 911 on my cell phone, I raced for the window.

This was New York—I could be sliced and diced by this crazy woman by the time it took police to arrive.

I shouted "Help!" out the window as the 911 line rang and rang and then I got an inspired idea, remembering what I'd been told at a self-defense class to shout in an emergency: Don't shout help because no one wants to get involved.

Instead, I screamed, "Fire! Fire!"

❖

The sin ye do by two and two ye must pay for one by one.

—RUDYARD KIPLING, "TOMLINSON"

5

❖

Cursed. That's how I felt about my life. A computer geek bill collector disgraces me to the whole city and a wild-eyed woman tries to ventilate me with a letter opener—all on the same morning.

Some sort of biblical retribution for a life not well spent?

Bad karma for something I did in a past life?

Did I offend those three goddesses the Greeks called the Fates?

Someone who didn't like my art advice tormenting me with a Gypsy's evil eye?

A woman paying me back for sleeping with her man by sticking pins in a voodoo doll?

Getting involved with the gold mask of that Babylonian queen that's said to have caused more misfortune than God smit Egypt with?

The list seemed endless.

I didn't know the source of the damnation, but it seemed obvious that I was throwing snake eyes and it wasn't even Friday the thirteenth.

After I screamed "Fire!" I shouted to the maniacal woman on the other side of the door that the cops were on their way.

❖

As I cautiously went back to the door with a butcher knife in hand and looked through the peephole, I didn't see any sign of the crazy woman.

I guess telling her the cops were coming scared her off, but I wasn't about to open the door to find out if she was still there ready to pounce on me.

Screaming fire and yelling hadn't helped, of course.

No one came to my rescue, but that was no surprise. Sometimes living in New York made me feel like I was on a deserted island even though I rubbed elbows with people every time I left my apartment.

Finally, a 911 operator came on that sounded like she learned her English in Bangladesh—or maybe she was in Bangladesh for that matter—and took my report.

The first thing she wanted to know was whether it was a "domestic dispute." I assured her that I had no relatives who wanted to poke holes in me with a letter opener.

Knowing my blood hadn't been spilled and the assailant wasn't in sight meant she wasn't going to waste officers on someone who survived, so I told her that the crazy woman was still somewhere in building looking for victims.

I took some deep breaths to get my nerves under control while I waited for the police.

The whole thing was bizarre.

My computer ends up trashed, a complete stranger tries to poke holes in me . . . what else could happen today?

Morty jumped on the bed and went back to his usual spot. He had dove under the bed when I started yelling for help.

I grabbed the white envelope.

My name had been written in pencil on it.

The printed writing was neat and legible. Probably written by any older person because it wasn't the way people usually wrote today. They mostly scribbled when they had to actually write something since they spent most of their time using a computer keyboard or texting.

Also, there was no return address. And who used pencils anymore?

❖

People still wrote with pens, but addressing an envelope in pencil? I wasn't sure I even owned a pencil.

It occurred to me that a bill collector might have come up with a clever way to get my attention.

Inside the envelope was a newspaper clipping with a phone number at the top, written in pencil again, with the same neat and legible writing, and what appeared to be a poor photocopy of an article from a pseudo-scientific magazine.

I didn't recognize the phone number.

My first suspicion of the natty handwriting was a bastard named Henri Lipton. I thought I had gotten rid of him two years ago when his London antique gallery had gone up in flames with him in it.

No such luck.

Like the devil that comes to call to make a deal with you when you are at your weakest level, Lipton had returned from the grave a few months ago and offered me a job.

My mistake was accepting it. I soon realized that I shouldn't have let my need for money get in the way of survival. But how can you refuse a chance to make a buck when you desperately need it?

The clipping was one of those society page photos of people in evening dress chatting at what I assumed was a society or charity affair.

The photo had been trimmed down to just show several women standing together. I could make out some hieroglyphics on the wall behind the women. I couldn't see much of the glyphs, but was sure they were a modern reproduction.

The written description that ordinarily would have appeared beneath a newspaper photo wasn't there, but I recognized the woman in the center, a dowager of London society, Lady Candace Berkshire Vanderbilt.

Anyone involved in Mediterranean region antiquities would recognize her name.

As a museum curator with a particular interest in Egyptian antiquities, I knew quite a bit about her because her grandfather, Gordon Nelson Vanderbilt, had been one of the wealthy backers of Howard Carter.

Grandfather Vanderbilt, along with Lord Carnarvon and others,

❖

had financed Carter's search for a pharaoh's tomb back in the 1920s. Carter had found King Tutankhamen . . . and the rest was history.

Of course, part of that history had to do with the mummy's revenge: Lord Carnarvon died soon afterwards from what was thought to have been an infected mosquito bite, Vanderbilt croaked the following year from food poisoning, and the curse of the mummy was off and running.

Vanderbilt also incurred considerable controversy because his wife was seen at a society gathering wearing an ancient Egyptian necklace, raising suspicion that it belonged in the Tut collection, even though he had claimed that he bought it on the open market.

His wife drowned when she fell and bumped her head in a bathtub and the newspapers had a field day again about the curse.

The current Mrs. Berkshire Vanderbilt had the necklace on in the picture. Somewhere along the line she had married a British lord and became a lady. I was surprised she was wearing it because I'd read she donated it to the Smithsonian, but the picture could have been taken before she gave it to the museum.

Nothing about the picture, other than it had been sent to me with a mysterious phone number, grabbed my interest. There was nothing new or sensational about Mrs. Vanderbilt or the necklace. The curse stories were decades old.

I studied the picture, wondering why it was sent to me.

Who sent it was another question.

And was there any money in it for me? And Morty. The damn cat had gone "green" and ate only fish not on the mercury or endangered species list. He used only biodegradable cat litter.

Studying the picture, I realized that the woman Lady Candace was talking to was also wearing a necklace that looked familiar to me.

I got out my magnifing glass and took a closer look. I recognized the necklace because I'd seen it before.

The Isis necklace.

The last time I'd seen the necklace was at the Egyptian Museum five or six years ago, where it should be. It had been part of the Tut exhibit.

How did the necklace get from the museum to this woman's neck?

The more I looked at the picture though, the more I realized that this necklace belonged in a museum, not on some rich woman's neck.

Someone obviously knew my weakness for protecting antiquities.

The title of the magazine article deepened the mystery: *"The Mummy's Revenge After Howard Carter Looted the Tomb."*

❖

6

❖

Howard Carter was the Holy Grail of archaeology. He lacked a university education in archaeology, yet gained a reputation as an outstanding archaeologist and Egyptologist even before he made the most stunning antiquities find in history. And he didn't just make a lucky find—he spent more than thirty years digging, bringing up a lot of dry holes along with some good finds, before he hit the jackpot.

The word "looting" and Howard Carter's name were also not in anyway synonomous: artifacts were his babies and he treated them with a rare reverence and respect.

I'd worked and studied antiquities for half my life and I never heard a bad word about the man.

The magazine that carried the mummy's revenge story was little more than a tabloid with scientific pretentions. I'd seen it near the checkout at grocery stores, with glaring headlines about ancient aliens and farm girls who have two-headed babies.

I would never have read the article if it hadn't come with an intriguing picture about the Isis necklace.

❖

The article began with tantalizing details about the curse of the pharaohs thrown upon those who violated their tombs. Hollywood characterized it as the revenge of mummies and turned it into a cottage industry after strange events made the news following the opening of King Tut's tomb.

The first event revolved around Howard Carter, a snake, and a canary.

Soon after opening the King Tut burial chambers, Carter sent an aide back to his house to retrieve something. As the man approached the house, he heard what he called a "faint, almost human cry." As he came to the entrance, he found a cobra curled up in the birdcage that hung there. It had Carter's canary in its mouth.

The cobra was the symbol of Egypt's pharaohs and the incident set off speculation that the ancient curse that was supposed to punish those who defiled the resting places of kings had struck.

To the Egyptian workers at the dig, Carter had not been killed by the cobra because he had handled the opening of the tomb with great care and reverence. But they wondered who the revenge would be reaped upon.

The legend grew as unusual deaths occurred among a group of people that had some association with King Tut's tomb. Some of the deaths occurred among those directly involved with Howard Carter and the excavation, but some people had merely been visitors Carter permitted onto the site.

The first strange death came within a few months and it was a sensational one: Lord Carnarvon. With his death, the curse became front-page news.

The exact cause of Lord Carnarvon's death wasn't known, although they believed he died from blood poisoning after a mosquito bite had become infected from shaving with a rusty blade. They fastened on that cause because the doctors couldn't come up with an exact diagnosis.

During his last moments, Carnarvon was heard mumbling Tutankhamen's name.

If that wasn't enough to throw fuel on the fires of the curse, when he died in Cairo during the wee hours, the lights in the city went

❖

inexplicably out—and two thousand miles away at his estate in Britain, the peer's favorite dog howled inconsolably and died within minutes of his master.

Lord Allenby, Britain's high commissioner for Egypt, demanded an explanation for the mysterious power outage, but his power plant engineers weren't able to supply one.

Within months, Egypt's first native Egyptologist and Egyptian Museum curator, Ahmed Kamal, and American Egyptologist William Henry Goodyear, both with a connection to the site, were dead.

In another strange twist, Aubry Herbert, Lord Carnarvon's brother, died six months later—also from blood poisoning. Aubry was only forty-three and Lord Carnarvon was fifty-six.

His death was followed by that of an Oxford archaeologist who had entered Tut's burial chamber with Carter. He hung himself, leaving a note that said he had "succumbed to a curse."

More deaths came; some seemed natural, some strange, but all were blamed on the curse. One scholar died attempting to rescue a book from his burning house. It was the Egyptian *Book of the Dead*.

That nearly a couple dozen people with some connection to King Tut's tomb died over the next six or seven years didn't appear on the surface to be significant.

However, when the ages of those who passed away underwent statistical analysis, the results supported the fact that the death rate was far above the norm. Throw in some strange circumstances, including the death of Lord Carnarvon's wife allegedly from an insect bite, and it makes one wonder if the spirit of the boy king wasn't reeking havoc on the invaders.

The article's premise was that the long-dead pharaoh was taking his revenge not just because his tomb had been opened, but also because it had been secretly looted by Carter and his cohorts.

The theft had occurred at the tomb, soon after the realization that a major find had in fact been made and before the Egyptian government inspectors had arrived.

In a very famous moment on November twenty-sixth, Carter had a

❖

hole made in a wall that was exposed after stairs leading to it were excavated. The hole only revealed a pitch-black empty void.

To determine if the empty space was a room, Carter stuck a long steel rod through the opening. Deciding the area was large enough to be a room, he next extended a candle through the hole and stuck his head through the opening.

That was when Lord Carnarvon, who was behind him, asked Carter the famous question. The article had excerpts from Carter's own account, which said "as soon as one's eyes became accustomed to the glimmer of light, the interior of the chamber gradually loomed . . . with its strange and wonderful medley of extraordinary and beautiful objects. Lord Carnarvon said to me, 'Can you see anything?' I replied to him, 'Yes, it's wonderful.'"

It was an extraordinary moment.

Egyptian tombs had been picked over for thousands of years and not a single intact tomb had been found. Archaeologists were lucky to find even broken fragments left behind by looters and conquerors.

It was also an extraordinary moment for Howard Carter who had come to Egypt thirty-one years earlier as a seventeen-year-old artist. Great photography was still in its infancy and Carter was first employed to reproduce the wall etchings by hand.

He learned archaeology and Egyptology hands-on by working at the sites and stayed in the profession for the rest of his life.

Carter had been working for Lord Carnarvon for about fourteen years, without making a major discovery, when he found the boy-king's site.

What he saw told him that he had made a discovery of monumental importance. He wrote that he was struck dumb with amazement, that as objects took shape in the dark mist, his first impression suggested the property room of an opera of a vanished civilization. He saw "strange animals, statues, and gold—everywhere the glint of gold."

What a thrilling moment for a treasure seeker, which is what an archaeologist is, even if the treasure is to be placed in a museum.

The first person to set eyes upon the treasure in nearly four thousand

❖

years, Carter reported that he had experienced "the exhilaration of discovery, the fever of suspense, the almost overmastering impulse, born of curiosity, to break down the seals and lift the lids of boxes . . ."

As a treasure seeker myself, I was electrified just reading about it.

Peeking inside, Carter realized that he was only looking into the tomb's antechamber—the actual burial place and treasure room, with their untold riches, would be beyond that.

Carter stated he and Carnarvon went home that night and that the tomb was opened the next day when inspectors from the Egyptian department that supervised antiquity sites arrived.

According to the article, the exhilaration that Carter and Carnarvon felt at seeing what they realized was just a small part of the most amazing antiquities find in history was too much for them.

They had to see what was beyond, in the burial room where the pharaoh was entombed and the treasure room where the wealth that would give him a kingly existence in the next life was stored.

So they returned surreptitiously that night. And created a controversy as to what had been—or might have been—removed before the site was fully cataloged.

The article stirred a vague memory of having read before that there had been a nighttime secret entry of the tomb.

It also pointed out that a few weeks after the incident, Lord Carnarvon admitted to a London reporter that they had come back during the night and enlarged the hole in order to get into the antechamber to examine the artifacts there firsthand, but he claimed that they had resisted the tantalizing temptation to go beyond into the burial and treasure rooms.

The temptation would have been irresistible.

I suspect that's why they did it in the middle of the night. It had nothing to do with the fact that the Egyptian antiquities inspectors were arriving the following morning. It just may have been a seduction these men who spent their lives searching for riches were unable to resist.

Personally, I saw nothing wrong with their entry, even if it was done secretly. They weren't tomb robbers. The two of them returned in the middle of the night to get another look at their exciting find. Besides, they had dutifully notified the authorities of the discovery and the incident took place in 1922, before many of the strict rules laid down by the Egyptian authorities were created.

I think it would be more amazing if these men hadn't succumbed to the temptation to see firsthand what was in the antechamber and beyond.

Another important factor had to do with whether there was evidence that the tomb had ever been violated by looters in the past.

The contract between seekers like Carter and Carnarvon and the Egyptian government had recently been changed. In the past, any antiquities found were divided equally between the people who discovered them and the government. However, the contract had been changed to include a clause that if a tomb was found completely intact, all of the antiquities would go to the government with some payment for the work done by the excavators.

Carter put years of work into the excavations and Lord Carnarvon put the equivalent of millions of dollars into financing the projects, so no doubt they wanted to see if there was evidence of past entry by looters.

However, the article focused on the fact that some of King Tut's artifacts ended up in the hands of the men and some museums, inferring that they had been removed that night before they were officially cataloged.

A number of museums today have items that are alleged to have come from the boy king's treasures and Carter himself had items in his possession when he passed away in Britain years later.

As for the museum pieces, although there were rumors that Carter provided some of them, it was also just as likely that pieces made their way out of the Egyptian Museum and into the black market for antiquities through theft. There were even allegations that Egypt's King Farouk permitted some items to be taken, perhaps as a magnanimous gesture.

My bottom-line feeling after reading the article was that not everything from the Tut collection rested in the Egyptian Museum.

❖

I picked up my cell phone and hesitated for a moment, staring at the phone number.

Did I really want to get involved in a mystery in which a museum piece was stolen—again?

I took a deep breath and dialed the number.

❖

Death will slay with his wings whoever disturbs the peace of the pharaoh.

—WARNING ON CLAY TABLET FOUND
IN KING TUT'S ANTECHAMBER

7

❖

A man's voice answered almost immediately, as if he had been waiting for my call.

"Thank you for calling, Miss Dupre."

"And you are?"

"My name is Dr. Mounir Kaseem. I was hoping that the picture would arouse your interest. I would very much like to meet with you and discuss utilizing your services."

His English sounded slightly British, but with a Middle Eastern inflection. I guessed he was Egyptian, not an unlikely combination considering many well-off Egyptians had been educated in Britain, not to mention that he'd dropped an article on Egyptology on me.

Saying he wanted to hire me made him solid gold. As long as he paid, I didn't care if he was a serial killer wanting me to keep tabs on his victims.

Trying to keep the desperation out of my voice, I asked, "Is this about the Isis necklace? Has it been stolen?"

"I wish to retain you for a related matter."

❖

"What related matter?"

"Something I'd prefer to discuss in person with you. Would you mind joining me for lunch?"

I let the request hang in the air for a moment as I pretended to mull over my busy schedule.

"I might be able to do lunch. But I need to know a little more before I rearrange my schedule to meet with a new client. Who referred you to me? And what are we meeting about?"

I was too proud to ask up-front, *What's in it for me?*

"I can't tell you exactly who recommended you. I called the Egyptian department at the Met and asked for the names of top experts in the Eighteenth Dynasty era. I was given three names and chose to contact you after learning that you have experience in recovering looted artifacts."

I had worked for the Met eons ago, and I had recently left business cards with some old acquaintances there in the hopes of getting some referrals.

As for my recovery of looted artifacts, he obviously didn't know the entire story or he would've hung up and run the other way.

"Why don't we meet at the most notable Eighteenth Dynasty artifact in America?" he said. "Shall we say the obelisk at one o'clock? I have already made a reservation at the Russian Tea Room at two. Would that be satisfactory?"

How could I refuse? I was a little curious though why he wanted to meet me at Cleopatra's Needle first.

The Tea Room was an excellent choice—it inferred that he had good taste and that he had money. I didn't get to eat at pricy restaurants very often anymore. However, something he said puzzled me.

"You intimated that the Isis necklace had been stolen. I'm sure I would have heard about it if it had been taken from the Egyptian Museum."

He chuckled. "I was being facetious. It was stolen from King Tut's tomb along with all the other Tut treasures. I will explain the mystery of the necklace when we meet."

"One o'clock is fine."

❖

"Good. I suspect by then you will have solved the mystery of the Isis necklace."

"Before you hang up, perhaps you can solve a mystery for me. Who's the woman that tried to murder me this morning?"

"Tried to murder you?"

"Didn't you send a woman to slip that note under my door?"

"No, I sent over a bellman from my hotel. It was quite early and I told him to slip it under your door. You say someone tried to murder you?"

"Right after I picked the envelope off the floor, I opened the door and a woman tried to stab me."

I omitted the fact that it was with a letter opener.

I imagined the gears working in his head as he thought about what I had said.

"I know nothing about this. It is a complete surprise to me. I wish to talk to you about authenticating a rare artifact, not murder."

I believed him.

There were two compelling reasons for my faith in his honesty and veracity: I desperately needed the work and he didn't know me well enough to want me dead—I hoped.

I also had a third reason.

Like everyone else in New York, I had three locks on my front door to keep out people like a madwoman wielding a lethal letter opener.

So it could be a coincidence that a Middle Eastern woman, probably Egyptian, tried to kill me after a Middle Eastern man, also probably Egyptian, had an envelope slipped under my door about an Egyptian artifact.

Yeah, that worked.

Funny thing—the broker I am, the more logical and reasonable the completely irrational can sound to me.

After we hung up, I turned to Morty to let him know things were looking up. He had become spoiled eating organic cat food while I subsisted on fast food with saturated fats and artificial ingredients that were created in a test tube.

"We're going to be in the chips, Morty!"

He eyed me suspiciously, then went back to sleep.

❖

8

❖

It occurred to me that if I was really going to sound knowledgeable about the artifact Dr. Kaseem wanted me to evaluate, I should know what it was so I could be prepared to answer his questions.

I redialed him from the recent calls list on my phone and got nothing— no answer—no ringing; the call just seemed to fade into oblivion.

That was odd.

Even odder on a day that I had fallen out of bed and into the twilight zone.

I tried the number several more times as I was getting ready just to prove to myself that my instincts were right: No one wanted to hire my services; it was just some trick to lure me out of my apartment—no doubt a mob of my creditors would be waiting in the park to hang me from the obelisk.

I also wondered if the woman who tried to stab me might be another out-of-work art investigator who wanted the job even more desperately than me.

❖

I got a dry chuckle out of that one, but it sounded more like a death rattle than a laugh.

I didn't know if Mounir Kaseem had any interest in women, but just in case he was rich and wanted personal attention, I took extra care to look more attractive than desperate, but the lack of a callback number had sent my paranoia soaring.

"Something's up his sleeve," I told Morty.

Why couldn't things be simple?

❖

THE HEART SCARAB

The scarab . . . possesses remarkable powers, and if a figure of the scarab be made, and the proper words of power be written upon it, not only protection of the dead physical heart, but also new life and existence will be given to him to whose body it is attached.

—SIR WALLIS BUDGE, *EGYPTIAN MAGIC*

9

❖

Other than rocks and dirt, Cleopatra's Needle was the oldest thing in Central Park. An Eighteenth Dynasty pharaoh named Thutmose had it built more than 3,500 years ago.

That kind of time in history is hard to imagine without putting it into context—it was before the rise of classical Greece, long before the rise of the Roman Empire, fifteen centuries before the birth of Christ. And now the monolith commissioned by a pharaoh and placed near the banks of the Nile was in Central Park, New York City, USA.

The most militant warrior-pharaoh in Egyptian history, Thutmose would have turned over in his sarcophagus if he knew the nearly seventy-foot-tall granite obelisk had made its way thousands of miles from the Nile Valley to the heart of Manhattan.

Why they called the shaft of stone and its sister statue in London "Cleopatra's Needle" rather than "Thutmose's Needle" was a mystery to me, but reason enough for the mummy of the militant pharaoh to throw a curse this way.

The obelisk was about a hundred blocks and several hours from a morning of chaos with a computer store geek and a madwoman, but I was pretty sure I hadn't left behind some of the insanity.

It would be too much of a coincidence that I'd get a message under my door to meet with a client and had opened the door to find a frazzled woman intent upon sticking a letter opener in my throat.

The man who asked me to meet him at the obelisk in the park had been genuinely surprised when I told him a woman had just tried to slice and dice me, but I had to admit to myself during the long subway ride that there had to be a connection.

The monument's plaza was deserted, giving me a chance to catch my breath. Due to my current financial situation—broke and desperate—I had almost run from the subway stop on East Eighty-sixth out of fear I'd be late. In the old days I would have taken a taxi from my apartment.

Obelisks were right up my alley not only because I was an expert on Egyptian and other Mediterranean artifacts, but the ancient land of the pharaohs with its exotic mystery and magic has always been my prime interest in antiquities.

I went up to the obelisk and offered my condolences to Thutmose III for the misnaming of his monument.

"Sorry about the name, old chap, but Cleopatra has more sex appeal. You can blame Shakespeare and Cecil B. DeMille."

I felt bad that most of the inscriptions on the stone's surface were getting weathered. The pollution and acid rain in the city had taken its toll on the monument; it would have fared better had it stayed in the clear dry desert air of Egypt.

A middle-aged man with the olive tan of the southern Mediterranean came slowly walking in my direction, keeping an appraising eye on me all the while.

He was well dressed in a conservative, old-fashioned, gray worsted wool suit, a white shirt, and a British school tie.

My first impression from his short-cropped salt-and-pepper hair, flat stomach, and the way he held himself erect with his shoulders pulled back was that he was a military man.

I smelled affluence, too.

❖

He grinned at me. "Only a true lover of antiquities would speak to a stone monolith."

"In this town, it's not unusual to see people talking to brick walls—it just depends on what they've snorted." I offered my hand. "How do you do, Dr. Kaseem?"

He gave me a dead fish handshake.

My dad had always taught me to give firm handshakes when I was introduced to people. "It reveals character," he said. But he never told me what a limp one revealed and I suspected firmness was sometimes a cultural thing.

Not all cultures were into shaking hands and some foreigners, especially older Middle Easterners, are caught by surprise even today when a woman offers her hand. I figure that's their problem, not mine, and I give a firm handshake even to a limp one.

"Have you solved the Isis necklace mystery?" he asked.

"I think so. The tip-off wasn't the necklace or the beautiful gowns the women were wearing, but the wall with glyphs behind it. The party took place in a room at the Egyptian Museum that I've been to a number of times where they hold special events. I don't know why the woman was wearing the Isis necklace, but I assume it is still at the museum where it belongs."

"Very good, I'm impressed. And yes, it is the Isis necklace. The woman wearing it was making a substantial donation to the museum and was permitted to wear the necklace at the party."

"I hope you're not going to tell me that she has since had an Egyptian cobra appear around her neck that bit her as part of King Tut's retribution?"

He smiled. "I get the impression that you believe any retribution from the ghosts of the Nile are solely creatures of Hollywood."

I gave that a little thought as we meandered around a bit, looking over the obelisk.

He reminded me of Omar Sharif, the Egyptian actor who starred in *Doctor Zhivago* years ago. Kaseem looked to be in his late fifties.

"The mummy's revenge is obviously the stuff of movies," I said, "but I have to admit that spooky things did happen after King Tut's tomb was

❖

opened, especially Lord Carnarvon dying so soon and mysteriously. What do you think? Did the boy king lash out murderously with a curse?"

"I believe there is a curse. Not upon the thieves who stole our history, taking pieces like this magnificent monolith of Thutmose, but upon my own people. Our heads should be held down in shame for permitting foreigners to rape our land of historical treasures for more than two thousand years."

"Foreigners didn't always just take them," I said. "Most often they were sold to them by your people."

"Yes, exactly, and it is shameful that my people did such a thing. The result is that there are thousands of our artifacts scattered around the world. Every time I come to New York, I come to this park and visit Thutmose's obelisk. Then I go to other exhibits where many of our artifacts are kept."

He nodded at the Metropolitan Museum of Art a stone's throw away on Fifth Avenue, which had a stunning gallery of Egyptian antiquities.

"I do the same," he went on, "when I go to London, Paris, Berlin, Istanbul—our history is shattered and scattered and it is our own fault. That is the true curse of the pharaohs—we are a damned people because we permitted foreigners to take our historical treasures."

"I hope you weren't planning on hiring me to get the City of New York to ship this 250 tons of granite back to where it belongs on the Nile?"

"You think the city would object to me packing it up and taking it home?"

"You probably would not make it through airport security." I gave him a studied look. "You brought me here to test my reaction to the fact that so many historical treasures have been taken from your country?"

"Actually, I already know that you have supported the return of antiquities to their country of origin. But I don't have much time in the city and I thought it would be a good place to make your acquaintance and visit the monument myself."

He checked his watch. "If we grab a taxi, we should be able to get to the restaurant before they give away my reservation. And," he said, giving me a grave look, "you can tell me more about this incident that happened at your apartment on the way over."

❖

10

❖

She's in danger . . .

It wasn't a complete thought on the part of Fatima Sari as she followed at a distance and watched Madison Dupre and Mounir Kaseem as they walked to Fifth Avenue to flag down a taxi.

Fatima Sari was small, thin, and fragile. Dark blotches under her eyes and an almost panicked look on her face revealed that the source of her physical deterioration was due to mental suffering.

Having a sympathetic response to the danger she sensed to a woman she had tried to stab hours earlier was not a contradiction to Fatima. Her thoughts were jumbled, her reasoning meandering; she had no clear and concise notion why she wanted to kill the woman earlier and yet now was concerned about the woman's safety.

Even more havoc was created in her mind and body because she knew her thinking was warped and she couldn't do anything about it. She had been told that the woman was a danger to the artifact she had been sworn to protect, but she couldn't focus on exactly what danger the woman posed.

❖

Things she thought she saw weren't always there; conclusions she had reached—like trying to stab the woman—didn't always make sense after she did them. Fatima realized she was losing her grip on distinguishing between the real and the imagined. Worse, she felt as if someone else was getting more and more control of her thoughts and actions—a voice and messages telling her what to do, what to think, who her enemies were.

A voice that called herself Sphinx.

In Fatima's culture the sphinx was both a creature of myth and legend, a sacred beast that the pharaohs of old had called upon to defend the land when enemies were at the gates.

A still-rational part of Fatima's brain knew that the person who gave her commands over the phone was not the stone representation of a sphinx, but to her fogged brain, the woman appeared to have the spirit of the sphinx as she told Fatima that it was her duty to get back the sacred amulet that had been stolen from her.

Even if it meant killing the enemy who kept her from it.

She had struck out at the Dupre woman, too, because she was on the constant edge of panic, ready to flinch and bolt at any given moment—or to lash out with a deadly weapon.

Her friend Fuad tried to tell Fatima that her thinking wasn't straight because she had been drugged. She trusted Fuad, yet knowing that her mind was twisted because of something that had been slipped to her didn't make her thinking any clearer.

In the beginning, there had been a battle for control in her head as she struggled to clear her thoughts, but that war had been lost.

She still felt a compulsion to warn the Dupre woman about Kaseem . . . warn her that he was a dangerous man . . . warn her to stay away from him . . . but she didn't know why she felt that way. It hadn't come from Sphinx. Instead, it was a random thought flowing in her mind that she wasn't able to focus on.

Fatima had positioned herself earlier behind some bushes in Central Park and watched as the two of them walked around the obelisk.

She had not been ordered by Sphinx to go to the place and watch them; she no longer had any communication with Sphinx because Fuad

❖

had warned her that the woman who called herself by that name meant her harm.

To keep herself from being commanded by the woman, Fatima threw her cell phone in a trash bin. It had not occurred to her that doing so would cut her off from the only voice of reason left in her life, her friend Fuad.

After she had tried to stab the Dupre woman, Fatima had gotten on a subway and rode aimlessly, finally thinking clearly enough to wait near the hotel where Mounir Kaseem was staying and follow him as he left.

Arriving at the obelisk behind Kaseem, she missed her chance to talk to the woman and warn her about Kaseem. That the woman would have been terrified of her had not penetrated Fatima's hazy thinking.

You have to warn her, the voice in Fatima's head said.

At least that's what her logical mind was telling her, what little she had left of it.

Standing at a safe distance, Fatima couldn't hear what was being said between the two of them, but the voices in her head wouldn't shut off. They seemed to be getting worse instead of better. She wished they would stop.

As she waited, never taking her eyes off Kaseem and the woman, Fatima mindlessly took out a bagel from her bag, removed the wrapping, and started chewing on it. She wasn't really hungry but it gave her something to do as she focused on them.

She never used to be frightened, but now everything appeared dark and dangerous to her. Dread and fear always consumed her mind now and try as she might she couldn't shake off those feelings.

Fatima kept wondering who was going to creep up behind her and finally put her out of her misery. She welcomed death; at least she would finally have some peace. From the constant voices in her head. From the constant paranoia she felt.

Kaseem and the woman left the area and started walking toward Fifth Avenue to a line of taxis waiting for customers.

The voices in her head urged her to follow them.

She knew where they were going.

❖

Kaseem was staying at a hotel that was frequented by Egyptians and employed many Egyptians as staff. One of the clerks was her second cousin. Fatima convinced the girl to advise her of any requests that Kaseem made to the front desk.

After learning of his reservation at the Russian Tea Room and sure that he planned to meet the woman she'd attacked earlier, Fatima had changed her clothes and wore a scarf so that she wouldn't be instantly recognized.

Now she waited until they had gotten into the taxi before she took the next one in line.

❖

11

❖

"I enjoy the quiet elegance of the Tea Room," Mounir Kaseem said after we were seated in a red booth at the West Fifty-seventh Street landmark. "I have fond memories of the times my wife and I enjoyed meals here years ago, before she passed away. Have you been here before?"

"Oh, many times. I enjoy the memories, too—not my own, but those that other people have left behind."

He raised his eyebrows and smiled. "You experience other people's memories?"

"Not specifically, but I feel their aura. I believe people can pick up vibes from places and things. Sometimes when I handle an artifact I get a feeling that someone imbued it with strong emotions. Years ago in the Egyptian Museum I handled a necklace that had belonged to a queen who had died more than two thousand years ago. I nearly dropped it because I felt a vibration when I held it in my hands."

"Perhaps the queen was murdered wearing it."

"I like to think the necklace still possessed some of the strong love between the queen and the pharaoh who gave it to her."

❖

I diverted the conversation away from my feelings about objects because I didn't want him to think I was a crazy. We discussed the weather and traffic in the taxi ride to the restaurant, but not the attempt to stab me. He also hadn't yet volunteered why he had contacted me and I fought to keep my impatience in check.

"Dr. Kaseem, are you a scholar? A doctor of medicine?"

"I'm a professor of Egyptian history. And, I'm afraid, on sabbatical from my country. I also served in my country's armed forces. My criticism of the Egyptian government has made it necessary that I live in exile."

Exile? That was a word you didn't hear much anymore. Sounded more like a term used when a king is banished from his country rather than someone who leaves to keep from being arrested for political views. Egypt had an authoritative government. In its entire history, it had never been a true democracy, though any regime that could keep peace and prosperity was supported by most of the people.

I noticed a slight tic in his left eye every so often when he talked and wondered if it was just a nervous twitch or due to some other symptom. I had eye spasms once in a while; mine were mainly due to stress and fatigue.

"You will have to pardon me," he said, "if I come across as something of a fanatic about my country's history and the pieces that tell the story of that history. As I said, I am impressed by your own attitude toward antiquities. I find that money alone is only a short-term motivator."

I resisted telling him that money lacked strong motivation only to those who had plenty of it.

"Having reached the pinnacle of your profession," he said, "I assume you have visited Egypt more than once and have acquired a great deal of experience examining our artifacts."

A polite way of asking for my qualifications?

"I've been to your wonderful country three times, including an internship that allowed me to stay three months. In terms of my background, I have a master's degree in art history and undergraduate degrees in both art and archaeology. Before starting my own company, I worked for museums and private collectors. I'm an expert on Mediterranean antiquities in general, but my main interest has been in Egyptology. I'll be happy to provide a curriculum vitae."

"That won't be necessary. What I've been told by others is more important than one's own assessment. But I am curious as to why you studied archaeology. Was it your original intent to become a scientist?"

"I considered it—and did fieldwork in Egypt, Israel, and Jordan. I love the idea of recovering antiquities so they can be preserved in museums and enjoyed. But the reality of being hundreds of miles from the nearest restaurants, spending most of my time sifting through desert sand and shaking the scorpions out of my shoes before I put them on in the morning, wasn't my cup of tea. I'm afraid that my idea of camping out on sand is a deluxe room facing the beach.

"I studied archaeology because of my father's encouragement. He was a college teacher but also a frustrated adventurer who would rather have been playing Indiana Jones saving antiquities for museums than lecturing behind a podium. But knowing how archaeologists worked actually helped me in appraising antiquities because it gave me an insight as to the environment that artifacts were in for thousands of years as opposed to fraudulent reproductions being produced on a daily basis."

"Yes, that would be valuable experience."

"What piece are you looking for?"

"Are you familiar with the Heart of Egypt?" he asked.

I nodded. "Familiar enough to know that it might not exist."

The Heart of Egypt was a scarab, an amulet cut from stone or gem. It didn't look like a heart but as with all scarabs, it was a representation of the dung beetle that the ancient Egyptians believed were sacred and had magical powers.

I had my own scarab on a gold chain in my jewelry box, next to my bracelet with a cartouche on it. Like any good tourist, I bought the two amulets at Cairo's medieval Khan el-Khalili marketplace. My name inscribed in hieroglyphics on the bottom of the cartouche identified that I was its owner. Naturally, I never questioned how the marketplace engraver managed to find the right glyphs for "Madison Dupre" because

❖

that would have taken the fun out of buying "ancient" magical artifacts for less than the price of a tube of lipstick.

Unlike the small scarabs that could be pinned on clothes or worn as a necklace, a heart scarab was larger, about three inches long to mimic the size of the human heart. It's significance came into play after death.

To the Egyptians of the pharaohs' time, the human heart not only epitomized the power of life, but was the source of both good and evil acts and thoughts, literally the source of a person's conscience.

One's heart was considered a source of potential trouble after death because it would be questioned about the person's actions during life in a process called "Weighing of the Heart."

Osiris, the god of the dead, questioned the heart about the owner's past and the heart had to disclose the truth.

If the heart divulged bad acts or thoughts on the part of the person, Osiris ripped out the heart and threw it to a beast that devoured hearts instead of permitting the person to proceed into the paradisiacal afterlife.

The beast, Ahemait, was part lion, part hippopotamus, and part crocodile. Once Ahemait feasted on the person's heart, the person went to the dark and dreary Egyptian version of hell instead of paradise.

To ensure that one's heart didn't rat them out to Osiris, the clever Egyptian embalmers removed the deceased's human heart and replaced it with a sacred heart scarab.

The substitute scarab was inscribed on the bottom with a magical spell from *The Book of the Dead* so Osiris wouldn't realize it wasn't the real heart.

Unlike a real heart, the heart scarab would lie about the person's sins.

Wouldn't we all like to have one of those?

❖

12

❖

"As I'm sure you know," Kaseem said, "King Tutankhamen's mummification was slightly different than other royal mummies of that era. While the brain was removed through the nose, and the liver, stomach, and other innards also extracted, it was customary for the heart to be left in place with a heart scarab placed over it."

"Yet Tut's heart was removed," I said, digging a long way back for that recollection. I was an expert on artifacts, not history, though the two often went hand in hand. "A scarab with a heron carved on it was found on the body."

"The heron scarab was not a heart scarab," Kaseem said.

"I agree. The heron scarab was placed over his abdomen," I said, trying to get up to speed on the controversy about Tut's heart scarab. "And you're right. While some people have called it a heart scarab, the heron scarab was found in the wrong position in the mummy wrappings."

"There is no heart scarab in the Tutankhamen treasures in Cairo," he said, "but there was one found when his tomb was uncovered by Howard Carter and his team of archaeologists."

❖

The heart scarab had not been mentioned in the article Kaseem had slipped under my door, but I knew a little about the controversy.

"A dispute raged at the time about whether the heart scarab was stolen," I said. "Some said there never was one."

"I think you would agree with me," he said, "that Tutankhamen's lack of a heart scarab is troubling, to say the least. He was buried with all the pomp and riches of a pharaoh. He had suffered a crushing chest blow that damaged the heart so severely they may have taken it out when the lungs and other innards were removed. But could it be true that he wasn't given a heart scarab to keep him from being devoured by Ahemait, the beast? Rubbish."

I agreed with him. The lack of a heart scarab was puzzling.

"I know there were rumors of a heart scarab being found," I said, "but my recollection is that it never appeared on the list of treasures recovered at the site."

"It never appeared on the inventory because it was pocketed by one of the key people at the site. One of the laborers actually observed Sir Jacob Radcliff with the scarab. The laborer's story changed when he suddenly found himself in possession of more money than he would have otherwise earned in a lifetime."

More facts about the controversy were coming back to me. "Wasn't there also a dispute between Carter and his British financiers, Lord Carnarvon, Sir Jacob Radcliff, and the Egyptian government over the division of the treasures?"

"A bitter dispute. During that era, because my country was so desperately poor and under foreign influence, it entered into contracts with wealthy foreigners, mostly French, British, and German, to excavate archaeological sites."

"Fifty percent was the standard terms at the time," I said. "Half to the discoverers and half to the museum in Cairo."

"Yes, it depended on how intact the tomb or site was when the foreign excavators found it. If evidence showed that the site had been previously invaded by looters, the foreigners were allowed to keep half of any artifacts found. If there had been no previous entry, my country had the right to keep everything."

"And Carter claimed there was evidence that King Tut's tomb had been entered twice before by looters, so they had a right to half the treasures."

"Yes, the outer area of the burial site had been entered in the distant past, but obviously King Tutankhamen's burial chamber had not been discovered and entered by thieves because the incredible treasures in it were all still intact."

I remembered now why the controversy about the heart scarab and other artifacts arose.

"Carter and the wealthy men who financed the dig," I said, "were angry about the government's refusal to accept the fact that the site had been previously robbed."

"They were greedy. They didn't want to help uncover my people's history. They were thieves of history who coveted our treasures."

I didn't agree with him that foreigners who legitimately obtained artifacts from poor nations in the past were all a bunch of thieves. They were operating under what the rules were at the time, not to mention that the artifacts ended up well preserved in museums for the most part, rather than being left to the elements and in careless hands.

Much of what we have from antiquity would have been destroyed long ago if museums in the wealthier nations had not preserved them.

In a way, financing archaeological digs in search of buried treasures had about the same risks as the wildcatters had drilling for oil in the early days—most of the holes turned out to be dry because the site was chosen based upon a wing, a prayer, and a lot of guesswork.

A small opening often no bigger than a doorway had to be found in thousands of square miles of desert landscape. More often than not, even when a tomb was found, it had already been looted.

My own objection was that so much looting was still taking place because there were private collectors and museums willing to look the other way in order to get prize pieces.

I felt all artifacts acquired illegally should be returned to the countries of origin.

Since Kaseem was such a fierce advocate of his country and his version of history, I refrained from giving him my opinion.

❖

"So a witness claimed, at least initially, that he saw Radcliff with the heart scarab," I said. "I take it Radcliff wanted something nice from the site before it all got shipped off to the museum in Cairo."

"Exactly. He simply put the scarab in his pocket and returned to Britain. There was no law, no customs inspections as there are today."

"Your article mentioned the midnight visit and the belief that other items were taken."

"Yes, but the most valuable piece of all the Tutankhamen treasures was the scarab."

"Why? There have to be many more dazzling objets d'art in the collection than the scarab."

"For its magic."

13

❖

I kept a straight face because I thought his answer was comical, but asked him a serious question.

"Do you believe that the scarab has magical powers?"

He gave me a deep, throaty chuckle. "Absolutely, but not the way you might think. The magic lies in how it affects people. Egypt is a poor country with a rich history. For two thousand years, since the days of the Roman Empire, Egypt has been trampled by invading armies who stole from it, and the most prized pieces of Egyptian history were looted and taken to foreign lands. No doubt foreigners would have taken the Great Pyramid and the Sphinx had they been able to move them."

"The exception is Tut's treasures."

"Yes, and you must appreciate the effect that the discovery had on my people. When the tomb was found there was enormous pride and patriotism and identification with the greatness and glories of our past. The boy king's heart came to be called the 'Heart of Egypt' and symbolized all the greatness that we once were.

❖

"During that era of colonialism, a nationalistic movement arose determined to drive out the foreigners who controlled our country and rebuild the country's greatness. It was galvanized by the discovery of the incredible tomb. The theft of the heart scarab, the most sacred object belonging to King Tutankhamen, had a disheartening effect on my people. As time went on we remained first under the heel of foreign governments and then in the hands of corrupt officials because the people had lost hope.

"Our greatness has been taken away from us. I want it back for my country."

I was getting the picture.

The magical power of the scarab had to do with a person's thoughts and not its spiritual force.

"You believe the scarab's magic will once again galvanize the people of your country into achieving their potential."

He spread his fingers on the table. "Their *great* potential. What's stopping my people is their unwillingness to rid themselves of a government that keeps most of them poor."

Years ago a Cairo taxi driver told me the government kept control in the poor country by keeping the price of rice down—something Marie Antoinette and hubby Louie could have done to keep their own heads.

"Where is the scarab now?" I asked.

"Radcliff brought it back to his estate in England and housed it there in his private museum. Over the decades it had only been brought out to show a few private friends because to display it publicly would cause an uproar and an admission that it had been stolen from the tomb. Radcliff's great-granddaughter, Heather, came into possession of it and agreed recently to return it."

That caught me by surprise because it would have been major news in the world of antiquities.

He chuckled at the look on my face.

"But not publicly. Each of Radcliff's heirs have perpetrated the fraud by failing to admit to possession of the scarab. Not only would a public admission hurt Heather's family's reputation and her own, but many items Sir Jacob acquired during his time in Egypt and other places in

❖

the Middle East would come under scrutiny. To avoid publicity, a ruse was decided upon."

"What was the ruse?"

"The assistant curator in the Radcliff museum agreed to remove the scarab from the vault where it was kept and return it to Egypt. However, she would never admit where she obtained it from, although everyone would know that it came from the museum."

"I suppose it isn't stealing if the Radcliff woman agreed to it. Something went wrong?"

"Yes," he said, "something did go wrong or I wouldn't be seeking your services, would I? The scarab was actually stolen. A gang of thieves apparently learned of the scheme and intercepted the assistant curator at a hotel in London before she was to go to the airport."

I nodded, finally realizing where I fit into the grand scheme of things. "Now they want a ransom."

It was an educated guess. With world-class art, there was a thin line between "priceless" and "valueless." When a well-known art object was stolen, there was no market for it—except back to the original owner or their insurance company. It was an accepted practice to negotiate a price and exchange with an "innocent" go-between for return of the item.

The go-between who brokers the deal is, of course, usually a member of the gang of thieves, but one who didn't actually participate in the theft.

The sword of Damocles that hung over the stolen item was that the thieves threatened to destroy it if the ransom wasn't paid.

"They have demanded a great deal of money," he said.

"How much?"

"Five million American dollars."

I shrugged. "There are pieces that go for dozens of times that. The Egyptian government should pay it."

"The government is not involved. I am a poor man but I have raised the money among some wealthy patriots."

I almost scoffed out loud at his "poor man" statement. I deliberately looked at his ring.

He fingered it with his other hand. "I see you are admiring my

❖

ring," he said. "The ring is a fake. The vanity of a poor man imitating a rich one."

Was this a test?

"It's not a fake," I said. "It was once worn by a king and is probably worth a down payment on a 747."

The ring had a cobra with wings on it, a design that King Farouk was famous for wearing in his jewelry. No one else had worn that symbol, which was a takeoff of the cobra crowns the pharaohs wore.

Farouk was Egypt's last king and went into exile in the 1950s on the heels of a revolution.

"It was part of King Farouk's crown jewels," I said.

"How do you know it's not an imitation? What do you Americans call it, a knockoff?"

"It's hard to define. Some art appraisers refer to it as a ping going off in their head when something is real. I don't hear pings, but I do get a feeling that tells me when something is real. But when the fake is really good, it takes a while to see it."

In art terms, a "fake" made to fool buyers usually doesn't mean the object is a reproduction of an original piece, like making a copy of da Vinci's *Mona Lisa,* which everyone knows is hanging in the Louvre. Instead, the fake would often be a painting done by the counterfeiter in the style of da Vinci—the fraud is in passing it off as an original da Vinci.

That made many fakes extremely hard to sort out because a good counterfeiter can mimic the style of great works of art right down to the chemical compounds of the paint and the age of the canvas.

I told him about Howard Carter's theory in determining whether an artifact was a fake.

"Carter sat it aside in a spot where he would pass by or be able to glance at it once in a while as he went about his work. He paused to look at it several times a day. If the piece got better the more he looked at it, he knew it was genuine; if it got worse, he decided it was a fake."

"Very clever," he said. Then he gave me a sly smile. "You're right. The ring was a gift from the late king's family for services I provided."

"You should have asked them for the nickel."

❖

"The nickel?" He gave me a puzzled look.

"King Farouk owned a 1913 Liberty Head nickel, one of only five of its kind known to still exist. One of the nickels recently sold for nearly four million dollars."

Four million dollars for a nickel. Paintings selling for hundreds of millions. Chinese vases going for tens of millions. Collecting had become the sport of billionaires.

And I was counting pennies to keep my cat in free-range chicken.

His eye started to twitch again as he stared at me. It made me wonder if it wasn't a lie detector.

"How would you go about authenticating the scarab?" he asked. "Can it be tested to determine its age?"

"Not as you might imagine. Radiocarbon dating, measuring how old an object is by how radioactive its carbon content is, only works on things that were once living—like wood and paper. It can't be used to test mineral objects like stone. The heart is probably made of lapis lazuli."

It was an easy guess. Lapis lazuli was a rich, sky blue, semiprecious gem. Although not as valuable as precious gems like diamonds and rubies, it was easier for the ancients to cut into desired shapes than harder stones.

"Yes. And I have been told that counterfeiters are able to take the same material and duplicate the heart, making it extremely difficult to tell if it's a reproduction. Stone does not change over time, especially if it has been sealed in a tomb for thousands of years. Isn't that true?"

"Hard stone like lapis lazuli, marble, and limestone wouldn't materially change under those conditions. But other clues can determine if it's ancient. Lapis lazuli is a rock, formed from different minerals. Even though pieces of it from mines in different parts of the world may look similar, no two deposits of it have exactly the same chemical makeup."

"Ah, yes, like DNA and fingerprints. It has to be examined by a chemist?"

"Yes. Records, testing, and geological surveys have identified many of the pits and mines that were used by the Greeks, Romans, and Egyptians for the marble, clays, and other materials to make objects. Chemical analysis can reveal what site the piece came from and whether that

❖

source was one customarily used to make the type of piece we're examining."

He shook his head. "There would be no time to subject it to scientific analysis. Obviously, the thieves are not going to permit anything more than a quick examination done in a secret place and under the most stringent circumstances."

"Then you would have to gamble on its appearance alone. But there are clues that help. A stone object made for a pharaoh will be of the finest material available to the ancients.

"The lapis lazuli that your god-kings preferred came from Afghanistan, where it's been mined for thousands of years. It's intensely sky blue and has just a slight dusting of tiny pyrite particles, what we call fool's gold. I can tell by looking at the piece whether it's of the quality used by royalty."

"But a good forger would know to use the best Afghan lapis lazuli?"

"True, but there's more to consider. Like the type of tools they used. Modern tools, even hand tools, make subtly different impressions than the stone, copper, and bronze tools that were used during the time of the pharaohs.

"The patina, the outer coating that appears over time on an object, also has to be examined because it can reveal the age of an object and where it's been kept. Obviously, items kept sealed in a tomb have a different patina than those buried in the ground or exposed over the eons to the elements."

"I've been told that forgers can duplicate the patina to appear aged."

"They can try. Microscopic examination can usually show whether the tarnish has developed over thousands of years or was just put on recently. Now you're going to tell me that there won't be an opportunity to examine the piece under a microscope, right?"

"Unfortunately, that is the case."

"Which brings the situation down to the most basic test of the authenticity of a piece of art: gut reaction—what it looks like . . . feels like."

I realized he was already aware of everything I had told him. Any expert he spoke to could have pretty much told him the same thing.

❖

"You already knew that it would come down to an opinion based upon a quick examination," I said.

"Yes, I confess I did. The other experts I spoke to made the same conclusion. With so little time, complete reliance would have to be on the instincts of the person making the examination. As you pointed out, the gut reaction of what the expert sees and feels."

"Which is why I am particularly interested in hiring you. No one I spoke to had any actual field experience with antiquities as you did working at archaeological sites. And in this case, because the scarab has never had the intense scrutiny by experts that all the other Tut pieces have had, there is nothing to compare it with."

I wanted to get across to him that if there was nothing to compare it with, and no time to take tests, there was no guarantee of success.

"Modern reproductions are often so good that it's not uncommon for experts to come up with different opinions as to whether an object is genuine—and that's after subjecting it to scientific tests. It's not uncommon for pieces to be declared genuine and revealed to be a fraud years later," I told him.

"I'm aware of that. Which is why I have come to you. Most art professionals learned their trade from books and working in museums. You have actually done fieldwork and that impressed me. Not only was the object stolen from a dig, but it's been kept in seclusion over the years rather than being exposed to different environments."

He paused and leaned toward me across the table. "I have great faith in my own powers of judging people and situations. My gut, as you put it, is telling me you would be the right person to take on a mystery that began nearly a century ago."

And my gut right now was telling me to get up and walk away.

Not all the pieces were connecting, especially the ones about returning the scarab to Egypt in secret and the Egyptian government not being involved in either the attempt to return it or coming up with the money to ransom it.

Even though my gut was telling me to walk away, my brain was screaming that I needed the money and it was the only game in town at the moment.

❖

"So you want me to authenticate the scarab before the ransom money changes hands," I said.

"True."

"And every other expert you talked to turned you down."

He smiled and folded his hands together. "You're right again. No one is eager to assist me."

"Frankly, Mr. Kaseem, there are easier ways of making money than getting involved with a gang of art thieves. The scarab isn't going to come with a stamp of approval on it proving that it came from Tut's tomb. It's not something you can glance at or even spend an hour examining and be sure it's genuine.

"It's almost impossible to authenticate a piece without having precise information about it and even then three experts may come up with three different opinions."

He started to say something and I talked past him.

"The examination is going to take place in secret without the expert even knowing where they're at. If it turns out it isn't the real scarab, or the expert is unsure or needs more time to examine it, the person could likely get their throat slit. Sometimes the expert gets killed just because they saw too much even when an exchange is arranged."

I didn't add that the only person dumb enough to consider such a thing would have to be broke and desperate. Someone like me.

"I understand completely," he said. "Even though I spoke to a number of experts in Europe, I did not attempt to retain any of them because they all expressed the same concerns you have. I came to New York because your name kept popping up as a person with unique qualifications."

"What happened to the three names you got from the Met?" I threw back his lie with a smile.

"I lied, of course. In fact, some of the experts who mentioned you inferred that you had, shall we say, more than average experience with stolen artwork—from a unique angle, of course. Since you have dealt with thieves before and have been instrumental in returning historical treasures to their proper domains, I'm sure you are the right person who can help me."

"Those experts who spoke of my unique relationship with looted artifacts probably forgot to mention that I was the one who went into the line of fire to return looted pieces while they did nothing."

"Which is why I am here." He leaned across the table, grabbing hold of my eyes with an intense gaze. "I have seen the scarab. I have even held it in the palm of my hand. I thought it was going to burn a hole in my flesh. It needs to be returned to my people, Miss Dupre. It won't take much. We have the money. We—"

"I would need data—pictures, exact measurements—"

"We have all that waiting for you in England."

I looked away and sighed, not from boredom but with a mixture of remorse and regret that I had to deal with thieves to pay the rent.

"A short hop over the Atlantic," he said, reaching into an inside pocket and pulling out an envelope and laying it on the table. "Inside is a ticket to London and your first payment. Twenty thousand in cash. Another twenty when it's returned to us."

I stared at the envelope.

For sure, I'd gone to more dangerous places than merry ole England for less money.

"You'll have to add another zero to your figure if I succeed in getting the scarab returned to you."

"That is satisfactory."

I reached across the table and took the envelope.

I didn't know why, but my hands were sweaty, as if my body knew something I didn't know. But it didn't matter. After all, Britain was a civilized country. What could go wrong?

❖

14

❖

When we left the restaurant, Kaseem stepped into a cab waiting out front and I started walking toward the nearest subway. Even though I had the money for a taxi, I'd get home faster on the subway.

Kaseem told me contact had been made with the thieves but no examination of the scarab arranged. I was to check into a hotel in London and wait until he called me with the details of the meeting.

I was already nervous about meeting with the gang. For sure the meet wasn't going to take place at a London equivalent of the Russian Tea Room. Being searched—everywhere—and blindfolded and shoved into the trunk of a car for a ride to a dark and lonely place was not just the stuff of movies, but the way paying ransoms to recover artifacts commonly came down.

I couldn't leave for England without getting a sitter for Morty—keeper or even guard was a more accurate description for what it took to handle him than "cat sitter." He was a ten-pound feline who thought he was a four-hundred-pound tiger.

I called my friend Michelangelo and told him I needed "someone to

❖

take care of my pussy." Being in the chips, I invited him for dinner at my favorite Little Italy dive.

I admit I was shameless in letting him think I was talking about sex, but a girl has to do what a girl has to do these days when even schoolkids are sexting.

I stopped at a bank on my way to the subway station.

I didn't put the whole amount in my bank account, only a thousand of it; the rest was going home with me.

The last time I put a big chunk of money into the bank, the government got their greedy little hands on it. I still owed them money, not for back taxes but for the criminally insane penalties and interest they levy when you can't pay all your taxes at once.

I wasn't putting any more money into my account than necessary to meet current bills.

I also wasn't going to hide my cash in the refrigerator. That was a stupid mistake not to be repeated again. Who would have guessed that the guy I picked to watch Morty for me on my last trip out of town would help himself to my cold cash in the freezer? He seemed like a nice guy who liked cats . . . I had even bought him his favorite bottle of rum.

No, this time the cash was going in a place where no one would ever think to look. The toilet tank. In a sealed plastic baggie.

What thief would think to look there?

I thought the idea was inspired.

I JUST MISSED THE train by seconds after I walked down the stairs of the subway station and zipped my MetroCard through the turnstile. The next one wasn't due for another ten minutes.

I checked for any weird and crazy characters lounging about. I always did this when I was in a subway station. Call me paranoid, but if I saw any weirdos I'd get as far away from them as possible. I had already run into one crazy person today.

So far so good.

I picked a spot and waited, thinking about the good old days when I rarely rode the subway. It was a status thing to takes taxis or be picked

❖

up by a car and driver even if it took longer to get anywhere on the streets above. I had a good paying job then.

Back to reality here: at least I had picked up a new client and I was going to England and maybe even Egypt. That's what I was thinking about when my eye suddenly caught sight of a woman staring at me.

I froze.

Oh shit—it was her.

I wasn't 100 percent sure since she was dressed differently and there were thousands of women in the city with a similar age, build, and ethnic background. Other women with an alike appearance were in the station, but what keyed me on to her was that she had paused close to me, making the short hairs on the back of my neck fan.

I stood with my feet cemented to the ground debating what to do. I still hadn't gotten a look at her face because I was avoiding staring at her. I could run for an exit in the small station without passing her.

Don't panic, I told myself.

She wasn't making a move toward me, probably because there were other people around. Of course, this was New York, a city famous for its refusal of the average citizen to come to the aid of crime victims. And the cops sometimes weren't much more helpful. The woman could slice and dice me on the platform and people would simply step around the blood.

I heard the rumbling noise as a train was approaching the station. I didn't know if that was a good sign or not. Train cars were smaller now, making it harder to avoid someone out to stab you. I sure as hell wasn't going to get into the same subway car with her.

I started edging away, I hoped subtly, as if I were getting in position to board.

The woman turned toward me. She was sweating. It was warm in the subway station, but not uncomfortably hot enough to break out in a sweat.

She also looked tired, no, more than tired; she appeared fatigued, even wasted. Something was definitely wrong with the woman, but she didn't look threatening, just appeared all worn-out, as if she had been struggling with life's demons and not winning the war.

❖

There was something else about her. A hint of hysteria from life or drugs, I didn't know which.

I still wasn't sure it was her and I didn't want to make eye contact with her even if it wasn't. I learned that lesson soon after I had arrived in New York for my first curator job.

I'd had the misfortune to make eye contact with a bag lady on the street who humiliated me by yelling for the whole world to hear, "Doesn't a lady know she's not supposed to pick a bugger out of her nose?" I wanted to crawl under the nearest manhole cover and hide.

After that I never made eye contact with crazies.

I edged farther away and my movement seemed to galvanize her into action.

She started toward me, rambling almost unintelligently. "It's cursed . . . it's taken my soul—it'll take yours. Run! Get away now!"

The light of the oncoming subway train was in sight now and the noise began blocking out most of what the woman was rambling about as I backed away.

She got so close I put out my hand to hold her back, not to push her away but just to keep space between us.

Her rambling in English had now reverted to Arabic. With the noise and my limited understanding of Arabic, I wasn't making out what she was saying.

I continued to back up and suddenly realized that I was still dangerously close to the edge of the platform.

The woman looked startled for a moment, looking past me, as if she had seen something that frightened her. She screamed and lunged at me. I put out my hands to stop her from hitting me and she veered and ran off the platform as the train roared in.

In a split second the train was there and she was gone.

People were screaming.

I was one of them.

15

❖

"You didn't know the woman? Never saw her before this morning? And she never tried to attack you at the subway station?"

It was the third time the subway cop asked me about the woman who ran in front of the train. The incident at my apartment hadn't been entered into whatever the police used for a database and I had to fill him in on the letter opener attack first.

"She didn't appear to be trying to attack me," I said. "As I told you, she struck me as delusional. I don't know what she was trying to do. She just kept jabbering about a curse—look, I don't know. I seem to have had the bad luck to run into her."

"Luck? She showed up at your apartment this morning and then again at a subway station halfway across the city?"

I was being evasive, of course. I had money in my pocket that was as vital to me as life support to someone in intensive care. If I told this cop that a man had given me twenty thousand dollars this morning and there had to be a connection between him and this crazy woman, he would take the money, at least the nineteen thousand I had in my pocket.

❖

I had taken Kaseem's word that he didn't know anything about the woman but having her show up after I left him at the restaurant was too much. She might have followed me and she never mentioned Kaseem.

Being broke made me easily persuadable and seemed to have gotten to the point of it making me brain-dead stupid.

If I gave the cop a reason to arrest or search me, he'd also find the money and it would end up wherever the nation's largest police force stuck cash evidence so it was lost forever.

The subway cop didn't exactly instill me with confidence, either, as to his ability or my own ability to sweet-talk my way out of anything. He seemed to have that pit bull mentality that sinks teeth into an idea and never lets go. Right now he was clamped on to the notion that the woman and I had a history.

I didn't blame him, but it wasn't true.

Detective Gerdy may have been a regular cop, but subway cop was how I'd come to think of him after a hurry-up-and-wait bureaucratic routine that had taken hours.

I felt horrible for the poor woman who ran in front of the train, but now I wished I hadn't identified myself at the scene as a witness because four hours later I was in a police interview room that smelled of stale cigarettes and the trans fat from greasy French fries and spicy buffalo wings. Trans fats were outlawed in the city and smoking wasn't allowed in public buildings, but the smell had probably added a coating on the chipped paint over the decades.

A patina of killer fat and cigarette smoke that a few thousand years from now some art appraiser would examine to see if the grimy table in the room was a real artifact.

I sat on a grimy chair across the grimy table from the subway cop and tried to sound credible. I was tired and exasperated.

"Officer, I've already told you three times that I didn't know the woman." I gave him a smile. "Look, I'm hungry, tired, traumatized, and have a cat that's probably shredding my couch because I haven't gotten home to feed him dinner and I'm too humane to declaw him even though he's keeping me in the poorhouse buying furniture. Can we wrap this up soon?"

"I'm moving on it as fast as I can. A woman is dead. We have to cover all the bases."

From the looks of him it was going to take a while.

His belly hanging over his belt with a shirt spreading apart where one button was missing, sports jacket too tight and so far out of fashion the polyester finish would have been a fashion statement on a stud, slacks wrinkled and faded at the knees, shoes scuffed—he looked like a guy who life had left behind and who couldn't run fast enough to catch up.

He also needed to cut the hair in his nose and ears. And lose some weight.

Once in a while he'd look up from a report he was reading and shake his head a little, causing his jowls to jiggle.

I was ready to reach across the table and grab the papers and find out what the hell he found so interesting.

The body was still warm, literally, so the police bureaucracy couldn't have produced much paperwork. I got the impression that he thought if he kept me here long enough, I'd confess to something out of sheer boredom.

I considered it just to get the hell away from him, but I didn't know what crime to confess to.

Failing to stop a suicide?

Was that a crime?

I wasn't trying to be insensitive, but at the moment I was more concerned about the money in my pocket that my hand kept brushing to feel the reassuring bulge. So far he hadn't searched me, but the night was still young.

A uniformed subway cop had called the poor woman a "splatterer," but I guess that wasn't being insensitive, either. Millions of people ride the subway every day and a few of them end up accidentally (or on purpose) falling, tripping, jumping, or being pushed in front of the oncoming trains.

One of the terrible truths I'd learned in my thirty-something years was that people commit suicide because sometimes life is worse than death for them.

The woman had been out of it, maybe even tired of living. She might

❖

have just wanted to lay down and die but some thought spinning in her head about a curse was keeping her body moving.

Suicide had been the first thought from the cops who talked to me and other witnesses at the scene. But after giving the uniformed cops a statement, I had been shuffled to this detective whose nose and ears needed a haircut.

While he read at a snail's pace, I tried to occupy my tired mind with the view I had through a grimy plate glass window to a large room with government-issued gray steel desks that had probably been requisitioned back before my parents were born.

Cops of all size, color, sex, and race were at desks talking on phones or talking to each other—no one seemed to be reading anything, just talking, no one except the cop who had me trapped as though he had a foot holding down my tail.

"Very strange," he said, jiggling his jowls.

"What is strange?"

"A woman you don't know tries to stab you this morning and then hours later starts talking to you about a subject you didn't understand or couldn't hear. One moment this woman is talking to you, the next she's flying off the platform in front of a train."

I sucked in a breath and bit my lower lip to keep my sanity intact and then attempted to express myself without totally antagonizing him and thereby delaying my exit and jeopardizing the money in my pocket.

"I don't know that I'd call it strange in a city with eight million people. You hear about people every day that are so devastated by life or drugs that they end up street crazy. You must deal with them every day."

"Actually, I was referring to the coincidence."

"What coincidence?"

"You and her both being there . . . right at that moment . . . and you've never met each other before this morning."

"The woman probably got the notion in her head that I was someone else. Maybe someone who stole her husband. So she wanders around my building until I open my door. Then she follows me when I leave. Or maybe we just happened to be in the same subway station at the same time."

❖

He nodded, his jowls jiggling. "Interesting."

I lost it.

"Excuse me, but what is so interesting about it? I was in the wrong place at the wrong time, when a poor sick woman decided to end it all. End of story."

He wasn't buying it.

"Look," I told the subway cop, "it's too bad that this woman didn't get help with her problems, but she was obviously miserable. For some people, dying is better than living." Which pretty well described my feelings about being trapped in this interview room with this detective. "I have things I have to do. There's nothing else I can tell you."

"Hell of a coincidence."

"There's that word again. What's so hard to understand about 'I don't know her'? Never saw her before this morning. A complete stranger, as are most of the millions of other people in the city."

Staring at me, his wrinkled face, wide nose, and watery, red-veined eyes reminded me of a sad bloodhound.

I felt sorry for talking so callously about the poor woman and I needed to go to someplace sane and have a drink.

I got up, ready to leave, but paused, not wanting to be rude. I was beginning to feel sorry for him, too.

"Detective, I really don't know the woman. I'm not even sure it's the same woman who was at my apartment."

A lie, but a good one. How would they prove that it was the same woman? I just as well could have run into two crazies on the same day. It wasn't out of the question.

Let me tell you, any juror in New York City would sympathize with that contention.

I decided to beat the drum on the premise that it was an entirely different woman than the one that had wielded the letter opener.

"The more I think about it, I'm sure it wasn't the same woman." I locked eyes with him. "When you get the report I gave to the policeman at my apartment this morning, you'll see that it's not the same woman. The description is different."

The clothes were certainly different.

❖

"The woman in the subway approached me because I made the mistake of meeting her eye. You know as well as I do that you should never do that with a crazy. Then she went running in front of the train. That's all I know. Can I go now?"

"Have any business dealings in London or Egypt?" he asked, ignoring my question to leave.

"Not—not really."

I rubbed the sweat from the palm of my hand on the money bulge.

"Sounds like you're not sure."

"Why do you ask?"

"Her name is Fatima Sari. She had an Egyptian passport. Flew in yesterday from London."

I tried to keep a poker face but my guilty conscience got my tongue wagging.

"I've never heard of her. I did talk to someone, not this woman, about an Egyptian piece recently. But that's all. I'm an expert on antiquities. I've dealt with Egyptian artifacts hundreds of times. But like I keep telling you, I don't know this woman from Adam."

"A complete stranger speaks to you, someone you've never seen before, and you just happen to be in the wrong place at the wrong time. . . ."

"Exactly."

Was he finally getting it?

"And she has your business card in her pocket."

"*What?*"

He holds up a business card. "Madison Dupre, Art Inquiries—"

"That's my card."

"Unless there's another woman with your name and information, I guess it is. This woman you keep saying you don't know is carrying your business card when she just happens to be in the same subway station as you are and just happens to end up in front of a train after talking to you."

He gave me a sad look. "I guess with seven billion people on the planet, it was inevitable one of them would be carrying your business card when they accidentally bump into you and get killed in a New York subway station after trying to fillet you earlier with a letter opener."

❖

My heart was in my throat.

"It's a coincidence, that's all."

I sounded desperate even to myself.

His cell phone rang and he answered it. "No shit? It showed that?"

He gave me a meaningful look, letting me know the call concerned me. "Get it over to me so I can take a look."

I had the feeling that he had been told something I didn't want to hear.

"Interesting," he said.

I didn't want to, but I had to take the bait. "What now?"

"The security camera at the station shows you giving her a push."

16

❖

The meeting with the woman had gone well, Kaseem thought. She appeared to have accepted him as he presented himself. And nothing he had told her had been a lie. His only fraud was by omission—he didn't tell her she would be killed after authenticating the artifact. If the thieves didn't kill her, which he assumed they would, he would have it done because he couldn't risk having a witness to his machinations.

That she would die carrying out the task meant nothing to him. He considered himself a man of destiny. The death of Madison Dupre would be collateral damage, one of many to come, as he put a plan into action that had been brewing in his head for nearly two decades.

Kaseem had not lied when he said that he was a scholar, though he was far more a soldier than a man of books. He, in fact, had a doctorate in history, but it was obtained in the narrow field of military history. And his degree didn't come from an ordinary university but from a military academy: the Egyptian Army War College.

He had also failed to mention that before his banishment from his

❖

country, he had been a general in the army. And that he had fled a firing squad after organizing a coup that would have toppled the government had one of its members not betrayed the plot to the authorities.

As a history student, he had studied conquerors, from the great Thutmose to Alexander, Napoleon, Hitler, and Stalin, asking himself what inspired the passions and fiery visions of conquerors like Alexander and madmen like Hitler.

It had been Hitler's style that most captured Kaseem's interest. Hitler had managed to galvanize millions of people despite the fact that millions of others considered him a raving lunatic.

He had studied the Nazi dictator, analyzing what was the "fire in the man's belly" that caused millions to support him when much of what he spoke were lies and exaggerations.

Hitler rose to power after the economic debacle and great depression that followed World War I. The Germans had suffered particularly hard, both from hyperinflation whereby it took a wheelbarrow full of paper money to buy a loaf of bread, and all the while having an overreaching peace treaty shoved down their throats.

Kaseem came to the conclusion that Hitler had talked to the German people as if they were a defeated sports team he was coaching, shouting at them about how they were possessed with the power and destiny to be masters of the world and giving them a reason for why they had not achieved their great destiny and an enemy to hate: the Jews had held them back, he ranted, raved, and shouted.

What especially interested Kaseem was the way Hitler mesmerized the nation not only with Teutonic legends of powerfully built, golden-haired heroes and heroines for the German people to emulate, but with religious magic and the supernatural.

A special unit of storm troopers called the *Ahnenerbe* was formed to search the world for archaeological treasures to prove the superiority of Hitler's imagined master race and to strengthen the people's belief in extreme nationalism.

In other words, the SS set out to find proof other than their own chest-pounding and ravings that they were the master race.

Seizing Austria, they took possession of the spear called the Holy Lance or the Spear of Destiny. Said to have been used to pierce the side of Christ on the cross, the blood-stained spear had been carried into battle by kings and emperors.

Other quests were for the Holy Grail, a cup with magic powers because it was used by Christ at the Last Supper, sacred stones and runes with mystical meanings from Teutonic tales, and even an expedition to the Roof of the World, Tibet, to find what their junk science told them would be Aryan ancestors.

That Adolf was a psychopath who killed himself after killing thirty million people and losing a war he started didn't matter to Kaseem. Nor did the bizarre Austrian's sex life that ranged from the suicide of his niece after she was forced into a sexual relationship with him to getting it off by lying down and having women piss on him.

Hitler had failed after conquering a vast territory because although he was a great talker he lacked a good military mind. He had only risen to a rank of corporal during his military service.

General Kaseem's worldview was that there were more than three hundred million people in the Middle East of Arabic descent and that Arabs had a proud history. Not only was Egypt of the pharaohs a world power in its day, but the great Middle Eastern civilization that followed, the Arabic followers of Islam, had conquered the lands and people from Mesopotamia to the Atlantic, replacing those cultures with the Arabic language and customs.

In its day, the Arabians weren't just the world's greatest military power, but the most advanced civilization on the planet in terms of science, medicine, and mathematics.

With several hundred million people in the Arabic world, a long-term enemy to hate and rally against, Kaseem had found his calling: to take power in the largest Arabic country, Egypt, and unite all other Arabs in the Middle East and North Africa under his command.

He also had an object with a proven ability to excite the masses: the Heart of Egypt.

As he told Madison Dupre, in the 1920s when nationalistic fever

❖

ran wild in Egypt, the return of King Tut's heart scarab had been a rallying cry to drive out foreigners and bring Egypt back to the greatness it once enjoyed.

General Kaseem was going to bring that cry back to a fever pitch.

❖

The old beliefs will be brought back to honor again. The whole secret knowledge of nature, of the divine, the demonic. We will wash off the Christian veneer and bring out a religion peculiar to our race.

—ADOLF HITLER

17

❖

I staggered out of the police station gasping for air like a fish flapping on a boat deck.

I couldn't believe it. It was no surprise that Kaseem had lied to me. I had already guessed that.

But going from a victim to a murder suspect in a flash had taken my breath away.

The whole world had turned upside down since I tumbled out of bed this morning.

The woman ranting about a curse had been right. There was a curse for sure and it had its arms around me and was squeezing me like a giant squid.

I was left speechless when Detective Gerdy dropped the accusation that I had killed the woman.

When I stopped hyperventilating I got out my cell phone and told Michelangelo to meet me in Little Italy immediately.

"What's the rush?"

"Murder!" I screeched.

I needed a drink—several of them—and a plate of carbohydrates and a chocolate dessert because I was burning up nervous energy faster than I could manufacture it.

My nerves needed wine and pasta and Michelangelo's help with the subway detective.

But before I met him I wanted to drop off the money that I had on me at my apartment. With my luck, I'd be mugged before I got a chance to hide it.

While I was there, I'd also pay the rent and feed Morty.

I wanted to see my landlord as much as I hated having an IRS audit but I needed to drop the money on him before he actually did serve me with an eviction notice.

THE DOOR TO ARNIE'S apartment was open. I knocked anyway as the smell of curry hit my nostrils.

"Arnie, it's Maddy. Arnie?"

"You have the rent?" he asked through a mouthful of food.

"Yes."

"Come in."

The last thing I wanted to do was step inside.

He was eating a piece of buttered bread. His T-shirt and work pants looked like they hadn't been washed since Marlon Brando wore them *On the Waterfront*.

Vaguely southern Mediterranean in looks, he had the bald head, thick neck, and petroleum barrel torso of a professional wrestler on a TV show.

Someone—no, *something*—was sitting on his couch. At first I thought it was a person, but then realized it must be a big doll or mannequin.

Arnie and the whatever appeared to have been sitting together watching one of the endless reruns of a cop and lawyer TV show.

I resisted the urge to ask him why he had it because I suspected the answer would embarrass me, or at least send me into a fit of laugher.

I handed him the money.

❖

He grabbed it greedily with his buttered fingers. "Why can't you pay on time?"

"Why can't you fix things around here?"

"I do."

"The lock on the front door hasn't been fixed."

He shrugged his shoulders. "It's on my list."

"You better make it number one on your list because some crazy person attacked me today."

"There are lots of weirdos out there," he said, counting the money with his greasy fingers. "Some of them get invited in."

"Yeah, but this one didn't get invited. I could've been raped and murdered! I should report you to the Building Department."

He looked hurt. "I keep you from being evicted and you want to make me lose my job? The owners say you're late too often, to toss you out. I told them you've just had a bad run but you're a good tenant."

Wow, I had no idea that he had been protecting me. I thought he owned the building. What a jerk I'd been.

"Thanks, Arnie. I appreciate it. And I was only kidding about the Building Department. Listen, I'll be gone for a few days and a friend will be coming by to take care of my cat."

"First you pay for the broken window."

"I didn't break the window. Someone threw a rock at it from the street."

"The glass was on the street, not in your apartment."

Good point. I should have watched more cop shows on TV.

I gave him the money and started to leave, but my curiosity got the best of me. I had decided the woman sitting on the couch was a robot.

"What is that?"

"Sheila."

"What does she do?"

He gave me a wide grin on his face. "Stuff my wife never used to do."

I gave him a disgusted look.

"How much did she cost?"

"Ten thousand dollars."

"*What?* You paid ten thousand for a sex toy!"

❖

He looked hurt. "She's not a sex toy. She's my friend."

I immediately felt sorry for him. Having to buy a friend. Poor bastard. He should have invested the money in a charm school class.

"Do you want to see what she can do?" He grinned.

I fled.

18

❖

Mike was already at the bar with a beer in his hand. I plopped down next to him.

"God, I've been to hell and back and the night's still young. I spent the day running from an ancient curse that won't be satisfied until it sticks pins in my eyes and drains my blood."

"I can tell you some horror stories, too," he said.

"I don't want to hear your horror stories. I have enough of my own."

"We can go back to your place, and you can tell me all about it in bed," he said, nuzzling my ear and working his hand up my thigh. "I know how to make you feel better."

He could but I wasn't in the mood at the moment. I ordered a glass of wine. And moved his hand away. "Not now."

Michelangelo's real name was Michael Anthony. He was a detective with the NYPD, head of their art theft squad. It goes without saying that as usual with my first encounters with police officers, my first meeting with Mike, about a year ago, was not pleasant—a rather nasty

❖

misunderstanding about pad thai noodles and looted Cambodian artifacts. But that's another story.

The news media called him Michelangelo because he was also a
painter and because his real name was vaguely similar to the great
Italian Renaissance artist. Having seen his artwork, the only similar-
ity between him and the real Michelangelo were their names. The guy
couldn't have made a living doing family portraits, but it wasn't something you'd want to say to a guy who packs muscles and a gun or two.

He claimed we had a "booty call" relationship. That was a modern
term for people who call each other up late at night when they can't
sleep and need sex but otherwise go their own ways the rest of the day.

I hated the description, it was cold and mean and bloodless, but I
had to admit that it was accurate.

"Okay," he said, "shoot. I'm all ears."

"I need my drink first."

After I got my Pinot Noir and took a few sips, I started to tell him
about the computer fiasco.

It was avoidance behavior. I needed to build up to being a murder
suspect slowly or I'd break down. Thinking about that poor woman was
also a bummer.

"I finally threw the damn thing out the window."

He thought the whole thing was hilarious.

"It's actually funny," he said after he stopped laughing.

"Bizarre is more like it. It gets better. Then I was attacked by a crazy
woman."

"What!" He looked at me and almost choked on his drink. "On the
street?"

"No! Inside my goddamn apartment building. Good old Arnie hasn't
fixed the lock on the front door yet."

"You should report that guy."

"Naw, he's not a bad guy really."

Then I told him about the attack on me.

"So you filed a report on this crazy woman."

"Yeah, but it won't do any good."

"They'll get her."

❖

"No, they won't."

"Sure they will." He took a gulp of his beer.

"She's dead," I said.

He covered his mouth as he started to spit out beer.

I told him about what happened that day without mentioning Kaseem by name or the fact I had had a big payday.

"I just finished having lunch and was on my way home. And there she was again."

"So she was following you."

"Evidently. The woman had serious mental problems. Something was definitely wrong with her."

"Whatever she was—drug addict, sick, demented, crazy—it's over."

"No, it isn't. They say I pushed her in front of the train."

He listened quietly as I described the grilling at the police station.

"This bastard cop is trying to hang me," I told Mike.

"Just because he considers you a person of interest in a suspicious death doesn't make him a bastard."

"Person of interest, suspicious death, your damn cop jargon has become bureaucratic double-talk. This guy is trying to prove the woman was murdered and that I did it. Maybe he needs a promotion, maybe he has a fetish for framing people, maybe—"

"Hey, calm down. The security tape will tell the story."

"He lied when he said the camera shows me pushing her. I'd be pretty stupid to sit here and lie to you I if did something that was caught on tape, wouldn't I? I didn't push her. I want you to get ahold of that tape before he destroys it."

"Your paranoia is running rampant. He's not going to destroy the tape, and he's not out to frame you."

I tried to keep from exploding and spoke as calmly as I could.

"The man told me that the security tape shows I gave her a push. *That is a lie.* Now, with all that logic and reasonableness you manage to maintain when it's not your tush on the line, why don't you explain to me how that could possibly be when I know I didn't push her and neither did anyone else?"

"I'd have to see the security tape—"

❖

"Bullshit! I just told you, she wasn't pushed. She jumped. Actually ran off the platform and in front of the train."

The woman had her back to the train when she suddenly bolted but I didn't speculate with him as to whether in her confused state of mind she even realized the train was coming. Right at the moment her suicide fit nicely because it eliminated any connection to me and the money.

"Okay, stay calm. Maybe he's pulling your string to see what you blurt out."

"Why would he do that? And don't tell me to stay calm."

"Come on, Maddy, pervs don't run up to cops and confess their crimes the minute we show up at the scene flashing badges. They need a little nudging, so sometimes we say there's a witness when there isn't or that they left their DNA before evidence is even tested, something to rattle them and get them to think they're nailed so they start incriminating themselves as they justify what they did."

I chewed on spaghetti Bolognese and tried to digest what Mike was saying, that the subway cop would lie to me so I would blurt out a confession.

"What about this guy who hired you—what does he say about the crazy woman?"

"I didn't get any answer at the number when I called after the incident."

"He probably had a cell phone that he picked up at the airport and dumped after he used up the time."

For sure, there was a connection between Kaseem and Fatima Sari, but I knew that he hadn't harmed her. She did it to herself. I wasn't ready to kill my one source of income by giving up his name to the cops, especially these days when a Middle Eastern appearance or name was liable to get you tagged as a terrorist.

He gave me a kiss on the cheek. "Don't get crazy about it. I'll talk to the guy, see what he really has. I have a great in—you've been a person of interest in so damn many art deals that have gone—"

"Call him now."

"He's probably not on duty—"

"He's always on duty, the guy has no life."

❖

I gave him Detective Gerdy's card. "His cell phone's on it. Call him now or I won't get any sleep tonight."

Mike started to leave and I grabbed his arm. "Where you going?"

"Outside, where I can hear better."

That was only half true—the bar was a little noisy, but he was getting far enough away to where the subway cop wouldn't hear me growling in the background.

He came back and slipped into the seat next to me and signaled the bartender for another beer.

"Gerdy doesn't have the tape yet, but he said he'll let me see it when he gets it. It has to be processed in forensics, so he'll probably get it tomorrow or the next day."

I didn't like his neutral tone. Something was wrong.

"Is he still claiming I pushed her?"

"He hasn't seen the tape, but he says that's what the video tech told him."

My life was spinning out of control, but I was suddenly calm. "What else did he tell you? That he's going to arrest me?"

"He said he was going to view the tape before he does anything, but because there's a foreign connection, he's coming to ask you to hand over your passport."

"What? Is he crazy? I'm not giving him my passport. Let him get a court order."

"It's standard procedure. If he arrested you, a judge wouldn't set bail unless you surrendered your passport because you do work that takes you out of the country."

Good God. Being arrested. Stuck in jail. I'd be homeless for sure when I got out if that bastard did that.

"This is insane. I didn't do anything. Some crazy woman tries to stab me with a letter opener and then jumps in front of a train. I didn't even know her name, never saw her before."

I hid my face in my hands.

"I don't know even know who I am at the moment. I should have stayed in bed this morning."

He squeezed my arm. "Don't worry, I'll help you. The forensics tech

❖

may not even know who you are on the tape. I'll take a look at it. In the meantime, don't talk to Gerdy without a lawyer present."

"Uh-huh."

"I don't like the sound of that, Maddy. . . . Promise me you won't do anything stupid."

"Would I do something stupid?"

"Do chickens have lips?"

❖

19

❖

I didn't do anything stupid until after I let him know I wasn't in the mood for any sex that night and went home just long enough to pack a carry-on and give Morty a hug and extra food and water.

I was on board a red-eye to London and the plane was starting to taxi on the runway before I called Mike and told him I left my apartment door unlocked and needed him to feed Morty until I got back.

"You have to take care of my pussy," I reminded him, deliberately loud enough so the guy next to me who was already trying to get friendly would hear that I had a man in my life.

When he asked me where I'd skipped off to, I told him the truth only because it would be so easy for the police to find out.

"London."

I cut off his questions. "That's where I've been paid to go, where the woman flew in from, and where I'll find the answers."

"Detective Gerdy will consider it an admission of guilt."

"Look at the security tape. If I gave that woman a shove, I'll put the rope around my neck myself."

❖

I hung up and turned off the phone to end his rebuttals and recriminations.

I smiled sweetly at the flight attendant who had told me twice to turn off my phone.

"Sorry. My baby's sick."

A little lie was better than getting caught offending a flight attendant nowadays because their job had gone from being nice to people to tyrants who order the captain to slam on the brakes and call airport security whenever a passenger looked cross-eyed at one of them.

Britain is a civilized country, I reminded myself again as the plane lifted off.

I shouldn't have a problem unless someone checks and finds out that the last time I was there I left in a hurry with a burning art gallery and dead bodies behind me.

CURSE OF THE PHARAOHS

After visiting Howard Carter and the tomb of King
Tut, anthropologist Henry Field wrote that Sir Bruce
Ingham, a friend of Carter's, had been given a mum-
mified hand to use as a paperweight.

A scarab on a bracelet attached to the hand said,
"Cursed be who moves my body. To him shall come
fire, water, and pestilence."

Not long after receiving the scarab bracelet, Ingham's
house burned down and then flooded after it was
rebuilt.

20

❖

Salisbury Plain, England

Fuad Hassan squeezed his cell phone tightly and whispered to himself, "Fatima, where are you?"

He snapped the phone closed and stuck it in his pocket when he got her voice mail recording again.

Fuad had not heard from Fatima Sari, his assistant, for two days now and his last conversation with her had left him shaken. He couldn't sleep, couldn't concentrate on his work as he worried about her.

For the last twelve years he had been the curator for the Radcliff Collection, a private museum founded by Sir Jacob Radcliff. The world's largest private collection of ancient Egyptian artifacts, it now rested in the hands of Radcliff's great-granddaughter, Heather Radcliff.

Fortunately for the museum, Heather, who knew infinitely more about the latest fashions than antiquities or anything else for that matter that required even rudimentary book learning, never strayed into the museum unless she was showing a visitor her unique collection.

The fact that she was very rich usually impressed her visitors, who were suitably complimentary about her knowledge of ancient Egyptian

❖

artifacts, even if she did call the collection's sarcophagus her mummy's bed.

She floated through a life in which the high points were sexual relationships with men and women, few of which lasted more than six weeks, and the quality of cocaine she sniffed.

In between attending parties in Manhattan, Paris, and London, she spent time trying to find out her purpose in life and why she was put on this earth. That quest to find the meaning in her existence had taken her from mind-spirit awakenings in the red rocks of Sedona to the white-capped Himalayas, all at great cost that produced little insight as to her place in the universe other than having done little to have so much.

Currently she was searching for herself in the Druid spirituality that many believed existed in Stonehenge and other megalithic circles and trilithons found in the Salisbury Plain that her estate laid upon.

To Fuad, whose life was dedicated to the protection and preservation of the historical treasures of Egypt's brilliant history, Heather Radcliff was a vain, foolish woman whose only redeeming qualities were that she paid him to oversee her antiquities collection and that she had absolutely no interest in it except to occasionally flaunt the brilliance of her objects.

The costume party at the Radcliff estate had already lasted several hours now and Fuad had gone into the garden to make his call to Fatima to avoid the possibility of being overheard by the two guards that had been hired to watch any guests that wandered into the museum.

He wanted the museum to be locked up that evening in order to keep out drunken guests, but Heather Radcliff wasn't about to keep her most famous possessions out of sight.

Fuad was frightened for Fatima, and also for himself, but he didn't know who he could trust at the museum. The two of them were the only foreigners employed on the estate. Their language, religion, Egyptology backgrounds, even their own rather timid, reserved natures, kept them from assimilating with the servants, gardeners, and other staff.

Keenly aware that their inhibitions had kept them from intimacy with each other, Fuad regretted that he hadn't pursued his feelings for

❖

Fatima. Had they married, he would have forbade her from assuming the task of returning the heart back to Egypt.

Now he wished that he had argued with her more about not going, persisted harder at trying to persuade her from getting involved. He should have taken up the duty himself to protect her.

Fuad hadn't felt right about it from the beginning. The sacred scarab should have been returned to the chest of King Tutankhamen in great fanfare, not surreptitiously.

He turned away, disgusted, as a woman burst out of the house with a man following her, throwing off their clothes as they raced for the pool through the garden, laughing and shouting.

That the costume party had a Druid "fertility" theme, a thinly disguised excuse for an orgy, offended Fuad but didn't surprise him. Heather Radcliff had recently "discovered" that in a past life she had been a goddess of fertility, which in her mind translated to sex.

Fuad found the lascivious horseplay between the guests not only offensive to his sense of decency but also juvenile.

Back in the museum wing, he nodded politely at the two guards who were arguing over a soccer match and went into his office to check the monitors to see if the guards or anyone else had secretly pocketed something while he had stepped out.

Nothing had been taken and he credited his own doubts about the honest nature of mankind for having never had an item stolen. As important as the security cameras were, anything small enough to be pocketed was housed in locked glass-topped cases.

The museum was one long gallery, occupying what had originally contained the manor's armory, military uniforms, and hunting equipment.

It was an eclectic collection that included several large pieces—a ram's-headed sphinx from Karnak, the mummified remains of a Twenty-sixth Dynasty high priest in his sarcophagus, a chariot from the Ptolemaic Dynasty—and many smaller pieces, such as weapons, jewelry, amulets like scarabs, gems, stones in the shape of animals, and the like.

The Radcliff Collection was dwarfed by the Egyptian galleries at the British Museum, New York's Metropolitan, and the Louvre, but it was unmatched by any private collection in the world.

❖

How a rich man like Sir Jacob Radcliff had been able to acquire an enormous collection of Egyptian treasures was a reflection of Radcliff's times and the history of archaeology.

It was a piece of history that Fuad reflected upon as he hid away in his small museum office and stared blankly at the security monitors. If the Heart of Egypt had been rightfully stored in the Egyptian Museum instead of secreted out of the country by Radcliff, Fatima would be safe now.

Unlike most of his fellow countrymen who wanted everything ever taken or stolen from Egypt—the incredible collections in the great museums of the world and the countless number of pieces held in private hands—returned to Egypt, Fuad had a sense of history and understood that much of the great treasures of Egyptian antiquity would have been destroyed long ago if the relics hadn't been stored in museums and with people who could afford to safeguard and preserve them.

Sir Jacob Radcliff obtained his artifacts by participating in the financing of archaeological digs in countries rich in antiquities and poor in material goods. In countries where artifacts made an eon ago had little meaning to people who grubbed every day for enough to eat, wealthy individuals and museums paid fat fees and fatter bribes for the right to "mine" antiquity sites.

That Howard Carter had been financed by Lord Carnarvon, Radcliff, and others was well known, but their efforts, leading to the most fabulous find of all—the King Tut treasures—was just one of thousands of times in which people of wealth put up the money to find artifacts and often took half—if not all—of what was found.

Two famous incidents before the King Tut find were Heinrich Schliemann's discovery of Troy and Lord Elgin's Marbles, the incredible collection of marble pieces from the Parthenon and other buildings on the Acropolis in Athens. Those artifacts, probably the greatest left from ancient Greece, now sit in the British Museum in London.

The process by which Sir Jacob Radcliff built his collection was utilized for a couple of centuries by wealthy foreigners in their efforts to acquire artifacts from Egypt and other poor countries: payments, often

❖

in the form of bribes, paid to corrupt officials and at other times to poor governments in need of the funds.

But wealthy foreigners came late into the game of looting Egypt. The country had been raped and plundered of its antiquities for thousands of years. The Romans did it, the Turks, the French, and the British, with wealthy American, German, and other European museums coming in and taking many prizes even after invading armies and colonial masters had grabbed what they could.

The Heart of Egypt happened to be one of those pieces.

However, unlike artifacts that lie in peace still buried in the desert or in museum galleries, the scarab seemed to have a life and spirit of its own. And Fuad feared that the spirit it housed had attracted men even craftier and more devious than robber barons like Sir Jacob Radcliff.

Although he and Fatima were both trained Egyptologists, neither of them had the personality or the fortitude to deal with the convoluted schemes that have shadowed what should have been the joyous return of the heart scarab to its homeland.

Fuad, a thin, small-framed, and gentle man, whose reach was confined mostly to his work, had an affection for Fatima that he never expressed to her. Although he was twenty years her senior, his feelings weren't of a parental nature, but he was too shy and timid to voice them.

Fatima had a less stable personality. Delicate physically and mentally, she was controlled by her emotions and was quick to cry and to become guilt-stricken when things went bad even if they were not of her doing.

It was her irrational reaction to the loss of the sacred scarab that worried Faud.

She didn't seem to be able to stay coherent when he talked to her. She was an emotional wreck over the scarab, but it went beyond that, as if her mind was fouled by drugs. And he knew she was not a person to so such things.

Fuad tried phoning her again, but the call went instantly into voice mail, where he left another message. Fatima's state of mind saddened and frightened him, but he didn't know which way to turn for help.

❖

21

❖

Heathrow Airport, London

My phone went off as I walked toward a currency exchange kiosk at Heathrow. I didn't recognize the area code or the number, so that meant it was probably my friend from the Tea Room.

"I heard what happened," Mounir Kaseem said.

"I experienced what happened. A woman first tries to kill me and then dies in front of me and a cop wants to know why I claim she's a perfect stranger when she has my business card on her."

"I know nothing about—"

"I don't believe you. She was Egyptian; she was connected to you and your attempt to recover the scarab. As soon as things go to hell, I can't reach you on the phone."

"I'm sorry—you must have tried to call me after I'd gotten rid of the phone when the minutes were up."

"All deals are off between us. And you're not getting a refund. I only came here to find out why that poor woman jumped in front of a train, not to help you." I hung up on him.

❖

I did it out of an angry impulse, but it was a good move because I wanted to see how he came back—if he did. Was it going to be with threats or answers?

My phone rang and I answered with a quick "What?"

"You're right. I did know the woman, but I didn't know that she was in New York or that she would attack you."

"I want more than excuses. Tell me about Fatima Sari. Why was she in New York trying to contact me?"

He was quiet and I let the clock tick.

"She is . . . was . . . unbalanced," he said. "Fatima was an assistant curator at the Radcliff museum."

"Is she the one you said took the scarab?"

"She volunteered to return it to Egypt as part of the little charade we had devised to keep from tarnishing the Radcliff name. When it was stolen from her, she became irrational."

His explanation didn't make any sense to me. "What do you mean, irrational?"

I waited out another long pause before he answered.

"Fatima believed in both the potential greatness of our country and in the power of the magic that has come down from the times of the pharaohs. I'm not referring to silly stories about mummy curses, but what we spoke about at lunch—the powerful effect that a symbol of Egypt's grand past can have on my people. The loss of the scarab was not a monetary loss to her as it might be for an art dealer or collector. It was an event that stabbed at her very being."

"Are you saying she went crazy from guilt?"

"Yes, I suppose that's a way of putting it. She felt her life was ruined, her career destroyed, and her passionate desire to participate in an event important to her country was taken from her."

"Did she take drugs?" I asked.

"Sadly, yes. I discovered only after the scarab was stolen that she had experiences with narcotics."

"Could she have been involved in the theft? As a participant rather than the victim?"

❖

"I considered that, but I doubt it. She was not the devious type. Perhaps I would know more if we had been able to report the theft to the police. But you can see the problem with that."

I could see his point. How would Heather Radcliff report missing something that she denied ever having?

"But why was Fatima trying to contact me? And kill me?"

"I honestly don't know. I suspect she overheard me saying I was going to hire you after I was contacted by the thieves."

"When did you see her last?"

"Just before I left for New York. In London. She was acting very erratic, unstable. I insisted she consult a doctor and she disappeared. For all I know, she got a flight to New York before mine."

"I don't get it," I said. "I can understand that she got my name through you, but why would she come to New York and try to kill me just because you were going to hire me to authenticate the stolen piece? From what you told me, she should have been pleased that you were hiring me to help get back the scarab."

I got silence for a moment before he answered.

"She may have overheard a discussion I had and misinterpreted what I was saying."

"Which was?"

"I was telling an associate that you were once . . . inadvertently involved in the theft of a national treasure."

I restrained myself from blowing him off over the phone. Unfortunately, I had been involved—*inadvertently*—in an infamous incident in which a national treasure of Iraq had been looted.

"What did you say that made Fatima think I could be involved in the theft of the scarab?" I asked.

"My associate had suggested that because of your background, you might have knowledge of the scarab incident."

"What? That I was one of the thieves?"

"Please understand, it was a call in which we were bouncing back and forth different theories and strategies. I had no idea that Fatima would misinterpret what was being said. Obviously, if I thought you were

❖

in any way connected with or knew anything about the theft, I would not have hired you to authenticate it."

I had to admit that the woman, out of her mind from grief and guilt, could have been suspicious of me after hearing me described as some sort of international art thief.

"What exactly did Fatima say to you before she jumped in front of the train?" he asked.

"She mumbled some stuff about curses."

I was deliberately vague because I didn't want him to know how little I really knew. And I didn't want to tell him I was literally on the run from the police because it would give him leverage over me. I was stuck in the deal because he could open doors for me to get answers, but I also wanted to get a bonus. I figured I was going to need it if I had to hire an attorney when I got back to New York.

"I regret you had to witness the tragic end to her life," he said. "You may, of course, keep the retainer I gave you and return home. However, I wish you would consider continuing with our arrangement. I don't want to sound melodramatic, but I'm sure poor Fatima would rest better if the scarab was recovered."

I had no intention of walking away from the deal. I needed the money now more than ever. But I had to grit my teeth to keep from telling Kaseem that at this point I was more interested in getting information that would clear me with the subway cop than him getting back the scarab. And I still wasn't completely convinced that Fatima would have reacted so violently when she heard I might be involved in the theft.

Wouldn't she have demanded that I give back the scarab rather than trying to stab me to death?

I shook my head in disgust. I didn't know what had been going on in that crazy woman's mind.

"If you are willing to continue on," he said, "I will have the next payment for you tomorrow."

"I want twice what you promised me. And I want it today, not tomorrow."

"I'm not in Britain. I flew back to Paris to take care of another matter. I'll cross over and meet with you tomorrow afternoon with your payment, double as you have asked. You have earned it many times over. In the meantime, I've arranged for you to have the opportunity to examine some pictures and a reproduction of the scarab at the Radcliff museum."

I listened quietly as he told me I was to meet an art dealer in Salisbury at the train station.

After I hung up, my jaws were tight. I was looking for answers and didn't like the ones I had gotten from Kaseem. Worse, I had the feeling that I was being led around by the nose.

Money, money, money. That's what it was all about. Like a dog chasing its tail, I had to run after the money in what was becoming a vicious circle.

22

❖

The taxi ride from Heathrow to Waterloo Station took me through a damp, gray, overcast London, with threatening storm clouds that fed my own sense of dread that my feet were sinking deeper into a morass. It was too bad, because London was on my short list of favorite large cities.

I followed Kaseem's instructions, catching a train to Salisbury, where he said I would be met by the Radcliff woman's art consultant. I'd been on the rail line before because stunning relics of antiquity were on its route—Stonehenge and the Roman ruins at Bath.

I laid my bag on the table with seats facing each other in the hopes that people would think all the seats were occupied. I wasn't in the mood for any companion.

I hurried to the lounge car to get a cup of coffee to help my jet lag, hoping my bag would still be there when I returned to my seat.

When I got back, I checked my smartphone for messages. There was nothing from Michelangelo; only two calls from bill collectors. I ignored those. I planned to send each of them something from my cash hoard when I got home.

❖

A man sat down across from me and I looked up and did a double take when I realized he was staring at me . . . not a polite stare but that look a cop gives you when he's wondering what you're up to.

He had a southern Mediterranean olive complexion similar to Kaseem's, but that didn't necessarily make him Egyptian because like everywhere else, Britain was multiracial.

"Say something," I said, "so I'll know if you're a British or an Egyptian cop."

He raised his eyebrows. "Is there a sign around my neck that identifies me as a policeman?"

Definitely Egyptian, though he had a British accent underlying his native one, a not uncommon trait for people who learned their English from a Brit.

"It's your eyes. You're trying to look into my head instead of my clothes. At the moment I'd much rather meet a man putting the make on a woman than a cop out for information I don't have."

The smile on his face broke up the stern look of officialdom.

Good-looking, maybe late thirties, tall, well built, with a few specks of gray in his black hair, he was wearing a stylish black leather jacket, gray slacks, and sunglasses. The boot sticking out into the aisle looked like handcrafted Italian leather.

I didn't know what the dress code was for Egyptian policemen, but his clothes showed more good taste than expense. The tip-off was his watch when he reached out to shake my hand.

The watch wasn't flashy and had a simple black band rather than the heavy Rolexlike creations that could tell you the time in Timbuktu and the weather on Mars.

"Rafi al Din," he said. "My apologies. I didn't mean to stare at you as if you were a piece of incriminating evidence. And I confess that I am intrigued by what is hidden in your mind and under your clothes."

Ah, a cop with a sense of humor. And sex appeal. With my luck, he was another Michelangelo who hid his artistic nature behind beer, hot dogs, and sports bars.

"Let me guess, you're an Egyptian policeman and you want to talk to me about scarabs?"

❖

"Amazing. You're psychic. Does your crystal ball tell you how soon we will become lovers?"

I liked this man. So far.

"It's giving me a warning not to trust a tall, dark, and handsome man who suddenly appears at my table. Perhaps I've developed a sense of heightened awareness over the years because police officers seem to take an unhealthy interest in my life."

"Perhaps it's because, as you say in your country, where there's smoke, there's fire."

"Apparently the smoke gets in their eyes and they confuse me for the guilty party. The fact that I am not housed in a supermax with serial killers and people who eat people seems to offend their twisted view of an orderly world."

He started to say something and I threw up my hands in frustration. "Okay. Enough clever sparring. Who are you? What do you want? And would you mind getting lost?"

"I am sad to admit that in some ways I am already lost. But I have a card which reminds me who I am."

He gave me a business card, English on one side, Arabic on the other. The English side confirmed his name was Rafi al Din and that he was an inspector with the Supreme Council of Antiquities. It showed a Cairo address.

The SCA was the Egyptian government unit in charge of its antiquity sites and artifacts.

"Very impressive," I said, "a card you could stop at any print shop and have knocked out in five minutes. Do you have anything that looks a little more official? A badge? Gun?"

"Of course."

He showed me a picture ID with him in a fancy military-looking police uniform. I couldn't read Arabic, but I was impressed with the official appearance of the uniform. He looked as sexy in his uniform as he did in the leather jacket.

"Is your job as an inspector similar to the British version of a police official—a cop that investigates antiquity thefts?"

"Yes. I have a few questions to—"

❖

I cut him off. "Before we get to your questions, how did you know I was in Britain, on this train? Better yet, why have you bothered to find out I'm even on the planet?"

I met his eyes, waiting for answers.

He leaned back and gave me a quizzical stare. "Are you always this aggressive with policemen?"

I smiled, as sweet as I could, in spite of being a long way from home, running from the police, and suffering from jet lag.

"Only the ones who are thousands of miles outside of their jurisdiction."

He shrugged. "I could, of course, request assistance from Britain's Art Theft division . . ."

"Why don't you do that? And in the meantime, go find another seat. The one you're on is reserved for a human being."

He held up his hands. "I surrender."

"Too late, I don't take prisoners. And I've been threatened by the best, so please try to be civil."

We stared at each other, me exasperated and ready to erupt, him trying to figure out how to approach without getting bitten.

Never able to stand silence, I spoke first.

"Look, you obviously want to ask me some questions, I have a few myself. We can either trade or we can talk about the weather. So let's start with why you're tracking me."

"That should be obvious. Fatima Sari. She was on a watch list we share with Interpol and the FBI. You went on the same list after the incident in the subway station. When you bought a ticket for London in New York, that information was conveyed to me and I got on a plane in Cairo."

I nodded. "And within seconds of calling to reserve a train seat after I got into the taxi at Heathrow, the reservation hit the wonderful World Wide Web and you bought a ticket to Salisbury."

"We live in a connected world."

"Isn't that wonderful—this digital age bringing us all closer together?"

"Like your shadow."

"A monkey on my back is more like it," I said.

❖

That got a chuckle from him. He had nice teeth, very white. And nice lips, full and inviting.

"I'm sorry I put you through so much trouble," I said. "Next time just give me a call and I'll tell you who I'm going to murder next."

❖

23

❖

I immediately regretted making a joke about the woman's death.

"Okay, you didn't need to come all this way to talk to me," I said. "Anything I have to say to you could have been done by a short text message that said, 'I know nothing.' So why don't you go back to Cairo and save your department all the money you're spending on a wild-goose chase."

"This is a serious matter, Miss Dupre," he said brusquely.

"To you, not me. Whatever poor Ms. Sari, you, the Egyptian government, or the ghosts of avenging pharaohs have going, I'm not a part of it."

"Why did you meet with Fatima in New York?"

"I didn't *meet* with her. If you have been in contact with the New York police, you already know as much about it as I do. She knocked on my door and tried to stab me, then threw herself in front of a subway train while babbling about something. I don't have the faintest notion as to why she chose me other than that it must have been a case of mistaken identity."

He raised his eyebrows. "Mistaken identity? She had your business card on her."

❖

"I wasn't referring to the fact that she didn't know who I was, but that she was wrong about what she thought I was involved in."

"What did she think you were involved in?"

"If you want to play games, please find someone else to do it with."

He held up his hands again, this time palms forward to ward off an attack. "Okay, you're right, we know that she was involved with an attempt to return a national treasure to my country. But what was she babbling about?"

"I don't know. She spoke a few words in English and then reverted to Arabic. Something about a curse." I gave him a blunt look. "But I'm sure you already know the answer to that. If you don't, use some of that wonderful electronic gadgetry that you're using to keep track of my every move and e-mail the New York cop in charge of the investigation."

"This is your idea of exchanging information? I'm sorry we got off on the wrong foot. I have already admitted that attempting to intimidate you with official authority isn't the best way to win cooperation."

"Oh, no, I intimidate just fine. I just don't know anything. And I've discovered that while lying to a policeman just gets their adrenaline up, they hate it when you really don't know anything."

"Please do me a favor and tell me what you do know—and don't assume I know everything already."

I leaned forward and tried to look sincere. Now I wanted the man to go away. "Okay, this is the truth and the whole truth. I opened my apartment door and a woman I never saw before tried to stab me. She never told me why and I don't know why.

"A few hours later I was standing in a subway station. A woman I had never seen before until she tried to stab me came toward me talking irrationally about a curse. Why she approached me and had my card on her, I honestly don't know. I had been consulted and retained by someone else about the scarab. I assume that was how she knew about me." I leaned forward and gave him a tight grin. "Satisfied?"

"Who retained you?"

"I'm not at liberty to disclose that. As I'm sure you know, art is a cutthroat business that operates under a veil of privacy."

"What has he hired you to do?"

❖

"I am not at liberty to disclose what *he*—or *she*—has consulted me about."

"Bedouins of my country would call you a dry well when it comes to information."

My turn to get exasperated again. "You see—it's history repeating itself. You assume I'm being deceptive because I don't know why the woman approached me and can't disclose my client's name. What's the nature of your investigation?"

"I'm not at liberty to disclose that."

"I guess that means you're lying."

He looked away, pursing his lips. I had the impression he was trying to keep from laughing.

"Okay, Miss Dupre—may I call you Madison now that we're old friends?"

"My old friends call me Maddy, but you can call me Miss Dupre."

"Maddy, as you have already guessed, my investigation revolves around a certain national treasure—"

"Why don't you just call it the Heart of Egypt? Isn't that what this is all about?"

He merely gave me a polite smile, but I got the drift. For whatever reasons, he wasn't able to reveal that he was searching for the Heart of Egypt even though he knew that I knew that he knew. . . .

It never failed to amaze me that I could be so smart and poor and the politicians running this world were so rich and stupid.

"Let's get down to the bottom line. Tell me what you want from me before my jet lag pulls my brain out of my nose like they did when they mummified your pharaohs."

"I will give you the laundry list. Who has employed you? What has he—or she—said to you about the Egyptian national treasure that is missing? In essence, tell me everything you know about the artifact, its present location, and what services you have been retained to perform."

"The answers to your questions are that nothing I am doing, have done, or plan to do, involve any violation of the laws of Britain, Egypt, or my own country."

❖

"That is simply being evasive. The New York authorities believe that Fatima Sari came there to ask your help in marketing the stolen artifact."

"Ah . . . you think she stole the scarab herself? Faked a robbery? Well, I can clue you in on this: the woman who tried to kill me, kill herself, or whatever she was doing, looked terrorized, and I can assure you that the person or persons who did the terrorizing were the thieves who took the scarab from her. If I were you, I'd be looking into a big league art theft organization, not the pathetic woman who threw herself in front of a subway train."

"Why do you have so much sympathy for a stranger who tried to kill you?" he asked.

"Because when I looked into her eyes, I saw fear. Now, if you don't mind, I'm going to close my eyes and try to get some sleep."

I got up and grabbed my bag to find another seat.

"Maddy, please, you're playing a dangerous game and you don't know all the rules or the players. You need my help."

"What are you offering?"

"Good advice. Tell me everything you know and return to New York where you will be safe."

"Rather than leaving it to you and the New York police to decide my fate, I think I'll stick with the Bible—knowing the truth is what sets us free."

"Please keep your seat," he said. "I'll find another."

A thought buzzed in my dense head as I sat back down. He hadn't mentioned Mounir Kaseem, but I was pretty certain he knew who had hired me.

I didn't know what that meant, but I did come to one conclusion about the conversation: my right knee was shaking and my heart was beating faster.

Something was said between us that triggered that primordial sense of fear that each of us have deep inside.

I thought about it as the train sped toward the strange and mystical Salisbury Plain where the Radcliff estate was located.

The Salisbury Plain was a somewhat bleak, windswept region with

❖

rolling hills, grasslands, and occasional stands of trees. The area was rich in history and archaeological sites, including Stonehenge, Old Sarum, a hill fort that was inhabited more than 5,000 years ago, and 2,000-year-old Roman roads.

Somehow it seemed appropriate that an ancient Egyptian stone that can stir the emotions of millions with its mystical allure would be found in a land haunted by the ghosts of Druids and Celts.

I had just started to doze off when I suddenly snapped awake, aware of what had been said that triggered the bone-chilling fear inside me— the look in Fatima's eyes. I saw hurt, anger, confusion, but most of all, a deep sense of horror and repulsion, as if she had been forced to witness the unthinkable. Or perhaps experienced it herself.

I had an insight about my own situation.

I was scared.

24

❖

The art dealer who met me at the Salisbury train station to escort me
to the Radcliff estate looked like he had slipped through a crack in time
from a more elegant age.

Sir Georges-Hamilton Edgeways was waiting for me as I stepped
off the London train. He didn't offer to shake hands, but tipped his hat
and offered his arm.

I surrendered my small carry-on to a porter he had arranged for
because I didn't want to offend his old-fashioned charm. Besides, after
dealing with a death, a lying client, and cops on two continents, I was
happy to be in the hands of someone whose eccentricities ran to fashion
and manners.

A chauffer-driven 1930 red Rolls-Royce Phantom II with black fend-
ers was waiting for us outside. The chauffer was also a throwback to the
1930s, right up to the snobbery he radiated.

The art dealer looked as much a period piece as the car in a vested
wool gray suit and derby hat, striped tie, a purple handkerchief erupting

❖

out of his breast pocket, and a gold watch chain. Gray spats over his black shoes finished off the vintage couture look.

The cane in his hand with a fancy ivory head seemed more of a fashion accessory than something used for walking. I was almost tempted to ask him if the cane had a secret sword.

I suppose the car and clothes were advertising badges. They certainly would make him memorable to his clients.

I'd heard of Sir Georges-Hamilton but had never dealt with him during my high-flying days in the trade. I'm sure he'd heard of me, but he pointedly didn't mention anything about the indelible impression on British art that I made when I ran from the most prestigious art gallery in the country as it was blowing up behind me.

Happy that my tainted past wasn't discussed, as we were chauffeured to the estate I learned a bit about the rich, pampered, and slightly odd Heather Radcliff who sounded like she had too much money, too many neuroses, and not enough common sense.

Regardless of whether you believed Stonehenge to be spiritually powerful, the stark landscape of the Salisbury Plain had a mystic, almost haunted feel for me and I wondered how Heather Radcliff felt about it.

I shared that question with Sir Georges-Hamilton.

"She spends most of her time in London, Monte Carlo, Manhattan, and wherever else people with enormous amounts of money and the hangers-on that flutter around them can be found. However, I do suspect that since she was born not too many miles from Stonehenge that is one reason she is, shall we say, eccentric."

"Heather's not married?"

"Not as of yesterday, but she is full of surprises. By the way, Lady Radcliff prefers to be called Isis. She has changed her name legally to Isis because she believes she is a reincarnation of the Egyptian goddess."

"Hmm . . . interesting."

"Quite."

Eccentric was his euphemism I guess for her being rich and crazy. One of the perks of being rich is that you can afford to be crazy, but since I was broke and needed her cooperation, I didn't offer that observation.

❖

"You won't meet Lady Radcliff until she gets out of jail this after-noon," he said matter-of-factly.

"Jail?"

He checked his watch. "About now she and a group of other Druids are attempting to reclaim Stonehenge from the government as their sacred temple for religious rites. They will be arrested, processed, and released. And fined later."

"Her claim of ownership is that she's a Druid? Isn't she an Egyptian goddess?"

"Both, actually. Isis and her fellow Druids believe that Stonehenge was built by Egyptian priests who brought the practice of Druidism to Britain."

That made about as much sense as her claim to being the reincarnation of a goddess.

"I don't recall a historical link between Stonehenge, Druids, and Egypt, but I imagine the authorities would strongly object to Druid rites at the site since the ancient Druids practiced human sacrifice."

"I wouldn't offer that observation to Isis. Her spiritual advisor has assured her otherwise."

"I take it her spiritual advisor isn't the archbishop of Canterbury."

"For a certainty. Ramses is an interesting individual," Sir Georges-Hamilton said.

"He must be, since he's named after an Egyptian pharaoh. Another case of reincarnation?"

"Quite. And direct lineage to a Druid high priest who Ramses says built Stonehenge."

"I should have thought of that myself."

He cleared his throat. "I wouldn't want you to draw any negative impressions of Isis. Though she has gotten some rather negative publicity while trying to find herself, she is quite a fine lady, generous to the community, and a supporter of art."

"Supporter of art" meant he had sold her something.

"I take it this Druid business isn't the first cult experience she's had on her journey of self-discovery."

"Unfortunately not. She was orphaned at the age of four after her

❖

parents died in a plane crash and literally raised by trust lawyers who hired a secession of nannies to ensure she never became too attached to any of them. Considerable efforts were also necessary to fight off relatives after her money."

She sounded like a cross between a sad Christina Onassis and a frivolous Paris Hilton.

"She proves one of the fundamental laws of nature," I said. "The richer you are, the crazier you're allowed to be."

There I went again, opening my mouth. But I let that sink in and then asked, "Is there anything else about Isis and her clan of Druids that I should know so I don't offend her?"

"Yes. As you know, Isis was a goddess of love. You should be aware that Lady Radcliff–Isis is openly bisexual and quite liberal about sexual activities. She believes that sexual activity should not be prohibited regardless of age, gender, or relationship. "

"How about the family pets?"

25

❖

Before we arrived at Radcliff House I tried to get information about Mounir Kaseem from the art dealer and was surprised when he told me that he had never met the man or spoken to him.

"Ramses is the person whom Mr. Kaseem dealt with in regard to the scarab," he said.

Sir Georges-Hamilton also carefully avoided all discussion about the scarab, obviously distancing himself from the mess.

"Fuad Hassan, the curator of the Radcliff museum, will be able to answer all your questions."

Another runaround. I thought about asking him why he picked me up at the train station if he wasn't going to give me information, but I suspected I already knew the answer—he wanted to clue me in on Isis so I wouldn't do something reasonable like looking shocked when she started discussing ancient Egyptian spells, human sacrifice, humping with a camel, or whatever else she and her menagerie of parasites and weirdos were into.

I GOT MY FIRST glimpse of Radcliff House after the limo passed through a gate set in a medieval stone wall. The palatial manor house of weathered brick sat at the end of a long, straight cobblestoned road. The style was mostly Tudor and a little medieval castle, with a large gable on the right side and a turret with a circular top and crenellations.

Big and solid, old and stately, it appeared to have descended from many centuries of high nobility, though Sir Georges-Hamilton told me that it was built in the early 1900s.

My knight turned me over to the butler as soon as we entered and did a disappearing act.

"Ramses will see madam in the library," the haughty butler said. He could have played the villain in a 1930s mystery novel revolving around a murder in the library.

I wondered how much of the Hollywood theatrics Isis had inherited and how much she had cultivated herself.

Ramses was seated behind a desk, studying what looked to be an ancient manuscript.

Short and slender, with grave, narrow features and a closely shaven head, his thin face and nose remind me of a hawk. He wore a dark black Nehru jacket, a hip-length tailored coat with a band collar named after the Indian prime minister.

He wasn't Egyptian, although his light copper complexion gave him a Mediterranean look—perhaps southern Spanish or Italian.

Ramses didn't bother looking up as I approached and didn't bother returning my greeting when I said, "Good afternoon."

I could see the manuscript he seemed so engrossed in was written in ancient Greek, a language I had studied as part of my expertise in ancient Mediterranean artifacts, and I was almost tempted to see whether he really spoke the language, which I doubted, but reminded myself that I needed the money more than putting down the rude man.

Instead, I spun around and walked out of the library.

No one was in the great hall and I shouted out loud, "Hello! Butler!"

The servant suddenly appeared beside me.

❖

"Will you call me a taxi?"

"A taxi, madam?"

"Yes, a taxi."

Ramses came out of the library behind me.

"What do you think you're doing?" he demanded.

I looked him squarely in the eyes and said, "Since I've gotten involved in this mess less than forty-eight hours ago, I've seen a woman killed and I've been questioned by police on two continents. I'm in no mood for rudeness."

His mouth opened and closed as he tried to find words and then he turned to the butler and snapped, "Go on with your duties."

He was still struggling with something to say to me and finally got out, "Come," as he retreated back into the library.

It sounded like a command you say to a dog, but at least he didn't say fetch or roll over. I knew I had to change my attitude toward him but it wasn't easy.

Back in the library, I held out my hand. "Madison Dupre."

He looked like he'd rather spit on it than shake it, but he gave me a moist, slimy-feeling paw. My sentiment about his handshake might have been affected by the fact that I thought of him as a cockroach that I wanted to stamp and squash.

Ramses seated himself back down behind the Greek book and stared up at me with the small, false smile and suspicious eyes of a snake oil salesman.

I realized he wasn't just an arrogant bastard but was also wary of me and probably putting on a false front. Perhaps the situation with the scarab jeopardized his position as head guru or whatever he was to Isis.

He had a good thing going here—living the high life was better than selling shoes or whatever he did before he got reincarnated as an ancient pharaoh, but it was a lifestyle that could quickly change if his wacko protégée decided she was bored with being a goddess and found something else utterly weird to make herself look ridiculous.

My father would have said Ramses was like an snarling old dog who had jumped on the back of a meat wagon and ready to go for the throat of anyone who tried to drag him off.

❖

Mentioning the police earlier had probably gotten his immediate attention.

"Did Sir Georges-Hamilton advise you on how sensitive Isis is?" Ramses asked.

I was tempted to say that he told me she was a bisexual nympho into bestiality, but I decided to be nice and keep it straight. I sat down in one of the chairs in front of his desk before I answered him.

"Yes, he did. I really don't need to bother Isis. I understand that she has a curator who can provide me with information."

"Unfortunately, she learned you were coming and wants to meet you. She wants to be reassured that you will not defame her family name in any way."

"I have no intention of even mentioning her family name to anyone. I've just been hired to examine the scarab. When it's found, that is. Has there been any news about it?"

Ramses started to say something and stopped when the goddess herself came into the room.

26

❖

"Ramses, is this the woman you told me about? The American art person?"

Isis had an overloud, shrill voice. She floated toward me and absentmindedly shook my hand.

"You-you're supposed to be at Stonehenge," Ramses stammered, surprised by her appearance.

Sir Georges-Hamilton was with her.

"The stupid police refused to arrest me," she said. "They gave me a ticket for trespassing as if I had been driving a car."

Isis was thirtyish, skinny, with a narrow nose, thin lips, and unmanageable blond hair that probably always looked like it needed to be brushed.

She struck me as a hyper person, a bit scatterbrained, and even a little melancholy when I looked at her doleful eyes.

I would have bet that she had never read a book in her entire life. It went with the territory of upper-class British women who were intellectually uneducated except for attending an expensive finishing school

❖

as Princess Diana had done. Unlike Di though, I suspected that Isis had not risen above her lack of education.

"My great-grandfather was a thief," she told me, without waiting for confirmation of who I was. "Most of my ancestors were thieves, too. That's how great fortunes are built, don't you think?"

I started to tell her I didn't think, period, about her great-grandfather, but Ramses interrupted me.

"But we don't want you telling everyone that, do we? You're supposed to pretend that it was never stolen by your great-grandfather like your family has always pretended."

"Have you found the scarab yet?" Isis asked him. "I should never have let it be taken out of the vault. If it was to be returned to its spiritual home, I should have been the one to do it, not that incompetent woman. Now she's dead and the police will be asking questions."

Ramses swept in between us. "Miss Dupre has been advised as to how to deal with the old rumors about the scarab and she has to get to work now, doesn't she, Sir Georges?"

The dapper art dealer picked up the cue and ran with it, taking me out of the library with a firm grip on my arm.

Once we were outside the room, Sir Georges-Hamilton said, "I will introduce you to the curator." He gave me a sympathetic look and shook his head. "Sad, isn't it? All that money and she's really quite miserable."

"No. Sad is being broke and miserable."

27

❖

The great-granddad of Isis really was a robber baron when it came to antiquities. That was evident the moment I stepped into the museum wing of the palatial Radcliff house.

"There are private collections all over the world," the art dealer told me, "but few this large and valuable."

Although I saw a few Greek, Roman, and Babylonian pieces, the main focus of the museum was Egyptian.

Sir Georges-Hamilton introduced me to Curator Fuad Hassan and then did another one of his disappearing acts. He apparently had learned how to avoid trouble by slipping quietly away anytime it raised its ugly head.

Fuad appeared scholarly and honest. I liked him immediately.

A little mousey and fragile, he was paper-thin, with olive flesh pulled tightly over small bones. Gold-rimmed glasses were mounted on a small, stubby nose. His eyes reminded me of a rabbit that sticks its head out of its hole to check for rain before venturing out.

❖

He seemed a little overwhelmed by life and probably retreated into a museum like a monk cloistered in a monastery.

"Quite a mess, isn't it?" I said.

His eyes flinched back as if I'd slapped him, but then he gave me a look of pure gratitude.

"Thank you. No one has described it so accurately. One of the great treasures of my country, of the ancient world, has been lost—*stolen*—and the people in this house talk as if it was just a knickknack taken from the local antique shop."

He instantly shut up and turned around, as if he was looking for somewhere to hide his head. This was probably the most insubordinate that he'd been in his life.

"How did this ridiculous deception get started?" I asked. I wanted to test Kaseem's version against Fuad's.

"Miss Radcliff was persuaded to return the scarab to Egypt, where it rightly belongs."

I noticed he didn't use the name Isis.

"How was she persuaded?"

"I believe her advisor convinced her that the scarab carried a curse that had doomed her family and the curse was now keeping her from being happy."

Jesus, I thought. The only thing keeping the woman from being happy was that she had so much money; she needed to get a life.

I could see how it came down—Kaseem got to Ramses, with money, and had him sell Isis the curse story. I didn't unload the garbage on Fuad.

"Why did your assistant, Fatima Sari, agree to be the one to carry the scarab back to Egypt?"

His features softened and I saw the concern in his eyes. He trembled as he struggled to get control of his emotions. He obviously must have had some special feelings for her to be so overcome with sadness. Poor bastard, he was probably in love with her.

Quiet, reserved, even timid, and quite a bit older than Fatima, he no doubt had been completely unable to deal with either his feelings for her or his failure to come and save her when everything went south after the scarab was stolen from her.

❖

My heart immediately went out to him. His assistant had been in trouble, in danger, alone, and from what I could see, more than half crazy. He had probably tried to help her but what she needed was a knight in shining armor and all he probably offered was pleas for her to come home.

"She was really a good person," he said. "She loved the artifacts of our country, called them her children. It was that love that would doom her."

"Because she agreed to return the scarab?"

"Yes, she was thrilled at the opportunity when it was offered to her. Knowing that she would be the one who returned one of our greatest treasures to Egypt mesmerized her."

If I had been in her shoes, it would have enthralled me, too. No one who loved art would pass up the chance to return a national treasure to its home.

He appeared ready to break down. "Fatima was . . ."

"Too idealistic? Naïve?"

"Yes, yes, that is exactly right, she saw people and situations too often as she thought they should be, rather than as they were. The world is full of people who are greedy and corrupt. She had no sins, no faults. She only wanted to do good."

"So what went wrong?" I asked.

He waved his hands nervously. "Everything. It was all being done in secret. My advice was for Miss Radcliff to present the scarab to the Egyptian ambassador in London as part of a goodwill gesture, but she was convinced that it would be an admission that her ancestor had stolen it in the first place."

I could see his logic.

"Everybody already knew that Sir Jacob Radcliff pocketed the scarab anyway, so why go through the pretense."

"Precisely. They acted like children playing a game rather than dealing with a priceless artifact. They sent Fatima out with it in secret."

"What about security?"

"Hired from an agency who provides guards for social events. They were not professional art security. They didn't even know what they were protecting."

❖

"No one I've spoken to has told me how the scarab was taken from Fatima. Do you know?"

He shook his head. "Not all that happened. I got a call from her, she was hysterical. No . . . not just hysterical, confused—"

"Drugged?"

"Yes . . . yes, for a certainty. She was confused, stumbling over her words."

"When did the theft occur?"

"Sometime after Fatima retired. Everything was fine when she went to bed. The heart was in the hotel room safe. But when she woke up, the safe was open and the scarab gone. And she was confused, dazed."

"She had no idea of who might have drugged her? Been in her room last? Had a drink with in the hotel lounge before she went to bed?"

"She was a good Muslim, she didn't drink alcoholic beverages. And even though I recognized that she had been drugged, she did not."

"What did she think happened?"

"She didn't know. Her mind was mixed-up, as if she had been given something so potent that it was still affecting her thoughts hours later."

"Days later," I said. "When I saw her, she wasn't coherent in her thinking process."

"I know. I called her cell phone many times. At first she answered and I could tell she was not thinking correctly. I tried to get her to come home or even just tell me where she was so I could come and get her . . ."

He stopped, emotion swelling in him. He walked away for a moment before turning back to me.

"She was a sensitive person, fragile both in mind and body. When she called me she was traumatized and not just because she had been drugged. I believe the loss of the scarab broke her mind."

When I saw the woman she was very thin, almost anorexic. I'm sure she wouldn't have shed that much weight in the few days that had passed since she had been drugged. Obviously whoever drugged Fatima gave her too much, not realizing the effect it would have on a woman of such slight build.

"Who else knew that Fatima was returning the scarab to Egypt?"

He threw up his hands. "The whole world. It was supposed to be a secret, but the servants and the gardeners knew it, which meant the grocer, the butcher, the baker, and so on also knew it."

The hurt etched on his face grew. He appeared ready to tear up. "When you last saw Fatima, did she . . . did she . . ."

"She didn't suffer, if that's what you mean. She was killed instantly. She probably didn't even know what hit her."

I liked Fuad and was tempted to tell him that he should get away from the Radcliff house and the insanity and intrigues as soon as possible, but he saved me the trouble.

"I will share a secret with you," he said. "I am leaving my job here as curator for the museum. I have given Miss Radcliff notice and will leave after she is able to hire another curator for the collection. I have been loyal to her despite everything that has happened."

"Have things changed since Ramses has come on board?" I asked.

He grimaced. "Very much so. He—he influences Miss Radcliff and I believe not in a beneficial way."

"That's probably an understatement. Have you heard of Svengali?"

He shook his head.

"He's a character from a novel. The name has come to characterize someone who dominates and manipulates another person for their own purpose. I see Ramses as her Svengali."

"He would sell the collection for a pittance and pocket the money," Fuad whispered. "He knows nothing about art. I'm sure he was paid to manipulate Miss Radcliff with that ridiculous story about a curse."

He turned away from me again. "I'm sorry, I probably have said too much."

"No, you've just told the truth about a bad situation."

"It's my duty to serve Miss Radcliff until my replacement is found. I must not be disloyal."

Pretty sure I had gotten all the information out of him about Fatima, I asked him what he could tell me about the scarab.

"I'll show you what we have."

He handed me pictures of the scarab, which told me little about it because they were not the professional shots a museum would have taken to identify the scarab in case it had been stolen.

❖

The heart was short, broad, and ugly, as all scarabs were.

I thought about the insect and its importance to the Egyptians as I looked at the pictures.

People who see a scarab for the first time find it strange that the personification of the dung beetle is a significant source of the mystery and magic of ancient Egypt, and that a bug who waddled in excrement was worshipped as the symbol of rebirth after death.

The beetle lived off the dropped excrement of animals, grabbing a piece of the stuff, forming it into a ball, and rolling it off to a hole in the ground or inside a dead animal where the dung was used as food. Eggs were wrapped in dung, too, for nourishment, so life appeared to come from the inanimate animal droppings.

Because it appeared to the Egyptians that the beetles were reborn from dead matter, and the way they rolled the round balls that were used to create life, they identified the beetle with Khepri, a god who rolled the ball-shaped sun across the sky during the day. At the end of the day the sun was swallowed by Nut, goddess of the sky, and reemerged from her womb the next day, mimicking the birth of beetles from dark mass.

Death and rebirth became a ubiquitous theme in the minds and art of the ancient Egyptians, with the death and rebirth cycle of the beetle symbolic of it. King Tut's tomb wasn't just rich in material possessions, but had been stocked with food and other provisions he would need when he was reborn.

"I realize the pictures are not of the best quality. Here," he said, handing me a scarab. "This is the most important item. Other than it being only a few years old, rather than a few thousand, it is an exact replica of the Heart of Egypt."

The scarab was made of the same grade of Afghan blue lapis lazuli with a brushing of a very fine gold pyrite like I had observed on the pictures.

"The surest way to tell if it's a counterfeit," I said, "would be to compare the pattern of the gold dusting with the pattern on the original. It would be impossible to make a model that had exactly the same pattern as the original even if it came from the mining site. Or even if it came from the same piece of rock," I added.

❖

"Yes, of course, the patterns would look the same to the naked eye, but a closer examination would show differences."

"Are there better pictures available?"

"There are, but I don't have them here."

I took a thorough look at the scarab he gave me.

"You know, this is an excellent reproduction," I said. "If you hadn't told me this was a copy, I would've taken it to be a three-thousand-year-old artifact from the tomb of King Tut."

Its connection to the boy king was obvious: Tut's name signed in hieroglyphics appeared on its back.

After examining it for a moment, I still had the same impression—that I was looking at a piece of antiquity. But as I had told Kaseem, reproductions are often so good they are extremely difficult to sort out. The counterfeiter who did this one not only used the correct Afghan stone, I had no doubt that a microscopic examination would show it was carved with the type of tools used in antiquity. Without the real scarab to make a comparison with, the key to revealing it was a copy would be a chemical analysis of the patina on the stone that usually formed over the ages.

"Howard Carter had a method for determining whether a piece was an artifact or a reproduction," I said. "He placed the item where he would see it during the day. After a few days he knew whether it was real or a fake.

"I think Carter would have reached the same conclusion I did about this piece—it looks real; nothing's screaming at me that says it isn't, so it'll take more than a brief examination to determine that it's a fake. Unlike Carter's day, there are lab tests we can do."

He suddenly gave me a small smile.

"There is a quicker way," he said and offered me a magnifying glass. "Something about the appearance of the scarab may tell you it is a reproduction."

I felt like a schoolgirl being tested, but he was a sweet little man and I didn't want to disappoint him.

"I'll use my own," I said, as I took out the jeweler's loupe from my purse and started examining the piece.

Nothing on the top or the sides shouted fake at me. On the bottom

❖

I found a tiny mark, a swirl, that would have been visible to the naked eye only if you knew to look for it. Even at that, making out the detail of the swirl required a magnifying glass.

I guessed the purpose.

"The reproduction is so good, the maker put a mark on it so you see a difference from the original . . . but not easily, you'd still have to double-check it under magnification. They used a swirl pattern so the mark could be distinguished from marks created accidentally."

He grinned and clapped his hands. "Yes, yes, it's a pattern that would not be duplicated accidentally by people or nature. I put it on myself. Not even the counterfeiter knows I did this."

"Is the weight also the same?"

"Exactly the same," he said.

"So the reproduction was made for public display?" I asked.

"Yes. Miss Radcliff used to show the real heart to guests. But after a couple of incidents in which robbers stole from private collections like ours, I convinced her to have reproductions of the most valuable and ir-replaceable pieces created for public display, while the real pieces were kept in a vault."

Reproductions were common among private collectors for the reason Fuad stated and for insurance coverage. With artwork selling commonly in the tens of millions, and even more than a hundred million for a single item sometimes, the cost of insuring the "priceless" was enormous.

Most collectors would have loaned their pieces to museums for safe-keeping and to let other people enjoy them, but altruism didn't appear to run in the Radcliff family.

"How many reproductions of the scarab were made?" I asked.

"From the original only this one, but there are many other copies in existence. You can buy them at any marketplace in Egypt, but they are tourist junk, with the appearance based upon conjecture because there are no public photos of the heart."

"No photos were taken back when Carter opened Tut's tomb?"

"There is a story that the heart was photographed, as were other items, but the pictures of items that never made their way to the Egyptian Museum were destroyed by the men who helped themselves to

❖

what they called mere tokens of the greatest archaeological find in history."

Photos of that era would have been black-and-white and of poor quality compared to the ones today. They would also have been evidence that the heart existed and was missing.

"Who made this replica?"

"A firm in Bath run by a gentleman with a rather colorful history. He was once imprisoned for counterfeiting a van Gogh that sold for millions. When he got out of prison, he turned his talents to making reproductions for legitimate purposes."

"Well, at least he put his talent to good use. Can I take this copy with me to compare it with the scarab presented as the original?"

"I'm afraid not. Miss Radcliff wishes to keep it here in the collection. She plans to show it to her friends after the heart is returned and a great deal of publicity is generated . . . to prove she had given up the original for the sake of the Egyptian people."

He didn't hide the sarcasm in his voice.

"Did the counterfeiter take pictures of the heart?"

"Yes, those are the ones I mentioned. He never had the heart in his workshop. He examined it here under my supervision several times and took pictures to use when he needed to."

"Good. I'm sure he would've taken really high-quality pictures. I'll need them. They should show the pattern of the gold dusting well enough to distinguish the original from a copy."

"I will call and have them sent over."

"I'd rather pick them up myself in Bath," I said. "It'll give me an excuse to have scones with clotted cream at the Roman baths."

I also wanted an excuse to talk to the counterfeiter. Fuad saw the scarab with a professional eye, but not even the best curator saw artifacts with the penetrating vision of an artistic counterfeiter. I wanted to make sure that Fuad was right and that only one perfect copy existed of the heart.

He showed me other scarabs in a glass case. I got the impression he was stalling for time as he gathered his thoughts. He stared down at the pieces in the case as he spoke.

❖

"The heart belongs to my people," he said.

"True. And you have a good chance of getting it back. The thieves can't sell a well-known work of art. Their only hope is to ransom it and that's why I was retained—to make sure the scarab is the genuine article."

"I know that you once fought to get a looted artifact back to the people of Iraq. Will you do the same with the Heart of Egypt?"

"That's my intention. I wouldn't have taken this assignment if I thought it would end up anywhere but where it belongs."

I had the feeling he wanted to tell me something. He started to speak and stopped as we heard the door in the other room open.

"Would you like to join me for lunch and continue our discussion?" I asked.

"Unfortunately, I am tied up here for the rest of the day." He gently put his hand on my arm. "Will you be in the area tomorrow evening?"

"I think so."

"There's a Druid fair near Stonehenge. Fatima and I used to go to it every year. We stand at the medieval tower overlooking the grounds and watch the people from above. Perhaps then we can talk some more."

"What time shall I meet you?"

"After dark," he said.

So we wouldn't be seen?

28

❖

I took the train to Bath, less than an hour's run, half expecting Rafi al Din, the Egyptian antiquities cop, to sit down across from me, but he didn't appear, much to my surprise. However, my gut told me he was still around . . . and not very far from me.

I tried calling Michelangelo to find out if he had any more information about the subway tape but he didn't pick up, so I left a message asking him if he was avoiding me.

Before heading out to see the counterfeiter, I checked into a small hotel and then paid a visit to one of my favorite places in Britain—the Roman ruins.

Aquae Sulis, the waters of Sulis, is what the Romans called the hot springs at Bath. Finding Britain's weather cold and damp, the conquerors from sunny Italy built a spectacular spa on the spot, the only thermal springs in the country. Though much abused and neglected over most of the last couple thousand years, the baths have now been restored.

The ruins come not only with history, but a place to have scones with

❖

clotted cream and strawberry jam, good British tea, and gentle music from violins and bass to listen to.

I was enjoying the music and scones when I got a jarring note—in the form of a chit, a rather old-fashioned way to convey a message.

The waiter handed me a scribbled note that read: "May I join you?"

"It's from the gentleman in the leather jacket," the waiter said, pointing to Rafi al Din, sitting in a corner behind me. He must have arrived after I had.

I smiled and nodded.

"I hope you don't mind," he said.

"Much better than a text message that sounds like it was composed by a nine-year-old computer geek. Actually, I expected to see you on the train."

"I had to do some business in Bath."

"And purely by chance ran into me here?"

He leaned forward and spoke in a faux-whisper. "I knew you were here because I'm a detective."

"So you talked to Fuad, who told you I'd come here. Which means you know I'm here to see the man who made a reproduction of the scarab."

It didn't surprise me that the Radcliff curator would cooperate, even secretly, with his homeland's antiquities department.

He shook his head. "Maddy, it's difficult for me to do my detecting if you are always one step ahead of me."

"I doubt that. What do you know about the counterfeiter? Fuad said he spent time in prison for fraud."

"That is about the extent of my knowledge, also. He makes copies for rich people so they can hide their originals from thieves. I'm sure it makes their insurance companies happy."

"Did your government ever attempt to buy the scarab from Isis?"

"We don't pay ransom. We requested the return of the stolen artifact on many occasions. There may have been some discussion about compensating the Radcliff family even though it had been stolen."

"In the antiquity trade," I said, "the word 'stolen' has different connotations than it does elsewhere. From Sir Jacob Radcliff's point of view and the others who spent years financing excavations in Egypt, your

❖

government violated their rights when it changed the terms of their agreement after the biggest find in history was made.

"I'm sure you know that almost immediately after the treasure was discovered, Carter and his colleagues became embroiled in a controversy with the government over division of the artifacts."

"We obviously have a different view of what occurred," he said. "By the terms of the concession agreement signed with Carter's group, if the tomb was found to be intact, my government could deny the excavators a share of the objects recovered. And since King Tutankhamen's tomb was in fact intact, that gave us the right to void the contract.

"Even though that was the position my government took, a large amount of money was paid to reimburse the concessionaires."

"An amount that didn't equal a fraction of the value of the find," I replied.

He was about to rebut my opinion but I didn't give him the chance to respond. "Don't get me wrong. I'm happy that Egypt kept most of the King Tut treasures. I'm just pointing out that it wasn't a case of greedy exploiters trying to get something they had no right to."

Rafi shrugged. "The dilemma in my country has always been the choice between bread and history. Every dollar spent on finding and preserving our antiquities is food out of the mouths of our people. That was how it was in the past and how it is even now—the majority of my people have little but the dirt between their toes while a small group of the rich live like kings."

"Unfortunately, that describes most of the third world."

Even as I said it, it occurred to me that "third world" is really a term that should be forgotten. Wide-scale travel and the Internet has made it one world.

"We can't afford to spend hundreds of millions of dollars ransoming antiquities from museums and collectors," he said. "Right now, besides the Heart of Egypt, the Supreme Council is demanding back the bust of Nefertiti from the Berlin Museum, the Rosetta Stone from the British Museum, and the Dendera Zodiac from the Louvre. Plus hundreds more around the world.

"Those are some of the greatest historical treasures in existence,

❖

but the scarab also has great political significance. It was discovered during a time when nationalism was rising in an attempt to throw off British dominance. Its disappearance has become a symbol of my country's loss of its heritage and political power."

Kaseem had essentially told me the same thing. I would have dropped Kaseem's name on him to learn what he knew about the man, but didn't dare betray the trust until I knew for sure that Kaseem had lied to me.

"I told you that the Supreme Council has tried on a number of occasions to get Isis, and other family members before her, to return the scarab to Egypt. Not willing to give up possession of one of the world's most precious relics, the family always turned a deaf ear to the request."

"Perhaps you should have tried another line of persuasion."

He raised his eyebrows. "Like telling her it was cursed?"

Something else he had learned from the curator.

"Someone beat you to that one, but since she's so superstitious you might have wrestled it from her if you told her you'd throw a curse tablet into the waters at Bath."

"A curse tablet?"

"A thin piece of metal with a curse scratched on it, usually asking the gods to damn an enemy. Archaeologists found a number of them here at the baths, but they were found all over the Greco-Roman world."

"I'll try to remember that when my supervisor fails to give me the promotion I deserve."

"Who do you think stole the scarab from Fatima?" I asked, not expecting an honest answer from him.

"If I knew, I would not be here begging for your help."

Begging? I tried to keep from laughing. It was more threats than pleas.

"Okay . . . but you must have a theory," I said.

"A gang of professional thieves? Colombian drug gangs have discovered that art is a type of international currency they can use to launder money with. How about an inside job? Perhaps the mummy itself returned for its heart. I will find out if Tutankhamen left his sarcophagus at the museum."

❖

"You know, Rafi, I was just beginning to warm up to you, but here you go again, reverting to cop talk and jokes to avoid disclosing anything. As long as your notion of sharing information is for me to tell you everything I know and you to tell me nothing, you can direct your questions in the future to the mummy."

I got up and he rose with me.

"Maddy, I told you we don't pay ransom. But we do pay finder's fees."

"How much do you pay?"

"That wouldn't be my decision. But I suspect that my superiors would not be adverse to paying a reasonable reward if the scarab was found and turned over to us. Did you have a figure in mind?"

"Not really. Besides, getting involved with thieves of an antiquity would make me lose my self-respect." I didn't add, however, that if Kaseem ended up cheating me out of my fee, I would not hesitate to get compensation from the Egyptian government.

"Rafi, I know you're just trying to do your job. Frankly, it would be a lot easier for you if you believed me. You think I know more than I'm letting on, maybe even that I know where the scarab is, but you're wrong, I don't. If by some miracle I came into possession of it, I would send it back to Egypt. Is that good enough to get you to forget I exist?"

"Absolutely. Will you have dinner with me now?"

"No. And you're lying about getting off my back."

"Yes, though I'm sure it's a very lovely back." He smiled.

I noticed his left earlobe was clipped. It added to his tough look.

"Gunshot?" I asked.

"Hungry rat when I was a kid," he said.

That piece of information told me that he reached his position through work and not family standing.

He had a scar across his nose. I didn't dare ask him about that one, but he volunteered when he saw me looking at it.

"Ex-wife," he said.

We each made an excuse about what we planned to do for the rest of the day and parted, though I at least told the truth about visiting the spa again.

❖

It has always struck me that the universe, Mother Earth, and life seemed to operate in circles, which I guess is why they say what goes around, comes around.

I knew the first time I met Rafi al Din that it wouldn't be the last time I saw him. I had a feeling as I left to visit the art counterfeiter that Rafi and I would circle around to meet again.

On one level, I didn't balk at the notion of seeing him again. He was an attractive man.

What always puzzled me about my choice in men was how many bad mistakes I made as I kept spinning around the circle of life, meeting and discarding men.

In my financial condition, I should be offering myself as a foot warmer to a man with a Rolls-Royce limo like Sir Georges-Hamilton rather than a cop who had gotten his ear bitten off by a rat and his nose busted by an ex-wife, who no doubt had adequate provocation.

29

❖

The counterfeiter's lair was a small, two-story Georgian-era box with decorative plasters on the front and an elaborate cornice capping off the front of the roof. The grayish brown brick building had a weathered patina that showed it was aging with grace even though its appearance as a whole needed a bit of a touch-up.

Curtains on the two windows of the second floor gave me the impression that he lived above his shop, while the large window in front looked like it hadn't been cleaned since the Napoleonic Wars.

I suspected he preferred it that way. Dirty windows suited the purpose of a man who worked in a secretive trade. So did the simple tarnished bronze plaque near the front door that quietly read, BOTWELL.

Duplicating rare treasures to protect them from thieves wasn't exactly the type of business someone advertises to the public at large. Nor would the customer want it known that they had a counterfeit made.

I expected Jeremy Botwell to have grim eyes and a prison pallor. Instead he was tall and lanky with a broad nose, thin blondish hair, and

❖

bright rosaceous cheeks. He struck me more as a schoolteacher than the criminal counterfeiter he had once been.

Criminals, of course, are also subject to the theory of law that what goes around, comes around. Which means most are repeat offenders. That made Botwell my chief suspect for masterminding the theft of the Heart of Egypt.

From what I knew about Fatima Sari, in an excited moment she might have told him about the plan to return the scarab to its homeland.

Botwell was dressed as an artisan: khaki pants, brown shirt, tennis shoes, all stained with paints and dyes.

I had arranged for Fuad to give Botwell exactly three minutes' notice that I would be picking up the photos. When I left the taxi a block from the shop, I called Fuad to tell him to make his call to Botwell.

The procedure had raised Fuad's eyebrows but he grinned when I told him why: I didn't want to give Botwell an opportunity to make a copy of the photos before I arrived.

The photos were on a laptop computer that Botwell had brought to the Radcliff museum and that Fuad had seen backed up on a flash drive. It wasn't a sure thing, but I planned to tell Botwell that Heather Radcliff had insisted that he turn over the photos to me and erase any copies he had.

Botwell had not been happy when upon entering I immediately asked for copies of the pictures and for him to erase all of the other copies while I stood by.

He looked ready to tell me to shove off, but I smiled sweetly and said, "I understand that Heather plans to have you duplicate quite a number of pieces. She just wants to make sure that hers are the only copies in existence."

The promise of money softened him enough to copy the pictures onto a flash drive that I had brought and then I watched as he erased the pictures off his computer and flash drive as we stood on either side of a wood counter on the first floor of his shop.

He claimed no prints had been made.

Fuad mentioned Botwell had an assistant named Quintin Rees

❖

who had helped produce the reproduction of the scarab, but I didn't see or hear anyone else in the shop as I was talking to Botwell.

"Does Mr. Rees have a copy of the pictures?" I asked.

"No," he answered immediately. "If that's all, I need to get back to my work."

"Actually, Miss Radcliff had a few other questions about the reproduction you made."

"I don't make reproductions," he snapped, "I make duplicate originals."

"Having seen your work, I don't doubt it. It would have taken a scientific test to determine that the scarab you made was a fake."

He scoffed. "It would have passed the test. I use stone from where the original object would have been quarried and get many slabs to make a perfect match."

I knew a perfect match wasn't possible when there are thousands of tiny flakes of gold-covered dust scattered in a piece, but I didn't correct him.

"I shape it only with the same type of tools used by the ancients. I do my own chemical analysis of the patina to make sure my mix will match. When I'm finished, God wouldn't be able to tell the difference," he said with pride in his voice.

Like all crooks—and ex-crooks—Botwell believed he was infinitely more clever than the rest of us. Apparently he hadn't been clever enough one time to stay out of jail.

"Was a second duplicate made?" I asked.

"No. Of course not. I never do that, I do honest work. I need to get back to work now."

I don't know why I bothered to ask the question, it just popped out, but his response pinged false in the lie detector at the back of my head.

"Is your assistant available? Miss Radcliff wanted me to ask him some questions."

"He's gone. No longer works here."

"Why?"

"Why is none of your business."

❖

I could see he was ready to throw me out if I asked another question. I had run the Radcliff promise of business as far as it would go.

It was time for another turn of the screw.

"Mr. Botwell, I know you do incredible work, and what I've seen was pure genius. But a problem has arisen. I'm a private inquiry agent—"

"Take your inquiries elsewhere."

"Who has been called in by Miss Radcliff to investigate the matter. Unless she gets some answers that satisfy her, I'm afraid her next call will be to Scotland Yard's Art and Antiquities Theft unit."

"I had nothing to do w-with-with anything," he stammered.

"So you knew about the theft?"

"Theft? What theft? I'm talking about the copy the woman wanted."

"What woman?"

"I don't know. She was Middle Eastern."

"Fatima Sari?"

"No, of course not, I know Fatima. It was another woman, but she had a dark complexion like Fatima."

"Egyptian?"

"I don't know. She came in one day and asked us to do a copy of the heart scarab. I wouldn't do it and sent her packing."

"You said she asked 'us.' She asked Quintin Rees, also?"

"She spoke to him first, yes. But I sent her packing."

I nodded and chewed on my lip. Botwell sent her packing, but what did Rees do?

"Your assistant spoke with her. Privately."

It wasn't a question.

Botwell surrendered.

"Look, I used to make things and sell them as something they weren't, but I found the perfect business for me doing it the honest way. I am straight, you understand. But that worthless scum has a drug problem and a drinking one. I was going to get rid of him anyway, but when I found out he talked to the woman on his own outside of the shop, I fired him immediately."

"Did he take a copy of the photos with him?"

"No."

His answer didn't sound too convincing.

"Tell me more about this other woman. Her name?"

He threw up his hands. "We weren't introduced. Never got as far as getting names."

"What did she look like?"

"I told you, Middle Eastern, dark hair, maybe in her late twenties. That's all I know. I told her no, showed her the door, she never came back."

"How did you know Quintin talked to her?"

"His wife. She called here in a rage saying Quintin had been out all night with some bitch who wanted him to make a copy of a scarab. His wife wanted me to tell her who the woman was."

"Did the woman say why she wanted the copy made?"

"Said she collects Egyptian stuff."

"I need to talk to Quintin. How can I contact him?"

"You'll find him in the gutter, rehab again, or on his way back to the gutter."

"Thanks for all your help."

I was on my way out the door when he said, "Hey, why don't you ask Radcliff's curator? The woman said Fuad sent her, but when I called him, he denied it. Lied to me, he did. I've lied enough times myself to know one when I hear it."

I was speechless.

"Shut the door on your way out."

30

❖

I dutifully shut the door behind me and walked up the street with questions, facts, and theories bumping into one another in my head like jalopies at a demolition derby.

Quintin was gone. He obviously made duplicates of the pictures. He'd made a copy of the heart for a woman. And Fuad might have sent her.

The question burning in my mind, though, was why the mystery woman wanted a copy of the scarab.

Was she one of the thieves, planning to tender the copy rather than the original when a deal was cut? For what purpose? No one was going to pay a second ransom if the thieves reneged on the promise to hand it over.

The more I thought about it, the more I realized that passing off the copy might work in some scenarios.

There were two very interested buyers for the heart—Kaseem and the Egyptian government. While the government would pay a hefty amount for the scarab, it wouldn't match the millions that Kaseem was willing to pay.

❖

Still, picking up another million from the government for the gang of thieves or herself would be clever. It could be done by offering the scarab to both Kaseem and the government at the same time. And collecting from both, passing one as the copy and the other the original.

If the mystery woman was in fact in with the thieves, she might even have planned a double cross with the copy: switch it for the original and collect the ransom herself.

My gut and paranoia were churning with conspiracy theories, but there were too many possibilities to nail one down.

I needed to find out who this mysterious woman was and why she wanted a copy of the scarab made.

I called the Radcliff manor house and asked to speak to the curator.

"Fuad, why did you tell me only one copy of the scarab was made?"

I took his stunned silence as an admission of guilt.

"I can't talk right now," he said in a hushed tone. "But believe me, please, I—I—"

"I know you would never do anything to hurt Fatima or keep the scarab from being returned. Who is the woman who had the copy made?"

"I can't talk now," he said in a barely audible tone.

"Fuad, I need to—"

"Tomorrow night, eight o'clock, at the fair."

He hung up before I could say any more.

What was that all about? I wondered. What had he gotten himself mixed up in?

Quintin Rees was my next objective. If I found him, I knew I could get all the information I needed because he had a habit and I had the money for his next fix.

❖

31

❖

I was in a taxi on the Royal Crescent, but too engrossed in a brown study to appreciate that the street is one of the most picturesque in Britain, when Michelangelo called.

"Thanks for returning my many calls," I said.

"Blame it on the time difference. You only call when this part of the world is asleep."

"Have you e-mailed me a copy of the subway tape?"

"I haven't got a copy yet."

Something in his voice told me that wasn't the end of the subject.

"What did that subway cop tell you now? That I pulled out a gun and shot the woman before she took her dive?"

"I saw the tape. It's inconclusive."

"*What?*"

I startled the taxi driver and he jerked the wheel.

"Calm down," Michelangelo said.

"What are you talking about? I told you I never touched the woman."

❖

"The problem is it's a small station with only one camera. The woman was between you and the camera. Your arm comes up—"

"I told you I never touched her."

"And I'm telling you that you can't see that on the tape. She's between you and the camera."

"Are you telling me that I'm in trouble because the damn city's too cheap to put more cameras in their subway stations? I want to see that tape for myself."

"I'm waiting for it. Gerdy said he'd e-mail me a copy when he gets it from forensics. I'll send you a copy when I get it. If Gerdy calls you, remember what I said about not talking unless a lawyer is present."

"Tell me what you saw on the tape."

"The woman has her back to the camera as she approaches you." Your arm goes out and suddenly she's careening toward the tracks."

"That's exactly what happened—but I never touched her. She wasn't even looking at me when she turned and ran at the train."

"I believe you. You know how punches are done in movies? A guy throws a punch at the other guy's face and they film it from the opposite side so the guy's head blocks a view of the punch. The fist doesn't get even close, but on film it looks like—"

I gave him my uncensored opinion of his Hollywood stunts analogy and I hung up.

"Just drive," I warned the driver, who shot a look back at me.

I thought about my next move.

"If I wanted to find someone and only had the name, where's the best place to start?" I asked the driver.

"Might try the phone book."

Now why didn't I think of that?

❖

32

❖

Quintin Rees lived in a neighborhood that wouldn't have qualified as one of the most picturesque in Britain even though the area was in one of the loveliest cities in a beautiful country. The building was a step or two down from my cusp of SoHo, Chinatown, and Little Italy flat, which was a few steps down from pristine.

Rather than calling myself and risking the ire or suspicion if a woman answered, I had the cabbie phone the listed telephone number.

"Disconnected," the cabbie told me. "Probably didn't pay his bill."

The cabbie and I were on good terms after I explained that the person on the phone I had used unladylike language on had been my cheating husband. The line always worked like a charm to rally men in my favor regardless of how often they cheated on their own wives.

"Looks like a place where most of the occupants are roaches," the cabbie said as we pulled up in front of the address.

From the appearance of the two guys hanging around a liquor store

❖

a couple doors down, the neighborhood wasn't Dickensian poor but crystal meth blighted.

"Don't go far," I told the driver.

"Rees" was scribbled in pencil next to the mail slot of apartment number 4. The building door was not locked and the apartment was on the first floor, down a dim stale hallway that needed a strong breath of fresh air through it to make it breathable.

A middle-aged woman answered the door. She looked like a poster child for the slogan "life's a bitch and then you die."

"What do you want?" she asked as soon as she opened the door and shortly before she was able to focus on me.

A wave of alcohol hit me. Maybe she used it for perfume.

"I need to talk to Quintin Rees."

"Piss off."

"I have money for him," I told the door closing on me.

The door popped back open immediately.

"You can give it to me," she said.

"I have to hand it to him."

"Piss off."

The door started to close again.

"I can give you something."

The door swung back open.

She gave me a long, bleary-eyed look. "What'd you want?"

"Information about a reproduction that Quintin did."

"He's not here."

"I'll pay you to tell me where he is."

"Let me see the money first."

I took a fifty-pound note out of my pocket and showed it to her.

"Where is he?"

"I don't know. That's the truth. He's been gone about a week. Said he had a big-paying assignment."

"What kind of assignment?"

"I don't know. He didn't tell me."

"When's he coming back?"

❖

"He won't be back until he's spent every bloody quid of it and then he'll be crying on me shoulder for more."

"You're going to have to tell me something about that assignment to get the money."

"I don't know any—wait, there was a woman, that's who he said hired him, it was a woman."

"What about the woman?"

"I don't know, just a woman."

"Middle Eastern woman?"

"Yeah, that's right, a Middle Eastern woman."

I made a mistake of suggesting it and couldn't trust her response. Sure that the well was dry, I gave her the fifty pounds.

I got exactly nothing from her except that he came into money and was MIA.

❖

33

❖

Quintin Rees hurried through the dark park to the place where the woman had told him the exchange would take place—her money for his work.

The area was cold and damp, with a light mist falling and a bit of fog gathering on the stretch of green that ran along the river. Used during the day by joggers and mothers with their kids, on summer nights there would be lovers strolling about, but on this soggy night it was lonely and deserted.

Quintin had asked to meet in a pub, but the woman had refused, saying that she didn't want to make the exchange in public.

He carried a small shopping bag and had his laptop strapped over his shoulder. The scarab he had made for her was wrapped in a towel and inside the shopping bag. He had done a good job on it despite having to make it in less ideal circumstances than the first one that had been made in Botwell's shop. But Quintin had done most of the work on the first copy and still had the pictures on his computer. That made the second one easier to reproduce.

❖

Botwell would know that Quintin had accepted the woman's offer to make the copy in return for a big payday the moment Botwell found that the rest of the lapis lazuli that he had obtained from Afghanistan was missing.

Quintin was sweating and it wasn't just because he needed a fix. The woman for whom he had made a duplicate scarab scared him. Not with words or threats, but with the stern presence she conveyed. But many things in life caused him discomfort and sent him to find a chemical or alcoholic relief.

He understood the compulsion of addiction better than most people. He had been enslaved to food, narcotics, alcohol, and fear almost continuously since adolescence. He had a talent to imitate art pieces with his hands, would have made a good sculptor and created original pieces if his creative juices hadn't been fried by crack and crank and wet from booze.

He nervously paced back and forth by a World War I statue of an infantryman where the woman had told him to meet her.

Quintin stopped and waited when he saw her coming. His body ached with the need to give it a jolt of pleasure and he had to fight the impulse to throw the bag containing the duplicate scarab at her and grab the money she contracted to pay and run for the closest fix.

"I have it," he said, showing her the bag as she approached.

"It better be good."

"It is. Better than the one I did for the Radcliff woman."

"Let me see."

"The money, give me the money."

"Yes, your payment."

She pulled a small-caliber revolver out of her pocket and shot him in the chest. As he staggered back, she moved forward and shot him in the forehead, then emptied the gun in his head and face.

She walked away with the bag containing the scarab, tossing the gun and Quintin's computer into the river.

❖

34

❖

I headed back to my hotel in Bath with my thoughts still tripping over each other as I tried to imagine how the subway tape could show me giving Fatima Sari a shove, while trying to concentrate on what appeared to be a mystery wrapped inside a puzzle in regard to the scarab.

I tried to get my head around Michelangelo's explanation that Fatima had gotten in the way of the camera leaving the impression that I had given her a shove.

I hated Michelangelo's contention that the camera didn't record the fact that I hadn't made contact with Fatima.

Knowing that I was on the run for something I didn't do gave me a knot in my stomach that made me feel like I'd been punched. And angry enough to punch whoever put me in the spot.

The problem was the list of suspects that seemed to be growing as I stumbled along trying to find answers.

So far all I knew about the woman who had hired Quintin the counterfeiter was that she was Middle Eastern, and probably Egyptian. Why

❖

she wanted a copy of the scarab was still at issue, despite my laundry list of possible motives.

The other thing I knew for sure was that the scarab theft was becoming more and more a murky morass. I felt as if I were in an Agatha Christie story where everyone present had motive and opportunity.

Even Fuad, who seemed to be innocence incarnate, was sitting on a secret, one that spelled out more involvement than he had let on.

I couldn't believe that Fuad was involved in anything criminal, at least not intentionally, but he was burning up not just with the loss of Fatima who he obviously loved, but with a load of guilt.

And I felt confident that finding out what that guilt was would open up a lot of doors and windows of the mystery surrounding the scarab.

FUAD'S HAND SHOOK AS he called the woman named Sphinx on his cell phone. The phone rang ten times before a computerized voice offered to let him leave a voice mail message.

"I need to talk to you," he said. "You told me getting a copy would help Fatima. Now she's dead and I have to tell the American woman. I'm meeting her at eight tomorrow night at the tower. Call me."

❖

35

❖

Flowers and champagne were waiting for me back in my hotel room along with a note from Rafi saying he would pick me up at eight for dinner.

I had the same room the last time I visited Bath. The hotel was on a slope and the balcony gave a lovely view of the river below. I longed to sit on the balcony and drink champagne and daydream about what Bath was like during Roman times and decided that was what I wanted to do tonight with Rafi.

I put the champagne on ice and ordered dinner for two from a restaurant recommended by the front desk—prime rib with Yorkshire pudding, horseradish cream, Brussels sprouts, and creamed onions.

My own choice would've been an Indian dinner from a restaurant down the street that I remembered had excellent food, but I decided that a traditional English dinner would be a better choice for Rafi, partly because there were some similarities between Indian food and Egyptian and the last thing anyone should want while traveling in a foreign country is to eat what they do back home.

Rafi also struck me as a meat-and-potatoes man and reminded me

❖

of Michelangelo—a guy willing to order champagne to finesse a woman, but after he gets what he wants heads for a sports bar to grab a beer and argue the latest game with his pals.

I need tender loving care, not sex, went through my mind as I soaked in a leisurely bath before meeting Rafi.

After two glasses of champagne, I was feeling a little buzzed and blamed it on the fragrant bath oil rather than the sparkling wine.

Had I been a decent woman the issue of sex on a first date wouldn't have even come up. It all went back to my theory of being raised bad because too often I let my desire for gratification overwhelm what should be at least minimal moral courage.

In other words, I shouldn't jump in bed with this guy until I can at least claim I have shared a little more intimacy with him than a hand-shake.

Come to think of it, I don't think we even shook hands.

I comforted myself morally with the fact that seduction has a long history in the intelligence-gathering sector. While I didn't delude myself into believing that Rafi would tell me what he'd learned about the missing scarab, a lot can be revealed just by the way he avoided my questions or asked his own.

Which is probably exactly what he was thinking about me.

B Y THE TIME R AFI knocked on the door, the champagne was chilled, minus what I had drunk, the table on the balcony set with hors d'oeuvres, and dinner was covered with silver hoods and ready to be served from a side table.

When he stepped inside, I got a whiff of a very subtle cologne, a really nice woodsy scent. I usually didn't like cologne on a man, mostly because they used too much of it, but Rafi's was just right, a hint of masculinity and oozing with sensuality.

"You smell really nice," he said.

We stared at each other for a long moment and all of sudden we were in each other's arms, kissing passionately, my breasts pressed against his chest as he pulled me hard against him. I could feel the

❖

bulge growing between his legs. He wanted me as much as I wanted him.

My dress came off a few seconds later and went flying somewhere. The only thing I wore underneath was a black lacy thong .

Our lips were still locked together as I undid his belt buckle and zipper and I'm ashamed to say my fingers didn't fumble in getting down to basics because they knew exactly where they were going and what they wanted to do.

I wrapped my hand around his throbbing phallus and squeezed, hard, up and down. Rafi waited to come, gentleman that he was. Instead, he grabbed my legs and pulled me up, mounting me on him as he stood, driving his stalk up again and again, pushing against my clit until I was moaning with pleasure when the orgasm came for both of us.

Before the night was over, we ended up having sex three more times.

Okay, I knew I would be mad at myself in the morning but, as always, I fell back on the alibi that in order to do these things, I had to have been raised bad.

36

❖

The next morning as I was soaking in the tub, trying to make sense of the scarab mess that I'd gotten myself into, and trying not to think about the mess I'd gotten my own life into, my cell phone went off.

I reached out and grabbed the phone where I'd laid it on the floor.

"What are you doing?" Rafi asked.

"Soaking in the tub."

"Want company?"

"Only if you have your own soap."

We chatted for a moment and agreed to meet for breakfast. After I hung up, I thought I saw someone go by the partially opened bathroom door.

I had closed the door most of the way to conserve the heat in the bathroom.

"Come back later, please!" I yelled, assuming it was the maid and regretted that I hadn't put the DO NOT DISTURB sign on the door. Then it occurred to me that it might not be a maid and that got my adrenaline going.

❖

I got out of the tub and wrapped a towel around myself and went into the bedroom. No one was there and I went to the door and opened it a crack to put the sign up, poking my head out to see if the maid was in the hallway.

The corridor was deserted.

No maid.

What the hell?

I swung around, looking over the room.

My purse was open.

I already knew the flash drive with the pictures of the scarab would be gone before I checked.

❖

37

❖

Feeling like a windup toy unable to turn in any direction but the one I was set on, I caught a train back to Salisbury to meet Fuad at the Druid Faire that evening.

I stood up Rafi for breakfast and checked out of the hotel. I left a simple message for him at the front desk: GTT.

Let him figure that one out. It meant Gone to Texas. Back in Old West days, the initials were left behind by people who were leaving town, heading out for a new life out West, or didn't want anyone to know where they were off to.

Rafi would not get it at all, which was why I left it. He was so in love with the Internet, he could go on the Web and find out what it meant.

My anger was directed at Rafi for a good reason. Someone had come into my room while I was in the tub and had stolen the flash drive out of my purse. He was the only one who could have done it.

I had only one key card to the room and it was still in my purse, but thieves and spies have developed electronic "skeleton key" cards—passkeys for doors using electronic cards.

❖

Which is why I had a lingering doubt about Rafi. He was a high-ranking Egyptian investigator for an important government agency that investigated contraband Egyptian artifacts all over the world. He would have access to an electronic device that opens a hotel-room door.

That left the question of how the intruder would know that I was in the bathroom and wouldn't see him.

Rafi knew I was in the tub. With the miracle of the interconnected world, he could have called me from just outside my room door, the wireless signal going tens of thousands of miles out to space to a satellite and beaming back down to me in the bathroom, before he entered my room as soon as we hung up.

It fit nicely, the electronic skeleton key and the call to me.

The only other scenario was a chilling one.

The person could have entered to get the flash drive and not cared whether I saw them or not.

I could think of only one reason why the intruder wouldn't care if I saw them or not—they would have killed me.

Had I barely missed getting killed because I was taking a bath?

Or had Rafi called me from the corridor and entered when he realized I wouldn't see him?

I liked the second scenario.

So why was the flash drive taken? To have the pictures so a copy of the scarab could be made?

No, my gut was screaming that the pictures were taken to make sure I didn't have them.

The quickest and easiest way to identify a reproduction is to compare the golden pyrite dust grain on the original with the fake.

Now I couldn't do that.

Someone was thinking way ahead of me.

I hired a taxi and spent the day checking out bars and dives for the missing Quintin Rees.

I came up with exactly nothing except for stares from a lot of men I didn't want to know better.

❖

38

❖

When I arrived in Salisbury, I checked into a hotel and rented a car, reminding myself to keep in mind the British did everything opposite to what I was used to when it came to cars and roads.

I took a run out to Stonehenge to reacquaint myself with the Celtic spirits before heading for my meeting with Fuad.

The Druid Faire sign at the entrance was illuminated by a flickering torch. It showed a raven sitting on a harvest moon, blood flowing down from where its talons gripped.

The Druid gods must have blessed the gathering because tonight a big bright moon smiled overhead.

The fair was laid out in a flat pasture and a long line of tents occupied both sides. Even at a distance I could see the "centerpiece" for the fair that Fuad had mentioned, a medieval stone tower about fifty feet high on a small rocky mound at the far end of the "street" created by the row of tents.

Fuad had told me the horse pasture was owned by Isis, but that she

❖

wouldn't be there because she was hosting a party for high-ranking Druids at her manor house.

The fair was similar to the Renaissance fairs I've visited back home, but this one had knights in armor, Roman gladiators, Druid priests in hooded robes, ancient Brits, and a Viking or two.

The smells were eclectic, too—Tibetan incense, good English horse manure, and the heady sweetness of marijuana were in the air . . .

Besides the historical themes, like all the fairs I've gone to there was the ubiquitous premise of separating people from their money. Booths sold cakes, hot drinks, and Cornish pasties; magic potions, powders, and spells for success at work, punishing your enemies, and wooing the one you loved; crystals and magic amulets you wore that brought good luck—there was even a booth selling Egyptian Druid magic, but I didn't see the Heart of Egypt among the scarabs offered.

I stopped for a moment and listened to the whimsical tune of a woman playing a harp and dropped a pound coin into her collection box.

I avoided a woman wearing a snake like a big necklace and smiled and shook my head at a fortune-teller who told me she had a secret to tell me, walked around a crowd watching a man swallowing a sword, and another group surrounding a woman blowing fire from her mouth.

A man in a hooded Druid priest robe came up beside me and in a stage whisper offered to sell me an enigmatic symbol that would reveal to me the secrets of life.

"No thanks," I told him. "It would take the fun out of living if I knew all of the answers."

A Merlin character carrying a staff, a man who was dressed either as an elf or Robin Hood, a fierce, bearded Arabic sheik with a falcon on his shoulder, a Druid priestess who looked mean enough to enjoy human sacrifice . . .

I know it's all corny and hokey, but I love the energy and excitement of circuses and street fairs, the people having fun pretending, even the hucksters trying to part me from my hard-earned money.

I was almost at the end of the street of tents when I looked up and saw the flash of a white shirt as someone fell from the tower ahead.

❖

By the time I reached the tower a large crowd had gathered around someone on the ground and I couldn't get close enough to see who it was. I asked a man who was pushing out of the crowd if he'd seen the person on the ground.

"A man's dead," he said.

"Was he Middle Eastern?"

"How did you know?"

"I'm psychic."

I looked at the faces in the crowd, moving quickly, hoping to spot whoever had given Fuad a push.

It occurred to me that I should get the hell away from the place before someone accused me of pushing him.

THE LOCAL NEWS ON TV reported that Fuad had been killed in the fall and that the cause was not yet ascertained, but that authorities were looking into the possibility of an accident or a suicide.

Things had gotten really ugly again. It seemed as if I had somehow kicked open Pandora's box.

I felt as if I had lost control, that events were spinning wildly around me. Since meeting Kaseem, I had gone from expensive tea to sheer madness in no time in New York. Now the insanity had followed me to England, right down to a woman with too much money and delusions of being a goddess.

Murder, madness, and greed swirled around me like a Mohave dust devil.

I didn't know where to turn, but I knew I couldn't go back to New York and face the subway suspicions with no answers and another "accidental" death hanging over me. And I couldn't call Rafi. I no longer trusted him.

Back at the hotel I found an envelope on my bed. It contained the second installment and a note that the third payment would be waiting for me in Cairo.

❖

39

❖

Cairo, Egypt

"Do I look like a terrorist?"

It was the first thing out of my mouth when security took me aside at the airport without clearing customs. I didn't get an answer.

Moments earlier, as I stood waiting in a slow line, I overheard someone mention that inspections were tighter because the U. S. president would be making a special friendship trip to Egypt to return an ancient artifact taken from Abu Simbel back in the 1960s and displayed until recently at the Smithsonian.

The object, a stone falcon, had been given to an archaeologist working as one of the advisors on the incredible feat of moving the colossal statues of Ramses from the rising waters that were created by the construction of the Aswân Dam. He in turn donated the bird of prey to the U. S. national museum.

I'd seen the piece at the Smithsonian and understood that it had been gifted by Egypt out of gratitude for aid in preserving the Aswân lake site, but I guess the political winds said that it was time to give it back.

I found it interesting that even my government was getting into the

❖

act when it came to appeasing the agitation of countries whose national historical treasures had been looted during colonial years.

I gave my passport to the clerk, idly ruminating on the international battles going on between museums and countries demanding their treasures back, when he startled me by saying, "You have to see a supervisor."

"Why?" I asked.

"He will explain."

And he did. My passport was being seized because I was on a watch list.

I almost laughed at the ludicrousness of it.

"Fine. Give me back my passport and I'll take the next plane out— to anywhere."

"You cannot exit the country until your passport is cleared."

"Cleared by who?" I asked.

"The Supreme Council of Antiquities."

Of course. Rafi al Din probably knew I had purchased a ticket to Cairo seconds after I selected my seat assignment. It was no longer a case of Big Brother watching; we all carried Big Brother around in our pockets.

That was all the supervisor could or would tell me despite my fuming. I demanded to see his superior.

"He's not here," he said. "You have to come back tomorrow."

"I want to see the supervisor's supervisor."

"Tomorrow."

I was fuming. Short of being jailed or murdered, losing a passport had to be the worse thing that could happen to a traveler. Having it seized by a government agency in a third world country that was both inefficient and nightmarishly bureaucratic was light-years beyond simply losing it. When things got lost in Egypt they ended up buried in mountains of paperwork, desert dunes, or only God knows where.

It scared the hell out of me.

Still furious, when I came out of the airport to flag down a taxi, I almost ran into a young Egyptian girl holding up a piece of cardboard with "Madison Dupre" scribbled on it in pencil.

❖

I guessed her age at about eleven or twelve, but she was thinner than the homegrown ones. A dark blue scarf covered her head and fell half-way down her back. Her shapeless white dress with long sleeves went all the way to her brown shoes.

She smiled shyly as I approached with a stern frown.

"Don't tell me," I said, "you're the shortest cop in Egypt."

She shook her head emphatically. "Oh, no, I'm not a policeman," she said in a naïve and sincere voice. "But my father is. He's waiting over there."

She looked to her left and pointed to where Rafi was leaning against a car parked at the curb with his arms folded.

He stood there with a grin on his face.

I had to fight my instinct to let him know exactly how I felt about my passport being seized in terms that would bring his manhood into question.

I kept my mouth shut because of his daughter.

He strolled over and extended his hand for my carry-on. "Let me take that for you."

"I think you've already taken enough." But I went ahead and gave it to him.

He loaded the luggage into the trunk and I got in the backseat with him. The little girl sat in the front seat with the driver, a woman who I immediately assumed was her mother and almost asked if she wouldn't mind breaking Rafi's nose again, this time for taking my passport, but his introduction to her proved I was wrong about the relationship.

"This is Lana, my deputy inspector, and you have already met Dalila, my daughter."

The young girl turned back and smiled.

Lana shot me a cursory glance, but gave no greeting. I didn't offer her one, either. She was about thirty, not unattractive, and my immediate impression was that she had the hard edge some women get when they've had to fight for survival because of a tough life.

I didn't like her. Which was fair because something in her demeanor toward me immediately signaled that I wasn't on her favorites list.

❖

"Are you mad at me for playing that joke with the sign?" Dalila asked, a little shyly.

Smart kid. She noticed the apprehensive look on my face.

"No, certainly not. But I'd like to poke out one of your father's eyes for taking my passport."

That got a jaw drop from Dalila and a harsh burst of laughter from Lana.

"You're mean," Dalila said.

"True . . . I get that way when someone goes out of their way to step on me."

Dalila looked to her father and then back to me. "He has a hard job to do," she said in a serious tone.

Cry me a river.

Her English was really good, without even the trace of accent that Rafi had. The girl was sweet and obviously loved her father very much. Which made her a poor judge of character.

I noticed that her face was paler than it should be and I couldn't see any hair where her scarf had pulled back a bit. She was bald underneath. Chemotherapy bald.

I immediately felt a pang for her. Children shouldn't have to fight for their lives.

"Dalila, I'm certain your father is a very fine policeman. However, police officers do make mistakes and he's made one about me. He's wasting his time harassing me because he's convinced that I know more about something than I do."

I turned from the girl and spoke directly to Rafi, who had been keeping a blank face.

"Why don't you give me my passport, turn this car around, and take me back to the airport? I'll go someplace where I'm welcomed, and you'll have more free time to catch art thieves like you're supposed to do."

"I didn't order your passport seized; my supervisor did."

He said it with too much sincerity. He was lying, of course.

"But he might release it if we reached an accommodation."

"I already told you. I won't disclose the name of my client. It's none of your business and the core of mine."

❖

"We know you're representing Mounir Kaseem. But what do you know about him?"

I shrugged. "He's a scholar of ancient Egyptian history. He told me he wants to make sure one of your country's prize treasures finds its way back here." I gave him a look. "Are you going to tell me he wants the scarab for himself?"

"Not at all. He told you the truth about wanting the scarab returned to Egypt. And he wasn't lying when he said he was a scholar of our ancient history, though not a university one."

"Great. Then we have nothing to argue about. Give me back my passport and I'll leave you and Kaseem to deal with the scarab."

"What's more important is what he *didn't* tell you."

Dalila turned around, sitting on her knees to face us, and held her chin with her hands. Her big brown eyes beamed with curiosity.

"There's always a catch, isn't there?" I told her.

She just stared at me.

I sighed. "Okay, what's the catch?"

"In a sense, Kaseem is an old Nazi, but one of the Egyptian variety. He was an army general, commander of a tank corps, and head of a military officers group who attempted to seize control of the country about fifteen years ago."

"Islamic extremists?" I asked.

"No, quite the opposite. Just as Hitler had a fascination for the mystical part of German history—the knights and heroes of Wagnerian operas or Teutonic myth—Kaseem's vision of Egypt has to with the days of the mighty pharaohs. He formed a secret organization of military officers, high-ranking public servants, and some wealthy men.

"Called the Golden Nile, the group believed Egypt was crippled by the continuous struggle of extremist religious groups against a government that lacked a vision of Egypt's potential greatness. They hatched a plot to seize the government with a coup, stamp out the religious opposition, and lead Egypt's eighty million people into a golden age."

"So, he's in exile because he's politically dangerous to the present administration?"

Rafi frowned. "He's politically to the right of Genghis Khan and

❖

dangerous to the world at large. He wants to make Egypt, the largest Arab country, a nuclear power and unite the entire Arab world. Your government fears that if he rose to power here, he would destabilize the entire region."

"So what's the punch line to all this?"

"We believe Kaseem wants the scarab—not to hand over to the our museum—but to use it as a symbol of his quest for power. In fact, the Heart of Egypt is the emblem of his Golden Nile party."

I could have told him that I had long ago been burned out, disgusted, and repulsed by politics and politicians so that I cared less about who ran Egypt or just about anywhere else in the world.

But I digested what Rafi had just told me.

Kaseem and his neo-Nazi Golden Nile movement wanted to use the scarab as their symbolic weapon of power. That didn't bother me much. I'm sure that if the present administration gets their hands on it first, they'll pose with it as a symbol of *their* power.

I didn't volunteer any of my cynical thoughts to Rafi.

"What do you want from me?" I asked Rafi, and then to Dalila, "You can interpret that as me asking your father, 'How do I get back my passport?'"

"Your cooperation," Rafi answered. "We believe Kaseem is in contact with the thieves who took the scarab and will be contacting you and giving you instructions. When he does, all you have to do is inform us. Agreed?"

"Of course."

He gave me an appraising look and asked his daughter, "What do you think, Dalila? Do you believe her?"

"I like her. But she's lying."

Sweet little child.

"Drop me off at my hotel. I need to get rid of an awful headache caused by jet lag . . . and police brutality."

40

❖

I entered through the front door of the Hyatt hotel and left from a side exit. I had no intention of staying somewhere that I could be found so easily. Besides, I was planning to take the next plane out of Cairo.

Nothing is impossible if you are clever enough, I assured myself as a taxi dropped me off at the American Embassy.

An hour later, after filling out enough forms to deforest Central Park, I was called into the office of Mr. Flem, the passport clerk.

He didn't bother turning from the computer screen he was staring at to say hello. I could see that he was involved in a very tense diplomatic situation—a game of solitaire.

He turned to acknowledge my presence on the planet after a notice popped up on his computer screen advising him that he had lost the game.

"One moment please," he said.

His fingers flew on the keyboard for what I hoped was a printout of a new passport for me.

Earlier while I had waited to be called in, I saw him smile and fawn

❖

over an American in a much more expensive suit than he himself wore and sternly address an Egyptian clerk who no doubt used his small paycheck to support a family.

Obviously Mr. Flem was the kiss-up, kick-down type who kissed up to superiors and kicked the unfortunates below him.

I wasn't sure if I should intimidate the weasel-looking little bureaucrat or butter him up. I decided to try sugar rather than vinegar, giving him a seductive smile in the hopes that it might make the weasel really think he could actually appeal to a woman.

"I'm really grateful that you're acting so quickly on replacing my passport," I said. "I have to get back to New York because of a family emergency. My little Morty is ill."

He didn't look up from the computer screen as he spoke. "You reported your passport stolen."

"Yes."

"That is not the information we received. The foreign ministry has advised us that your passport has been seized by the government because you are on a watch list." He looked up and said in a deliberate voice, "You lied on an official government form. That is perjury."

So much for sugar.

"Excuse me, my passport was *stolen* by an inspector of the antiquities department in order to get me to do his bidding."

He glanced back to the computer. "That's not the information I have."

"Really? Did you get your information from reading the back of those cards you've been playing?"

That dropped his jaw and got his bureaucratic dander up.

"Miss Dupre, you are—"

"An American citizen and a taxpayer"—not completely true—"and my passport was taken illegally." I leaned on his desk. "Tell me what reason that lying computer gives for seizing my passport?"

He read information I couldn't see and turned back to me.

"You are on a watch list."

"Meaning what? Does it say that I'm a terrorist? Murderer? What are the legal grounds for taking my passport?"

"You are in a foreign country—"

❖

"I noticed that the moment I got off the plane."

"You don't have legal rights."

"That's great. We spend billions of dollars on embassies and more billions on aid to Egypt itself so they can do what they like to Americans and you just sit around on your hands and let them!"

"Madam—you are being insulting."

"No. I'm being desperate. I demand a new passport."

"Regulations require that we review the basis for the seizure before issuing another."

"How long will that take?"

"Seven to ten days."

"That's insane.

"Those are the rules."

"You can pick up the phone and call over to the foreign office. They won't be able to give you legitimate grounds for keeping my passport."

"Those are the rules," he repeated.

I could see that when he stood on the rules, he grew in stature—at least in his own eyes.

I resented the smug attitude of the bureaucratic little bastard.

"By the time you people get through screwing around with your book of rules, I might end up in the Egyptian version of a homeless shelter—the gutter."

I could see from the glow in his eyes that he was about to play his trump card.

"Has it occurred to you, Miss Dupre, that even if you *were* able to bully a new passport from this embassy—which you will not—that it would be seized when you returned to the airport to fly out?"

No, it hadn't occurred to me.

"You have been a terrific help," I said.

"I will be the one that has to clear the reissuance of your passport." He smirked. "I can see right now that it's going to take much longer than the usual seven to ten days."

I shrugged, defeated. "Great. My passport gets taken for an undefined reason by an unidentified foreign government agency and you are perfectly willing to put on your boots and jump on my battered body."

❖

I smiled down at him. "Why don't you look up Kafkaesque bureaucratic jerk while you're losing at cards?"

THERE IS NO QUESTION about it—I have a big mouth and a habit of sticking my foot into it.

I could have sweetened Mr. Flem into helping me, but instead, I antagonized him.

Completely stupid.

Somewhere between a woman jumping in front of a subway in New York and a man flying off the side of a medieval tower, I lost my own common sense.

I couldn't have played into Rafi's hand any better than with my own big mouth and arrogance.

I needed to get back in control.

I took a taxi back to the Hyatt hotel where Rafi had dropped me off earlier, and then registered.

After I visited my room, I went back down to the lobby and left by the side exit again. I walked a block before I got into another taxi that took me to an inexpensive hotel where I stayed when I first came to Egypt as a poor student to see firsthand some of the wonders of the ages.

Called Queen of the Nile, the hotel was safe, clean—at least it was a dozen years ago—and the only thing glamorous about it was the name.

By the time I reached the hotel, I was too tired and angry to care whether I had been followed.

❖

41

❖

The Queen of the Nile was located in a district that had both apartment and business buildings. It had an unusual setup—the lobby was on the ground floor, but the guest rooms were on floors fourteen to seventeen with residential apartments in between.

It hadn't changed at all since the last time I stayed there. Even the front desk clerk who pretended he remembered me from the past when I said I had stayed there was the same.

Getting off the elevator that seemed breathless and gasping after it lugged me all the way up to the seventeenth floor, I was happy to see that the emergency device in case of fire, earthquake, or whatever hadn't changed either: instead of having in a glass case a button that sets off an alarm, a key hung on a hook in the case.

In case of emergency, you broke the glass, grabbed the key, and used it to unlock the stairway door so you could run down seventeen flights of stairs. I took a picture of the key at the time because it was such a unique "emergency" system.

Being tracked and harassed from New York to England and now

❖

Cairo by computers, security cameras, and God knows what else, I could appreciate the low-tech device. I just wished the rest of my life was so simple.

I sat outside on the small balcony, drinking tea that I had delivered to my room, waiting for my phone to ring. I was a pawn waiting for the next move, reminding myself that just like lambs, pawns were also often sacrificed to win.

The city of Cairo was spread out below me, a golden haze in the background that I preferred to think of as dust from the surrounding desert rather than pollution. I gazed around, thinking about the magic and mystery of Egypt—the people whom I found to be quite friendly and generous, the pyramids that were magical, the archaeological sites that have been uncovered, and the ones still buried and waiting to be discovered by treasure seekers with trembling hands.

For a moment I forgot all about the troubles dogging me and focused on the splendors in front of me as the chant of a muezzin broadcasted from a minaret calling the faithful to prayer floated to me across the rooftops.

It didn't matter that the call was recorded and sent over loudspeakers—it was still mysterious and exotic.

I was glad that I had come back to the Queen of the Nile rather than staying at a modern hotel. It had so much more character and charm, and the rooms were simple but clean. The place was also peaceful and quiet, especially up here on the top floor. Even the crier summoning Muslims to prayer five times a day added to the alluring atmosphere of the place.

I lost track of time until I heard the muted knock on my door. I opened it and found a small cloth bag hanging from the door handle. Inside the bag I found a cell phone and an envelope.

I knew right away what the envelope contained—the third payment—all in hundred-dollar bills.

Crisp, new, neatly pressed hundreds.

It took me ten minutes, my loupe, years of examining objets d'art, and comparing the bundle of nice, new bills with a used hundred that I got from the hotel front desk clerk to find out that the whole lot of them were counterfeits, including the bills I had with me from New York.

❖

I was livid.

Kaseem had dumped funny money on me.

I had been too broke back home to give the bills a close examination. Not that it mattered that I had passed counterfeit bills in the States— considering what the prison term would be in Egypt for doing it, and the condition of the prisons, I'd never live long enough to serve a second term in the United States.

What was the man trying to do?

A better question was how I had gotten myself into a position where every time I turned around since meeting him I was facing five to life.

Just as puzzling—*why funny money?*

It hardly seemed worth it to pay me what must be chump change to a man like Kaseem who's the head of a political party that attracts rich people.

Ten minutes later I got a call from Kaseem.

"I provided the phone because yours will be monitored," he said.

"Maybe you should also provide some truthful answers. You've lied to me about everything. My passport's been pulled and you can go to hell if you think I'll help you with anything."

"Miss Dupre—"

"I'm going to turn this phone over to the police and let them use it to track the number you called from."

"That won't do any good. My phone will be destroyed at the end of this call. For your own sake, you must listen to me."

He was right. I had to at least listen to him.

"Talk," I said.

"I'm sure by now you know that I am an Egyptian patriot."

I bit my lip to keep from calling him a damn neo-Nazi on the run from his country's government.

"Regardless of what you think of my politics, no one accuses me of wanting anything but the best for my country."

"Why don't you save the campaign speech for the next election. What are you going to do to get me out of the mess you've shoved me into?"

"I didn't intend for bad things to happen—"

"Yeah, right."

❖

"But we must deal with the situation. I have been contacted by the thieves who stole the scarab from Fatima. They have stated a price that is acceptable, but I have to make sure that the scarab is the real one and not one of the many forgeries floating around the city."

"And that's where I come in."

"Yes. You have received your third payment. However, I will double it if you examine the scarab."

I made a vague listening response and didn't point out to the lying bastard that he could afford to give a suitcase full of money since it was counterfeit.

"Once the scarab is in my hands, I will again double your reward."

Generous to a fault.

"And if the scarab turns out to be a fake?"

"Naturally, that wouldn't be your fault. You would be paid anyway."

"What do I do with the money? Use it to stay in hotels because I can't leave the country?"

"Neither. Once I have the Heart of Egypt in my hand, I will turn it over to the people of Egypt. When that happens, any attempts by the authorities to manipulate you will collapse."

"I see." I didn't see, and was straining to keep my mouth shut to find out if I could learn any more from him.

"I regret the situation about your passport, but that will be straightened out. In the meantime, you are being well paid for—"

I lost it. "You dumped counterfeit money on me. Is that what you call being well paid?"

"Counterfeit?" He sounded surprised.

"Yes. Every damn one of them.

"That can't be."

"Literally dripping wet from the printing press. You know what, Mr. Kaseem, I'm getting you out of my life. Don't call me again."

I hung up and turned off my phone and went back out to the balcony in the hopes that the fresh air and peaceful atmosphere could help make some sense of the situation.

Kaseem's plan was that I would come to Egypt and authenticate an artifact for him, an artifact that the Egypt government also wanted.

At some point, I was to meet with killers and thieves, examine the piece, and get away without being murdered.

And if I managed to stay alive and jumped all the hurdles, I would be rewarded with funny money and share a cell with God knows who or what in a Cairo jail.

All the downsides were easy to see. What I couldn't grasp was an easy way out of what I had gotten myself into.

If I went to Rafi and the police, they would simply make me do the same thing that Kaseem wanted from me. For free.

And I was certain that the Egyptian police would be much less efficient at keeping me alive than Kaseem would—at least until Kaseem got with he wanted. Besides, if I double-crossed him, he'd simply kill me and get another expert.

I wasn't between a rock and a hard spot, but swimming frantically between a shark and a crocodile.

No matter which way I turned I was damned.

Stuck in a foreign country.

With no help from the American Embassy.

As usual when I have nowhere else to turn, I do what comes natural to me: I put one foot in front of the other and take cautious steps ahead, but also am ready to bolt and run if I have to.

So plunging ahead, I decided I had to leave my room and find out more about the scarab.

My first stop would be the Egyptian Museum. And I didn't dare leave the counterfeit money to be found by Egyptian police during a search or by a hotel maid cleaning up the room.

I cut a leg off of a pair of panty hose, spread the funny money inside it, tied it around my waist, and put my blouse on over it—an old traveler's trick for instantly creating a money belt.

In the Middle East, I always respect a tradition of modesty in female dress, so the improvised money belt wasn't noticeable by the time I got fully dressed in a loose fitting blouse and a long skirt with pockets.

❖

42

❖

I gave the taxi driver waiting in front of the hotel the name of a tourist hotel within walking distance from the Egyptian Museum, rather than the museum itself so I wouldn't signal my destination. For all I knew, every taxi driver in the city worked for Rafi or Kaseem.

We had driven for several minutes when I realized we were not heading for the museum area.

"Hey!" I snapped at him. "Wrong way."

He turned in the seat and smiled, saying, "It's okay, okay," and held up a small piece of paper with the sign of the Golden Nile on it. "Camel Market. It's okay."

That seemed to be the limit of his English.

It wasn't okay with me, but I had two choices.

I could throw myself out of the taxi when it slowed going through an intersection or even when we came to an actual stop, which was usually in a confused herd of vehicles, and probably get run over by other cars on the jammed streets.

Or I could stick my head out the window and start screaming the next time we passed a traffic cop. I had no idea what good that would do me to shout in English at a cop who couldn't even follow the cab.

Dead or alive, I would attract a lot of attention. Not a good idea when I was carrying a life sentence in a stuffed panty hose leg.

I needed Kaseem and real money.

He needed me.

I sat back and hoped I didn't get murdered.

43

❖

I'd never been to the Camel Market at Imbaba, a suburb of Cairo, but had heard of it. That camels were still traded in the modern city whose metro area was bulging with twenty million people seemed amazing until you drove a few miles up or down the Nile and realized that as soon as you left the city you had taken a time machine back to medieval days.

The taxi let me off a short walk from the market, with the driver using a little pidgin English and sign language to let me know he'd wait.

His belief that I was coming back was reassuring.

The market resided in a field, a large empty space in view of severe concrete apartment buildings. Men dressed in turbans and galabiyahs stood around in groups and haggled over prices while camels stood around or laid about, hobbled and complaining. Camel feed was piled on top of a long single-story building in order to keep the animals from devouring it.

The dust, stink, and noise was a pleasant relief from the dust, stink, and noise of the modern city.

❖

A man dressed the same as the haggling camel merchants in the market came up beside me.

"I didn't know the money was counterfeit," Kaseem said.

"Uh-huh." I wanted to believe him. I needed to believe him.

"I was actually also swindled, for a much larger sum. Someone owed me quite a bit of money and chose to pay me in Iran's second official currency."

"Come again?"

He chuckled without humor. "The Iranians pride themselves on producing the finest U.S. hundred-dollar bills. I'm surprised you caught the fraud, though I'm glad that you did. The felon who cheated me will now have to pay twice. Just as you are being paid double."

He slipped me a thick envelope. "Here is your money. Did you bring the counterfeit bills with you?"

"As a matter of fact, I did, but I'll need to slip into a bathroom to retrieve them."

"I'll take you to one, but it won't be up to your Western standards."

I didn't buy his story about being ripped off.

During the taxi ride it had occurred to me that if he didn't have the millions necessary to ransom the scarab, counterfeit money seemed to be a perfect substitution.

Maybe he had been testing the money on me.

As we walked, he asked, "Have you ever been to the Camel Market before?"

"No, the closest thing I've seen are the camel races in Dubai."

"Ah, yes, in oil-rich Dubai millions are paid for camels that are raced or win beauty contests. The animals here will sell for a few hundred dollars apiece, a little more for the ones with the most meat on them. They're brought here to be sold to butchers."

"To be eaten?"

"Camel meat is cheaper than beef or lamb, and is especially important to poor people who can't afford the choicer meats. Many of the animals were herded here by tribesmen, often a thirsty journey involving hundreds of miles."

Like an Old West cattle drive, I thought.

❖

"You know a lot about the camel business."

"My family raised camels when I was a boy," he said. "I drove them here more than once."

Which meant that we had met at the market because he had old friends and family connections with it that would protect him from government agents.

"Do not trust the police agent, Rafi al Din," he said.

I kept from laughing. Rafi's and Kaseem's names were both at the top of my "Do Not Trust" list.

"Like everyone else in the government," he said, "the man is corrupt. He is not working for the people of Egypt, but for himself."

"So what am I supposed to do now?" I asked.

"Just stand by."

"For how long?"

"Maybe tomorrow, maybe the next day. Negotiations are being conducted to ransom the scarab. Once I am convinced that the people I'm dealing with actually have it, then arrangements will be made for you to examine it."

"Examine it where?"

"I don't know yet. Obviously, the thieves will choose the place. You will not be harmed—they want money, not blood."

That wasn't necessarily true.

It had occurred to me in Britain that the thieves might not want me as a live witness after I examined the artifact. Now that I was sure Kaseem had political shenanigans up his sleeve in which the artifact played an important role, I was a loose end for him, too.

He handed me another phone.

"Discard your other one. Keep this on so I can reach you when I need to."

We parted after I stepped into a small, unlit room, a so-called bathroom with a hole in the floor to do your business, and substituted the real money he gave me for the phony bills.

I kept the phone on—at least until the taxi dropped me a couple of blocks from the Egyptian Museum.

❖

44

I had used the museum as an instructor for me when I was a student. I learned more about Egyptology in a few months there than spending years in a classroom.

At the information desk I confirmed that Adara Zidan, an assistant curator who had been helpful to me in the past, was still employed in the museum's King Tut gallery.

"Is she here now?"

"Yes, but I believe she's on her lunch break."

I scribbled a note and handed it to the person behind the desk.

"Could you deliver this to Adara and let her know that I'd like to see her?"

"She should be back in another half hour."

"Fine. I'll wait for her in the gallery."

I remembered Adara used to eat her lunch in the employee lounge so I knew my wait wouldn't be that long.

I wandered around the Tut treasures. Not all of the 3,500 items that the museum had from the tomb discovery were on display, but to anyone who had seen any part of the treasures, they were dazzling.

From the research done to reconstruct the boy king's life, it's pretty certain he had a short life—he died at the age of nineteen, probably due to injuries from an accident. Despite his imperial position, he might not have been the happiest guy in the palace because he had some medical problems, including an overbite, a cleft palate, and scoliosis. Opinions of his death ranged from a chariot accident to a kick from a horse.

Two hundred pieces of jewelry were found at the tomb, despite the fact that the outer chambers had already been looted. Howard Carter estimated more than half of the king's jewelry had been taken in the earlier robberies, though the inner chambers were intact.

On display in the museum were two of the best-known Tut scarabs: a magnificent ornament in blue, green, red, and orange known as the pectoral scarab; and a simple black resin scarab with an inlaid figure of a heron, which has erroneously been called the heart scarab even though it was found at the wrong place of the body and did not contain the magic inscriptions from *The Book of the Dead* used on heart scarabs to keep the heart from confessing its sins.

After Tut's chest had been opened, amuletic jewelry and a beaded "bib" were placed over the area to cover where the sternum, ribs, and skin had been excised. There were also a dozen layers of other protective jewelry above the bib.

So much to live for, so short a life. The Fates had not been kind to him.

Adara came out and gave me a sincere hug, then took me back to her office for tea.

"You haven't changed, you're still beautiful," she said.

"Thanks, you're too kind, but I know I've gotten more haggard from the weight of life's problems."

"Haven't we all." She laughed.

She was still tall and thin, in her fifties, but with more gray in the head of hair she pulled back into a bun.

I explained I was in town only briefly to look at an artifact being offered by a private collector. She knew enough about the competitive,

❖

cutthroat nature of international art to keep from asking about the piece or the name of the collector.

"I was wondering if you knew a person named Fatima Sari," I said.

"Oh, yes, poor dear, we heard about her accident. She worked here at the museum for a while. Terrible thing. We were told she stumbled into a train in New York. You knew Fatima?"

"Only what I heard on the news."

I didn't volunteer that I was a candidate—the only candidate—for pushing her onto the tracks, but I had to come up with a reason for my questions about the woman.

"Was she working for the museum when she died?" I asked.

"Oh, no, she worked at the private Radcliff museum in England."

"Wasn't Radcliff one of Carter's backers? Something of a scandal about Radcliff and missing pieces during the Tut find?"

"A number of pieces were taken and even Carter himself was suspected of rewarding himself from the find. Radcliff's name of course pops up in connection with the heart scarab."

"Did Tut really have a heart scarab?"

"Of course he did, even the poor had one carved from wood. It's unimaginable that he would have been buried without one. But you don't have to look far to find it, I have it right here."

Adara reached over and took a scarab holding down papers on the shelf behind her and handed it to me.

I could see it was a skilled fake—steps above the stuff sold to tourists in the marketplace, but not something that would fool an expert.

"My mother bought this for me at the Khan nearly twenty years after I got my job here in the Tut gallery. She was so excited, certain that she had found the missing heart."

"Perhaps she did. A couple thousand years from now this piece will also be an artifact from antiquity and worth a fortune."

"That's what I told her."

"Have there been any demands made to the Radcliff heirs for the return of it?"

She shook her head. "I don't know; that sort of thing would come from the administration."

❖

Not wanting to raise questions about why I was interested in the heart scarab, I changed the subject, asking her about people I knew years ago and catching up on each other's lives.

I had established what I wanted to know—the museum was unaware that Fatima was bringing the heart back to Egypt. It was the sort of colossal event that couldn't have been kept a secret. News of it would have spread to the staff, especially Adara's group who would have the task of authenticating it. And it would've been leaked to the press.

According to Kaseem, Fatima had been only hours away from a flight to Cairo when the scarab was stolen.

I found it interesting that she was about to fly out from London when the theft occurred.

When did Kaseem plan to advise the Egyptian authorities that one of their greatest lost treasures would soon be back?

Rafi was right—obviously Kaseem didn't plan to have the scarab returned, at least not to be handed over to the museum.

What if the scarab hadn't been stolen? Where would it have ended up? On a chain around Kaseem's neck as he rode a white horse into Cairo?

"I assume you're going to run up to Luxor," Adara said, which was a good assumption about anyone coming to Egypt to see antiquities. "If you're curious about the heart, why don't you speak to De Santis, the Italian priest who's written a book about Howard Carter and the Tutankhamen find. He's at a dig in the Valley of the Kings."

"I've heard of him. What does he know about the heart?"

"He's fascinated by it, probably because it's a mystery connected to the original find. He's doing a paper on it for an Italian archaeological publication. I've heard he's going to present a theory that the scarab doesn't exist and has evidence to back it up."

"What's his theory?"

"We won't know until we read it in print. As you know, archaeology is just as cutthroat a business as other sciences."

"It gets even more interesting when beaucoup bucks and the egos of billionaires are concerned."

Or when the fate of nations are involved.

❖

I left the museum with a daring thought roiling in my head.

Why not go to the Valley of the Kings? It wasn't that far—I could be back tomorrow if I scrambled.

The notion kept jabbing at me as I walked.

It would get me out of Cairo, where I was feeling claustrophobic and choking on machinations, plots, lies, and deceits.

Kaseem had not been definite about when I would be needed. And I needed some different air to clear my head.

❖

45

❖

Luxor and the ancient sites of Karnak, Thebes, and the Valley of the Kings and Queens were scattered on the sides of the Nile River south of Cairo.

The area is so chockfull of glorious remnants of ancient Egypt that it has been called an open-air museum.

The Valley of the Kings was where Howard Carter made history when he found King Tutankhamen's tomb, and maybe where he ignited ancient curses and where Sir Jacob Radcliff stole the boy king's heart.

It was also where an answer to the puzzles and conundrums that had been bothering me might be found.

I walked some six blocks before I made up my mind.

I took a taxi to the big Ramses Hilton and told a doorman to find me a newer taxi with air-conditioning and a driver that spoke a fair amount of English.

Seated in the cab, I told the driver to take me to Giza to see the pyramids. When I was sure that we were only being followed by thousands of other cars, none of which stood out to me, I asked him, "Can you drive me all the way to Luxor?"

❖

"Yes. Tomorrow—"

"No, I need to go now."

He shot me a look. "Now?"

I fanned five hundred-dollar bills. "Yes. Now. Immediately."

"It is a long drive, eight hours maybe."

"I've made it in six. We leave now or you can drop me off at the next hotel and I'll find someone else to take me."

"I have to call my boss first."

"Go ahead. Call. But tell them that you're driving a man."

He turned around and looked at me, puzzled. He wasn't sure what to make of me. "But you are not a man," he said.

"I need to get out of town," I whispered. "I have a jealous husband in Cairo and my lover is waiting for me in Luxor."

"Ah," he said, his eyes lighting up.

Being a traditional Middle Eastern male, he understood completely what sluts Western women were.

He swiftly darted in and out of the utter confusion and tumultuous array of cars, people, and donkey carts loaded with fresh produce, looking straight ahead of him, as he maneuvered through the city unfazed by the congestion all around, not bothering to stop at traffic lights, unless a policeman happened to be posted at the intersection.

"I am a very good driver." He smiled, noticing that I had put on my seat belt.

I smiled bravely.

He might've been a good driver but I was also worried about the other drivers not getting out of his way fast enough.

He looked straight ahead and didn't worry about cars coming from the sides.

The only good part of getting killed in Cairo traffic is that it would be for a better reason than being murdered because my usefulness had been exhausted.

❖

46

❖

Driving south, following the Nile River, we left behind a bustling, noisy, congested city and entered a world of rural towns and villages that was much the same as the days when crusader knights fought the armies of Allah in the nearby Holy Land.

Small mud houses, women dressed from head to toe in black, and donkey carts hauling hay had not changed much over the centuries. Even the men wearing the ubiquitous galabiyah and turban found throughout Egypt looked medieval outside urban areas, as they had at the camel market.

And that about summed up my thoughts about the clash between fanatical Muslim terrorists and the rest of the world—not a clash between religions but a collision between the modern and the medieval. Women in New York wore high heels and the latest fashions, and the women we passed along the road wore wood sandals and shapeless robes. Cairo women fell somewhere in between the time scale.

I worried a little about encountering problems on the road, but I knew

❖

the infrequent terrorist attacks in Egypt were usually well-planned massacres that erupted in areas populated by tourists.

Besides the Egyptian Museum, Giza, and the Red Sea resorts, Luxor had also been hit some years ago at the stunning Queen Hatshepsut's Temple on the west side when six terrorists killed sixty-two people, including a British child and four honeymooning Japanese couples, before killing themselves.

Yet it was a relief to go to Luxor and back to the ancient world that I loved and understood better than my own time.

Nearly dark when we arrived, I checked into the Winter Palace hotel and gave the taxi driver money to get his own room, though I suspected he would return to Cairo that night or sleep in his car and return in the morning because the money I gave him for a room was more than he earned in a month.

The Winter Palace embodied Luxor's vintage hotel, an elegant remnant from the Victorian Age with an added modern wing. It had been the favorite hotel for visitors during the age of colonialism and the "watering hole" during colonial times for Europeans like Howard Carter whose house across the river was still standing.

The older part of the Winter Palace was built in 1886 on the banks of the Nile. It was here that Carter revealed to guests the incredible discovery of King Tut's tomb.

Originally built with an English ambiance, the hotel had been refurbished with modern fixtures and amenities but still emanated a European feeling of character and charm.

Surrounded by beautiful trees and greenery and teased by a breeze that took the heat off the night, I walked up the wide stairway and entered the tranquil jasmine-scented lobby. I immediately felt at home. The grand foyer reminded me of a luxurious palace.

I sat down in one of the lounge chairs and just soaked in the atmosphere for a few minutes, then reluctantly got up as I made my way across the lobby to have a quick peek at the lush gardens in the back and a gallery displaying old clothing and ancient artifacts.

The terrace overlooking the Nile and the West Bank was a perfect

❖

place for a spot of afternoon tea or to watch the sunset while you lei-surely sipped a cool drink, something I planned to do that evening.

I could've sat in the lobby for hours, in a comfortable chair, watching people go up and down the grand stairways, but I finally went to the reception desk and registered.

My room faced the garden. I opened the door leading out to a small patio and soaked in the view again. This was my kind of place.

A charming old hotel with beautiful surroundings and attentive hotel staff and service.

It was too bad that I had to worry about my next room in Egypt having steel bars.

47

❖

In the morning I woke up early and hired a caleche, a four-wheeled horse carriage to take me to the temple ruins at Luxor and Karnak so I could wander among the sentinels of the past before heading across the river to the Valley of the Kings.

A crowd of people had already gathered at the entrance of the Luxor temple.

I wandered through the complex, awestruck at the gigantic statues and the colonnade of stone pillars still standing.

During the Roman era, the temple and its surroundings were a legionary fortress and the home of the Roman government in the area. Now it was home to millions of visitors.

The lone red granite obelisk stood proud and mighty despite the fact its mate was now in France.

Before I left, I stood in front of the Colossus of Ramesses II sitting inside the temple, wondering what he thought of all these people intruding on his grounds, then I walked next door to the Karnak Temple

❖

Complex, considered to be the second most visited historical site in Egypt, after the Giza pyramids.

The temple used to be connected to its counterpart, the Luxor Temple, via an avenue of sphinxes, most of which, except for a few yards outside each temple, have been destroyed.

There was so much to soak in—the reliefs on the walls with their original carvings and colors, the gigantic columns, the obelisks, the other smaller temples, but I wanted to see De Santis before it got too late.

The entire area of Luxor, called Thebes in ancient times, included the city of Luxor itself, the ruins of Karnak on the east side of the river, and the city of the dead referred to as the neocropolis on the west side— the Valley of the Kings, the Valley of the Queens, and other mortuary ruins of ancient Thebes.

I preferred taking the ferry ride across the river to the west bank instead of the quicker and more expensive motorboats that lined the Nile. A bridge had also opened in the late nineties allowing land access from the east bank to the west bank.

Before I stepped inside a waiting taxi when I got to the other side of the bank, I arranged my fare with the driver. I didn't want to haggle about how much I owed him.

The west side had been the principal burial place for Egyptian pharaohs for about five hundred years, up to about a thousand years before the Christian era began.

It may have been greener a few thousand years ago, but today it was a barren wasteland—a place of hot sands and deadly snakes, about the last place that you'd think five dozen of the mightiest kings on earth would have chosen for their burial tombs.

While the surface was a series of dry, ugly hills, cliffs, and gullies, beneath the ground there had already been found some of the finest examples of ancient artifacts on the planet, including the Tut treasures.

Howard Carter's house, atop a hill, looked much like a mud-walled fort with a round roofed section that reminded one of an astronomy observatory.

Adara had told me that De Santis was working at a site called KV99. It wasn't a tomb excavation site, but what once had been a small "factory"

❖

that produced the paints used to color the hieroglyphic pictographs that covered the walls, sarcophaguses, and just about everything the pharaohs needed in the next life from water jars to dinner plates.

The site was up a steep dirt road far from the closest discovered tomb. Considering that not all the tombs had been discovered in the area yet, it might even be sitting on top of one.

I didn't know how to reach the priest other than making a cold call and that worked out well in my own mind because he might not have wanted to see me if I asked for an appointment.

The hotel concierge knew De Santis when I inquired about him. Since it was some sort of workers' holiday, the concierge said that it was unlikely there would be anyone around, but he mentioned that De Santis had a reputation of being a workaholic who spent most of his waking hours at the site so I would most likely find him at work.

The concierge referred to him as a monk.

The archaeological site itself was not being worked on when I arrived and I saw no one except an elderly Egyptian relaxing in the shade. No doubt the security guard for the site.

A large tent had been set up about fifty feet from the site.

I told the taxi driver to wait for me and flashed some money to show I could be generous. It was a long walk back to town.

"Imam?" I asked the guard, using the only word I knew that could indicate a priest in Arabic and got back an answer and a wave pointing to the tent.

Entering the dark tent, I found De Santis working at a table that held several small jars.

"*Ciao. Il mio nome è Madison—*"

"Yes, yes, they called me from the hotel," he answered quickly, "they told me you were coming. What do you want?" He didn't bother looking up but concentrated on his work.

His English was better than my clumsy Italian. I guess monks have cell phones, too.

"Ink used on hieroglyphics?" I asked about the dried, colored substances in the jars, trying to be friendly before I delved into why I was there.

❖

I recalled how the Ancient Egyptians made ink. They mixed soot with gelatin, gum, and beeswax to make black ink, and ochre with gelatin, gum, and beeswax for red.

De Santis was short and thin, with a closely cropped salt-and-pepper beard and shaven head. He smelled of ancient dust. And *vino da tavola*. Lots of the table wine.

"Yes. Are you an archaeologist?" he snapped.

He had a brisk, impatient, all-business personality. I wanted to ask him some questions about his work but decided not to take any more of his time than necessary.

"I'm an antiquities appraiser. Egyptian pieces are my specialty, especially the New Kingdom artifacts."

"Of course. The New Kingdom is everyone's favorite because the pharaohs were at their mightiest."

"I apologize for not calling. They didn't tell me at the hotel you could be reached by phone. Adara Zidan at the Egyptian Museum recommended I talk to you."

"Fine. You have come. What is it you request of me?"

I couldn't get the answer I needed without a shade of truth.

"I have a client who is being offered a scarab that the seller claims is the Heart of Egypt."

He snorted with derision. "Tell your client that he will be cheated because the heart does not exist. Are you familiar with Howard Carter and how the treasure was handled?"

"I know a little—"

He interrupted me in his brisk manner.

"When you hear talk of the curse of the pharaohs and people dying, the one person who truly deserved to be stalked and killed by an ancient curse was Radcliff. Carter himself was respectful of the pharaoh's treasures and his desire was always to protect and preserve them. But not Radcliff. He was driven by greed and ego.

"The man took many fine artifacts out of Egypt, and more than half of them did not come into his hands legitimately. Do you know how archaeological digs were financed in those days?"

❖

I nodded. "Half of the treasures went to Europeans who discovered the treasures, half to the Egyptian government."

"Radcliff had never helped finance a significant find before Tut, yet he gathered many fine pieces for his private collection."

"So he was buying them and shipping them home."

"Exporting them in violation of the law, as part of the black market in antiquities that has existed since my Roman ancestors set out to conquer half the world and bring home the best of it."

"So he must have been ecstatic when Carter found Tut's tomb."

"The whole world was blessed when Tut's tomb was discovered, except perhaps the ghost of the pharaoh himself. But you're right, because for Radcliff, it finally connected him with a legitimate treasure instead of buying from thieves and unscrupulous antiquities dealers and bribing customs officials to get them out of the country."

"Are you saying that the Radcliff collection is essentially all contraband?"

"Oh, almost entirely. Which is one of the reasons it has always been kept in a private museum. It started out private because Radcliff was too greedy and egotistical to share his collection with the world by donating it to a major museum or even starting a public one in his name. Until the day came when countries whose treasures had been stolen wanted them back from the people who took them."

"So Radcliff kept it hidden," I said. "But what about the heart? Isn't it exactly like Radcliff to have stolen the heart scarab?"

"It was exactly like him . . . had there been one."

"I know that Tut didn't have a heart scarab, at least none that was reported. But wouldn't that have gone contrary to a well-established tradition of providing one during the mummification process?"

"There are two things that rebut the assumption of so many that King Tutankhamen had to have a heart scarab. First, go back to why the heart scarab was important to the Egyptians."

He waited for an answer.

"Because . . . ," I began, pausing for a moment, "if the person's heart revealed sinfulness when questioned by Osiris, the god of the dead, Osiris

❖

ripped out the heart and threw it to Ahemait, the devourer of hearts and the dead person was denied admission into the afterlife."

He wagged his finger at me like a schoolmaster trying to drive knowledge into a child's head.

"If the heart revealed *wickedness*."

"Ah . . . so you're saying Tut might have been an angel—so to speak," I added.

"He was a youth, a teenager, apparently killed in an accident. His grieving mother or the priests may well have made a decision that he was without sin."

"Do you have any historical evidence of—"

"Yes, that's the second part. Howard Carter. Carter was an ethical professional. Like everyone else connected to the find, there was great disappointment when the Egyptian government ruled that Tut's tomb had not been opened before Carter's discovery and they were denied the customary division in which the discoverers took half and the government took the other half."

"And that apparently caused some of the members of the dig to help themselves to some items?"

"Yes, and they were allowed some things, but Carter would not have permitted something of great value like the heart scarab to be taken."

"Did Carter claim there was no heart scarab?"

"It was not noted in the inventory, so it did not exist."

"If you are correct and there was never a Heart of Egypt scarab, then how did the legend and stories about it get started?"

"That devil Radcliff. He took a scarab, one of many found at the site, nothing of great value. No one stopped him and it was just another piece that Carter and the government were willing to look the other way about because there was a great deal of anger and resentment that the government was unwilling to honor the agreement."

"How did it come to be called a heart scarab?"

The monk took a sip of wine and then paused. "I have water around here somewhere—"

"I'm fine, I have a bottle in my bag."

"Now. As I said, there was no heart scarab, so Radcliff filled the

❖

void. He intimated to people that he had King Tut's heart scarab without really saying it right out. It was an empty boast, but one that pleased him because he was so angry that he was not getting part of the richest archaeological find in history. There was a nationalistic political movement at the time, one intent upon driving the British out. When the rumors spread that King Tut's heart scarab had been stolen by a foreigner, there was much hue and cry.

"It put Howard Carter into a terrible position. You see, he had to keep insisting that there was no heart scarab, but couldn't say outright that a member of his consortium had started a baseless rumor. The Egyptian government also denied the existence of the scarab, but to no avail because the people wanted it to exist. And wanted to hate foreigners for taking it, much as they had skimmed off the cream of Egypt for a couple thousand of years."

"So you're saying that after Radcliff died, his son, rather than letting the world know his father was a fraud and liar, put the scarab away and kept mum about the whole affair. And that's been the attitude of the family ever since."

"That is what happened. There was a clue on the Tutankhamen mummy that solved the mystery for me. I am preparing a paper on it—"

He suddenly stopped and stared past me.

Two Egyptian men stood at the entryway.

One of them had a big nasty weapon, the sort of thing you see terrorists firing on TV news reports.

The man without the weapon pointed and said in Arabic, "That one."

The machine gun bucked in the man's hands and the boom of rapid fire filled the room.

❖

48

❖

"They were thieves, not terrorists," the police captain told me.

Sitting in the backseat of a police car on my way to Luxor's police headquarters, I was numb.

De Santis was dead.

"But they took nothing." I hardly recognized the voice as my own.

The killers had left immediately after shooting him.

It happened that fast. My ears were ringing when they left and still ringing when I had called the hotel and asked them to send for the police because I didn't know how to contact the authorities in charge.

My taxi driver wasn't there when I came out. Neither was the old man providing "security." Both had probably fled as soon as the killers stepped out of their car.

There was nothing I could do for the priest. A look of shock, even surprise, was imprinted on his features for eternity.

I put my scarf over his face to give him some privacy.

The first officers that arrived were patrol officers who spoke no

English and could not understand my attempt to explain what had happened.

Moments later the higher-ranking officer who I was now riding with arrived and told me he was taking me to police headquarters. He spoke English but asked me almost nothing.

As we drove, I finally demanded if he wanted to know what the killers looked like.

"When we get to the station," he said.

I laid my head back and closed my eyes. I needed a drink. A plane ticket home. And a passport in order to get onto the plane.

I suddenly woke up to the fact that we were approaching the Luxor airport. I had no idea where the police station was and assumed it was near the airport until the police car pulled up to a curb.

A man with a cell phone to his ear hurried toward us.

"What is this? What's going on?" I asked the officer.

"He will take care of you." He indicated the man coming toward us.

"Take me to police headquarters. Now!"

"A flight to Cairo takes off in twenty minutes. You can be on it or you can stay in Luxor for a great deal of time explaining to the police why you were at the scene of a murder."

I didn't have to think that hard about which option to choose.

My passenger door was opened by the man with the phone glued to his ear.

He handed the phone to me as I stepped out, keeping a firm grip on my arm while I listened to the voice on the other end.

"Are you familiar with the Khan?" Kaseem asked.

I was so irate I couldn't speak but kept the phone to my ear and permitted the man to lead me into the terminal.

"I have followers in Luxor," Kaseem said. "Even in the police. I was called after you reported the death of the monk. I notified the officer who drove you to the airport to get you out of there."

"What's going on?"

I knew I probably wouldn't get the right answers from Kaseem, and I was right. He ignored the question.

❖

"I asked, are you familiar with the Khan?"

Not even God was that familiar with the Khan el-Khalili, the medieval marketplace in Cairo's Old City.

"Enough to find the front entrance."

I knew more than that about the great marketplace in the Old City.

The medieval souq was a twisted maze of hundreds, perhaps even thousands of vendors. It was an endless labyrinth of narrow serpentine alleyways. A few steps off the beaten path and tourists need a guide to get back to their bus.

"That is all you need to know. You are to meet a blind beggar at the entrance at five o'clock. He will be selling bottle cap openers."

"Selling what?"

"Bottle cap openers. Twist-off caps are not that common in my country."

"And what am I supposed to do with this blind beggar? Exchange secret passwords? Let you know what's going on by speaking into my Dick Tracy watch?"

"The man will lead you to where you can examine the scarab."

"That's it? I just walk into the marketplace and a blind man with bottle cap openers will take me to a priceless treasure?"

How blind was this beggar?

"I didn't make the arrangements, the thieves did."

I restrained myself from pointing out that thieves weren't the reason my passport was pulled, he was.

A man was dead. An old monk, priest, whatever he was, had been murdered in front of me. Savaged by a spray of bullets that made loud popping sounds. And Kaseem acted as if I was returning from a Red Sea vacation. And there wasn't a damn thing I could do about it.

The police officer he sent to get me out of the investigation into De Santis's murder had expressed it nicely—get on the plane for Cairo or get stuck in Luxor, with many thousands of dollars in a panty hose money belt around my waist for which I had no explanation the police would like. And my passport had been pulled because I was on a watch list.

I wanted to tell Kaseem to shove his whole intrigue in a place where the sun didn't shine, but I was screwed no matter which way I turned.

❖

"What do you plan to do when I'm examining the piece?"

"What do you mean?"

"I don't want to get shot in a crossfire."

He chuckled without humor. "These people are not fools. They will be prepared for an intervention. The ransom money is being put up by patriots that can afford it. And this time the money will be real. I just want the scarab, not a gunfight in the marketplace that will attract the police."

I believed him—at least the part about not wanting to attract the police.

"Put the battery back into your phone," he said. "You might need it in a hurry."

"Ah, I get it. You're tracking me by the signal my phone gives."

He hesitated.

"You might as well tell me. I'm also being tracked by the antiquities police. You're not going to want them following me into the marketplace."

"Take the battery out of your personal phone."

"My phone's turned off."

"You still have to take out the battery. Most cell phones give off a signal that is easily tracked even when the phone is off. Taking out the battery kills the signal."

Once I was on the plane, I took the batteries out of my phone and the one Kaseem had given me and took two aspirins.

I tried to make sense out of why De Santis was murdered.

Did Kaseem have him killed because the monk was going to publish a scholarly paper hypothesizing that there was no Heart of Egypt scarab?

That just didn't compute because the scarab had always been more legend than reality. Besides, the poor masses of Egypt who believed the legend and would be galvanized about it weren't going to be reading Italian archaeological journals.

Did my presence bring killers to De Santis's door?

That made no sense, either. There was a very short time from when I asked about the monk at the hotel to the time the killers had arrived—hardly enough time to plan out a killing.

The reason De Santis was killed escaped me at the moment, but it was just one item on a long list.

❖

Two things, however, had not escaped me.

Kaseem never asked me what my conversation with De Santis was about, and something De Santis said about King Tut's mummified remains provided the clue that he had never had a heart scarab.

I tried to focus on the clue on the mummy, rather than drive myself crazy trying to think of the dead bodies that I had left in my wake since meeting Mounir Kaseem.

Trying to focus was all I could do because I kept thinking about the old scholar who smelled of wine and just spent his life with his head stuck in books and artifacts.

49

❖

The Arabs called their marketplaces "souqs" and the Khan el-Khalili was the biggest one in Egypt, and the most interesting and exciting of the ones that I had been to over the years.

I walked through the market watching the swarm of people, smiling politely and shaking my head at hucksters peddling "priceless antiquities" made in the back room of their shops and at tourists and locals haggling over prices that never seemed to have a set amount, while I warded off kids and beggars demanding baksheesh—all of these and more were part of the everyday rhythm at the Khan.

Just about anything under the sun could be bought here—from three-thousand-year-old antiquities looted in the past week to three-year-old AK-47s last used even more recently.

The market had served for six hundred years as a caravan stop, but camels had now been replaced by tourist buses.

The tourists didn't venture far because the endless rows of narrow, serpentine, and nameless passageways filled with tiny shops in the Old City were daunting.

❖

Not far from where the tourist buses unloaded, you felt as if you had stepped into the past—and you had. Although the merchandise no longer arrived in long caravans of camels as it did for hundreds of years, much of the marketplace hadn't changed since the Turkish pashas had ruled Egypt.

Daylight was passing, and the muezzin late-afternoon call for prayers was in the air as I entered the marketplace.

Even though I was dressed modestly—a scarf over my head, a shawl over my shoulders, and a long charcoal cotton dress down to my ankles—I wasn't exactly blending in as a local, but at least I didn't pulsate like a neon sign as a lot of tourists did, either, especially the women who insisted on wearing tight short-shorts in what was still a socially conservative country for the most part.

I walked leisurely through the ancient streets, pretending that I was listening to the peddlers hawking their goods with a babble of short phrases in languages they thought you spoke and that had some connection to your homeland.

"My cousin's in Texas," said one merchant as he tried to sell me "ancient" papyrus with hieroglyphics painted on it.

"Kein danke," I answered in German, hoping to throw him off, and he replied, *"Mein Vetter ist in Berlin."* ("My cousin is in Berlin.")

No doubt if I had spoken the language of a remote Brazilian jungle tribe some Khan vendor would know it.

The pungent odor of aromatic spices hit my nostrils as I walked near the area where big stuffed sacks of the fragrant substances were lined up next to each other. Every imaginable spice was displayed for your eyes and nose.

I had only walked for a few minutes when I saw the blind beggar, an old wizened man standing in the middle of an intersection of passageways. He had dozens of metal bottle cap openers attached to the front of his coat like war medals.

The bottle cap openers made him stand out for me like a metal-blazoned neon sign.

I started to make my way toward him when a boy who looked about twelve approached me and said in a soft, enticing voice, "Come, Maddy."

❖

50

❖

At first I wasn't sure I had heard the boy right.

He walked past me and then stopped and turned around when I hadn't followed him.

Then he said my name again. "Come, Maddy."

He had probably been taught the one phrase in English.

I stayed a few steps behind as he took me deeper into the midst of the ancient alleys and off the beaten track and into a tiny canvas-covered passageway.

As I followed, I slipped the battery back into the cell phone Kaseem had provided and also stuck my battery into my own phone.

It was time to let the world know where I was in case I needed help.

He paused in front of a small shop with inexpensive copper goods— fat coffeepots, bowls, and cooking pans were stacked in heaps.

An old woman in the doorway of the shop narrowed her eyes at me for a moment before gesturing me to enter.

I stepped into the shadowy, unlit interior that was also crowded with copper goods and warily looked around.

❖

She then led me into an open-air workshop in the back where a man and two boys barely looked up from hammering and bending metal into all shapes and sizes.

We passed through the work area to a door and went through it into another passageway.

I reluctantly followed her.

What was I getting myself into?

I was retreating farther and farther away from the outside world and, worse, I didn't have a clue where I was.

Not uttering a word to me, the woman kept going, leading me farther into the confusing, tortuous passageways, the sky growing darker as the shadows lengthened with the sun setting.

I was truly in the medieval realm of the Khan where no tourist ever ventured.

How would I ever find my way back?

What perfect timing. Making the rendezvous late in the afternoon, the passageways were dimmer, which disoriented me even more, but they were not so dark that I might refuse to go deeper into the maze.

I had been in the Khan dozens of times but I had no idea of where I was now, although the city's relentless honking of horns in the distance clued me in to the fact that I wasn't that far from an ordinary street.

The woman led me to a shop where tobacco for shishas, the ubiquitous water pipes, was sold. Besides a large selection of aromatic tobacco these places also sold pot and maybe a little hashish.

She gestured for me to wait and I stood and watched for a moment as a man on a stool outside the shop forced smoke through the pipe's bubbling water and inhaled it.

The woman waved me in and stepped aside as I entered, hurrying away.

The shop was dark, lit only by a dim lamp, and the air was thick with the sweet and pungent smell of scented tobacco.

The only person I saw was a man behind the counter. He pointed to a door at the rear of the small shop.

Just a gesture, not a word spoken. I was beginning to wonder if the world had gone mute.

❖

"All right," I said out loud to myself, "must be the door with the tiger behind it."

My heart started beating a little faster as I opened the door and stepped inside.

An old man with a long beard, turban, and galabeya robe sat at a small table. Nicotine juice stained the corner of his beard on one side of his mouth.

I immediately felt claustrophobic in the stuffy room.

A single naked lightbulb, dim and dusty, illuminated the cramped space.

On the table was a piece of red silk, the size of a handkerchief, laid over what I presumed to be the Heart of Egypt scarab.

My heart made it to my throat as I stared at the silk cover. This was the moment of decision.

"Come, Maddy," the old man said, motioning me forward with his hand and gesturing at the silk.

I quickly glanced around the room while trying to appear as if I wasn't nervous. A set of curtains were on the wall behind the seated man. I didn't see any movement, but the curtains would be a perfect place for someone to hide behind.

Looking at the man seated at the table, I was certain that he couldn't be the mastermind of an international art thief scheme or even a know-ing member. He was too much the small-time Khan merchant; probably the owner of the tobacco shop. He struck me as being used as a front, perhaps not even realizing exactly the role he was playing, who I was, or what was coming down.

He pointed again at the object. "Come, Maddy."

"Is that all your English?" I asked. "Speak English?"

He smiled and pointed again. "Come, Maddy."

I stepped closer to the table. "Take it off." I waved my hand to indi-cate I wanted him to remove the silk cover.

I was careful to look down and avoid letting him look at my eyes as he pulled off the piece of cloth, a trick that I learned talking to a rug dealer in Istanbul.

Avoiding eye contact was an old habit from the days of haggling

❖

over the price of art. It's done for the same reason that I suspect some poker players even wear sunglasses—just as other card players can "read" the tells on the faces and eyes of other players, your pupils can involuntarily open slightly when you see something you like, such as a choice piece of art, for example.

I was glad now that I did it instinctively because when I saw the scarab I'm sure my eyes would have betrayed me the moment the silk came off.

I stared at it, instantly petrified, almost paralyzed.

My God . . . the scarab looked real.

A pulse at my temple started beating and I kept myself from clearing my throat.

I hadn't really known what to expect—the Heart of Egypt in the flesh, or a scarab like the one Adara had gotten from her mother, something a step above tourist stuff.

The scarab on the table appeared to be the real thing—or as close to it as a counterfeiter could possibly get.

It looked exactly like the realistic reproduction Fuad had showed me and I had the same feeling as I did when I saw the reproduction— like Howard Carter I might have to walk around it for days before I would be able to give an opinion on its authenticity.

Despite the tingling excitement I felt inside, I kept a poker face on as I took a Maglite and my loupe out of my shoulder bag and set them on the table.

I was too nervous and excited to sit down, so I reached over and picked up the scarab.

The man said something to me in Arabic and gestured to a chair next to the table, which I assumed meant an invitation to sit down, but I smiled and shook my head back and forth. My instinct told me to stay on two feet in case I needed to leave in a hurry.

I first examined the scarab in the dim light, feeling its weight and texture in my hands. If I had been alone, I would have asked the dung beetle if it had lied for King Tut when Ahemait, the devourer of the hearts of the dead, questioned it about the boy king's earthly sins.

❖

Was I actually holding one of the greatest treasures of Egyptian antiquity? Or a clever knockoff?

Nothing about the feel of the scarab told me it was a replica, but the more I held it, the more I began to get a cold feeling. I wasn't sure why I experienced the sensation—the piece in my hand was a perfect match to the one I saw at Isis' private museum.

I began to examine the scarab with the loupe and flashlight, this time going over every inch of it, not only looking for any marks that revealed it hadn't been made with ancient tools, but also for a telltale mark like the one Fuad Hassan had put on the bottom of the scarab to ensure that a reproduction could be distinguished from an original.

Again, nothing showed that I wasn't holding in my hand the Heart of Egypt that had been sealed in a tomb with a pharaoh for more than three thousand years.

I was stumped.

I had gone from heart-racing excitement to a cold chill at the bone about the piece. Yet I couldn't put my feeling into a coherent thought. I had no laundry list of factors revealing the scarab wasn't the original heart; that it wasn't the piece removed from King Tut.

Then it hit me.

Pretending to still examine the piece with my magnifying glass, I took a sniff of it.

The mummification process for a pharaoh involved extracting the brain through the nose and removing the other organs. The heart was left in place, and a heart scarab was laid over the area, along with a wedjat eye over the abdominal incision, an ancient Egyptian symbol to protect the king in the afterlife and to ward off evil.

The chest and abdominal area was then covered with layers of linen wrappings adorned with jewelry, with each layer bonded with resin.

In Tut's case, that process had taken place thirty-three hundred years ago.

After the discovery of his tomb about ninety years ago, the heart scarab would have been removed from the dense wrappings that had been sealed with resin.

❖

Usually the scent of the piece would not have retained its flavor of "antiquity" after being exposed to the air for nearly a century, even if the scarab had been in an airtight case for most of that time. But being sealed for thousands of years still left a hint of antiquity on objects, perhaps just the dust that the cloth bindings had in them when the wrapping process was done.

As I sniffed it again, I realized it wasn't the dust of ages on the piece that I smelled, but a subtle hint of chemical odor—very faint, but the sort of smell you'd get from paint that hadn't fully cured.

That smell hadn't been on the scarab that Fuad showed me, but I detected the odor on this piece.

Shades of Quintin Rees.

I felt reasonably certain that what I was holding in my hand was the result of the "big-paying" assignment that the counterfeiter's assistant had gotten from a woman of Middle Eastern descent.

Another perfect example of a skillful expert at fraud. Except that the chemicals hadn't fully cured yet.

The old man said something and I smiled.

I guess he was asking me for my opinion.

I only had one thought. I would be murdered if I told the thieves their prize was a copy. There simply would be no reason to keep me alive and report back to Kaseem not to pay the money.

Now what the hell was I going to do?

❖

51

❖

Holy shit! The old man was giving me the kind of look Arnie gives me when I can't pay the rent.

He knew something was wrong.

With the language barrier, there was no way to charm him. Not that I could have anyway—as a Khan merchant, he would be a veteran of dozens of haggling negotiations used every day to survive.

My right knee started shaking, a telling sign that the last thing I wanted to do was tell a bunch of crooks that I was onto their game or that they, too, had been taken.

Either way, they'd blame the messenger.

"It's very nice," I said, giving him what I thought was a convincing smile and a little bow. "One of the great treasures of the pharaohs."

I was sure my eyes were neon-flashing *"liar!"*

He started up from his chair and I saw movement behind the curtains.

"Have to tell my client the good news!" I yelped.

❖

I quickly bolted out the door and raced through the small shop in a flash, hitting the alley in a run.

I flew by two men, running like a bat out of hell.

The men behind me yelled "Stop!" in heavily accented English.

My feet pedaled even faster with the cold feeling between my shoulder blades that a bullet was on its way.

Darkness had already fallen and most of the shops were closed.

Few people were in the alleyways as I raced by with the sound of heavy running steps closing the gap behind me.

I didn't know where I was but headed blindly in the direction of the traffic noise.

As I came around a narrow corner, one of the men behind me grabbed the back of my scarf. I twisted and stumbled and bounced off a wall, swinging wildly and screaming.

He got a hold of my right arm, but I clawed furiously at his eye, my fingernails digging in as deep as I could. He screamed in pain and let go and I started running again as his companion came barreling at me.

I brushed by a boy leading a donkey piled high with goods as I dodged around another corner. As I sped by, I slapped the donkey's rear and shouted at it, causing the animal to bolt.

The boy and his donkey thankfully got between me and the two men and I propelled into a run again, driven by blind panic and adrenaline.

I was in high gear now.

I ran as if all the hounds of hell were on my heels and I believed they were. Those two men had been posted outside the tobacco shop to make sure I didn't go anywhere, regardless of what I had found.

It was a "kill the messenger" plan for sure.

They would have let me call Kaseem—reporting the scarab as genuine, of course—and then cut my throat so I wouldn't be able to tell the police if I was caught.

I saw the lights of cars ahead and came charging out into the street, almost getting hit by a taxi.

Horns honked, drivers shouted and cursed.

I heard a bang as a car slammed into another, but I didn't care.

❖

The noise and attention were lifesaving—literally.

I stepped into the taxi that had nearly run me over.

"I'm being chased by an angry husband," I yelled at the driver. "Go!"

❖

52

❖

I was already halfway to the hotel when my phone rang. I had decided to go back to the Queen of the Nile where I stayed before.

Kaseem.

"You lousy, no good—" I was about to say son of a bitch, but he cut me off.

"Was it the Heart of Egypt?" he asked excitedly.

"I almost got murdered."

"But you didn't."

"You'll get an answer when I have what you owe me. If it's play money, I go to the police."

"You don't know who you are dealing—"

I hung up on him.

He called me back. I waited until the tenth ring to answer.

"If the money's under my pillow when I get back to the hotel in an hour, you'll get your answer. Otherwise I tell the police."

I hung up again and took the battery out of his phone and did some quick thinking.

❖

"Keep driving," I told the taxi driver.

"To where?"

"I don't care. Just keep driving."

When something wasn't working, or was likely to get me killed, I had to change my game plan.

I decided on two changes for my immediate situation.

I put the first one into effect by calling Rafi al Din.

"I'm in a spot of trouble," I said. "There are some people I want to avoid in Cairo. Any suggestions?"

"A goddess of fate has guided you to me," he said. "I'll pick you up in two hours. Be packed."

I didn't have that much to pack in my small carry-on suitcase. I purposely had not brought a lot of clothes with me.

"Where are we going?"

"It'll be a surprise."

"I don't like surprises."

"I'll be at your hotel in two hours," he said.

"No, I'll meet you. Tell me where."

"The train station. South terminal."

AN HOUR LATER I was back at the hotel and ready to put phase two into action.

I asked the front desk clerk how many porters the hotel had on duty.

"Two," he said.

"Good. I want both of them to come to my room to help me with my luggage."

The desk clerk stared. "Miss, you checked in with a single small bag."

"I'm afraid of heights. Both porters." I pointed at the other clerk on duty. "Him, too."

"But—"

His mouth snapped shut as I laid a hundred on the counter.

"You, too. Now," I said.

Five minutes later I retrieved my small bag, an envelope under my pillow that felt right but I didn't open.

❖

The five of us went back down to the lobby and I had all four escort me to the waiting taxi outside.

I didn't know if Kaseem would have money or thugs waiting for me, but I figured that having a crowd around would at least avoid me getting murdered.

I told the driver to take me to a hotel where I'd switch to a taxi for the train station.

When I got back to Cairo, I would check into the most expensive, crowded, and secure hotel in the city.

No more being sixteen floors from the lobby and what turned out to be a revolving door to my room.

I wanted plenty of company after today—a place where my screams could be heard.

I checked the envelope, taking a bill out of the middle and using my mini-flashlight to examine it. It looked real. They all looked used, too—a good sign.

Kaseem probably had my money all the time, but had tried to cheat me and pocket it.

I called him en route and he answered on the first ring.

"Phony as a three dollar bill," I said with some satisfaction, not caring whether he understood the American expression.

"It's not possible!"

He sounded genuinely shocked and I got some satisfaction out of that, too.

"It's the same as the Radcliff replica, beautifully done; they're the best forgeries I've ever seen of an antiquity. This one was a side job done by a guy named Quintin Rees at the counterfeiting shop. I suspect Quintin might have had his throat cut after finishing it. He's MIA from home."

"MIA?"

"Missing in action."

"Are you certain you haven't made a mistake?"

I wanted to laugh out loud.

"The only mistake I made was letting you talk me into this mess. It's a phony."

❖

I took the battery out of his phone and chucked it and the phone out the window.

I leaned back in the cab and closed my eyes.

What was the old expression—being put through the wringer? That's how I felt. As if I'd been splashing around an old-time washing machine and then hauled out soaking wet and put through the rubber rollers that squeezed the water out before the wash got hung out to dry.

It had been one hell of a day, and it wasn't over.

I still had to meet Rafi al Din.

He hadn't told me why he wanted me to meet him at the train station, but I had hopes of a jaunt over to a Red Sea resort, Egypt's Riviera. Anywhere, as long as I got out of Cairo while I was still alive. And still had money in my pocket.

Now I needed my passport. Any way I could get it.

Even if I had to do some things that a lady shouldn't have to do.

Fortunately, Rafi was good-looking. Just the type I hate and am attracted to—a tough cop, probably drinks beer and smokes ugly black cigarettes as he watches soccer after sex.

What can I say?

Maybe it was me.

Did I expect too much from a man? Was I looking for Mr. Right to come along?

Maybe my standards were too high. Did I have to settle for less?

No, I didn't believe so.

It had to be that I was raised bad.

Being desperate with killers and thieves after me didn't help, either.

❖

53

❖

A Mercedes with dark-tinted windows bearing the insignia of an Egyptian army general transported Mounir Kaseem through the dark streets of Cairo. He sat in the backseat of the car driven by an active duty sergeant who had been Kaseem's own driver when Kaseem had been a high-ranking military officer.

After midnight, the crowded, frantic pace and harsh discordance of horns had quieted.

When they pulled up to a private marina on the east bank of the Nile north of the Imbaba bridge, Kaseem got out. The driver didn't need to be told to wait.

The camel market was not far from the area.

Kaseem walked past two sentries standing guard with automatic weapons and up the gangplank of a large dahabeeyah, a luxury houseboat-yacht.

Dahabeeyah meant "golden boat" in reference to the luxury river boats of the ancient pharaohs. The modern versions were the idea of

❖

Thomas Cook, the British tourism pioneer, about a hundred and fifty years ago, and as often carried archaeologists up the Nile to digs.

The boat Kaseem boarded was a floating Egyptian Army Officers Club, reserved for field grade officers.

Tonight it was being used for a meeting of a clandestine group of officers who supported Kaseem's Golden Nile nationalistic political action group.

As the middle-aged officers were about to hold a meeting in which they planned to decide the fate of their country, a group of young women enjoyed cocktails, hors d'oeuvres, and gossip on the stern deck patio.

The women weren't the wives of the men, though some had most of the privileges of wives without the formalities.

Once the meeting was over, the young women would join the older men for drinks and later entertain the men privately in the twelve bedroom suites on the boat.

Although the men weren't exceptionally wealthy by Western terms, they lived rich and privileged lives: their homes were behind high walls in secure neighborhoods, their wives shopped in London, Paris, and Dubai, and their children went to elitist Egyptian prep schools before attending universities in Britain and America.

The men considered themselves patriots, though by most reasonable standards they would be considered extremists whose political views were not shared by most of the people of their country.

Their goal was not to bring democracy to the country, but to stop the growing influence of Islamic reactionaries who wanted to return the country to medieval societies like the Taliban in Afghanistan and the northern Pakistani tribal areas.

If they succeeded, they would be autocrats who enjoyed even more power and wealth. That was never far from the minds of any of them as they voluntarily involved themselves in conspiracies that would earn them death by hanging if they failed.

Kaseem had been their commander before he fled into exile. Even in exile he was still in charge. Of all of them, he was the most dedicated and the least interested in enriching himself.

❖

He was also the most fanatical and dangerous.

Waiting for him in the lounge were a commanding general of an armored division, a general recently forced into retirement, and three colonels who knew they would never reach general rank.

The five men who had been waiting for him welcomed Kaseem with a salute that he returned. Then handshakes and praises were exchanged, fresh drinks were poured, and questions were asked about the health of their wives and the state of their children's schooling, jobs, and marriages before they started the meeting.

Though unspoken, the men were impressed that Kaseem had the courage to return clandestinely to Egypt.

Also understood by all of men was that their families would suffer and be impoverished if any of them were discovered to be traitors.

When the social greetings were finished, they stared at him, as a group, waiting for what he had to say.

He raised his glass. And smiled. "A toast to the Heart of Egypt."

"Is it true? Can we see it?" one of the colonels asked.

"It is en route to the place where it will be used at the proper time. I didn't dare bring it here. We are all expendable, but the heart . . . it must be preserved until then."

Except for the retired general, the officers were nervous and cautious as Kaseem once again went over their plan to seize power.

A paramount issue with the men was the fact that others had tried it and failed, most notably when President Anwar Sadat was assassinated by army extremists during a military parade.

"We know what went wrong that day," Kaseem said. "The plot only involved junior officers who lacked the ability to deploy large forces. We have that ability."

"They had no plan for seizure of the government," the retired general told them. "That was the height of lunacy. They did not have a leader, as we do"—he nodded at Kaseem—"ready to declare a state of emergency and seize power, along with the troops to back up the seizure."

"You will command the necessary troops," Kaseem reminded them. "Preparation and readiness to strike are the keys. We will move quickly and get the rest of the army on our side. The word will swiftly spread

❖

that it is the Golden Nile that has acted. The core leadership of the army know that we are not terrorists, but patriots."

For another hour they talked and planned and refined the stratagem that they had worked on for years, one that they believed would flush out the old powers and bring in their new thinking.

When they had their fill of politics and whiskey, Kaseem called it quits, informing the group that it was time for him to return to his quarters and begin implementing his plan.

The old general, who had been Kaseem's commanding officer in a bygone day before Kaseem rose in rank above him, walked him to the waiting staff car.

They chatted about the government's plan to build huge megacities to reduce Cairo's twenty million or so population by diverting millions of its inhabitants to the new metropolises, a scheme already under way and generally considered doomed to failure.

It was innocent talk on the dock in case they were overheard and it was not until they were at the car that the older officer explained the real reason he had walked Kaseem to the car.

"My friend," he said to Kaseem, "tell me the truth. Do you really have the Heart of Egypt in your hand?"

"Why do you ask?"

"Because if you did, I believe you would have showed it tonight."

"There has been a minor setback," Kaseem said. "I didn't dare mention it because our colleagues are too squeamish to hear the truth. I know who has the scarab. We will have it when we make our move."

❖

54

❖

I had already downed one glass of wine and was working on my second glass as I sat in the club car of the sleeper train from Cairo to Aswân. Considering what I'd been through, a third one wasn't that far away in my mind, and it would put me to sleep.

Rafi and Dalila were drinking fruit juice.

The trip was more than five hundred miles, an eleven-hour train ride between the two cities, passing through Luxor on the way.

Most tourists traveled the Nile by boat between Luxor and Aswân, but the train was faster and cheaper. The town of Aswân didn't have much appeal to me—it wasn't the Riviera, Egyptian or otherwise—but it was a gateway to one of the most stunning artifacts in the world, the colossi of Ramses at Abu Simbel.

"Lana is waiting for us at Aswân," Rafi said. He was referring to the edgy assistant that picked us up from the airport when I arrived in Cairo. "She'll drive us to Abu Simbal."

He still hadn't explained the reason for our trip, but now that there were no killers in sight, I wanted to know.

❖

"So tell me why we are going there?" I asked, yawning.

I had come down from my hyperadrenaline and was starting to feel a little tired as I finished my second glass.

"Some fellahs digging an irrigation ditch near Lake Aswân have uncovered a burial tomb of a wealthy Twenty-ninth Dynasty merchant. It had already been looted, probably soon after it was created over two thousand years ago, but there was enough left behind for these poor peasant laborers to have become rich if they had had more sophistication."

It was an old story heard over and again in the antiquities-rich Mediterranean area—workers digging a ditch, a road, or basement stumble upon a piece of history and grab it for themselves rather than turn it over to the authorities.

There was little temptation for these men to turn in the artifact. Desperately poor, even the small amount they received from a local antique dealer could equal years of income for them.

The piece would then make its way up the food chain of antique dealers until the artifact finally got smuggled out of the country and sold at auction in London, New York, or Hong Kong, often for millions of dollars.

When everything went to hell, it would be the poor workers trying to get some extra food and necessities for their families who would end up getting punished.

"The sudden advent of having more money brought the workers under the scrutiny of the local police chief," Rafi said.

"Of course, he didn't get a piece of the action, so he busted them," I said.

Rafi looked at his daughter. "Isn't she cynical?"

"That's what you said, too."

"Whatever." I laughed. "It's a good reason to see Abu Simbel again." And for me to stay out of Cairo until I figured out how to keep alive.

"Well, Dalila, I think it's time you finish your schoolwork and then to bed," Rafi said, his way of telling me he wanted to discuss what had happened between me and Kaseem.

We had two cabins next to each other with a connecting door in between. Rafi was to sleep in one, Dalila and I in the other. I initially had

❖

the cabin to myself, but Dalila asked if she could share it with me and I said sure, we'd have a pajama party.

Not exactly the sleeping arrangements I thought would work to my advantage, but the girl seemed like a nice kid.

Before we talked business I wanted to know more about Dalila's medical problem. As soon as he closed the adjoining door, I asked Rafi about her condition.

"What is Dalila suffering from?"

He didn't say anything for a moment but I could see from the way tension gripped him when I asked that it wasn't something he wanted to talk about.

"I don't mean to pry—"

"No," he interrupted, "it just makes me angry when I talk about it because I'm so helpless. There's nothing I can do to help her. She always had a weak immune system and was always sick." He stopped for a moment to get his emotions under control. "She has leukemia. The doctors say she needs a bone marrow transplant. If they don't find the right donor soon, then . . ." He looked away and didn't finish the sentence.

The prognosis sounded bad. I could see the agony on his face as he talked.

He obviously wasn't a donor candidate.

"You'll find a donor if you keep looking," I said.

"It wouldn't matter even if I found one. I don't want to discuss it."

"I'm sorry." What do you say to a father whose daughter is going to die?

What would I do if I were in his position? Everything that was humanly possible, I thought.

I felt his pain.

It was cruel punishment for any person, knowing that someone you love is facing death and there's nothing you can do about it. You still hope for a miracle but know in your heart it won't happen.

I held back the tears that were about to come, and changed the subject. "I'm sure you want to know about Kaseem."

He cleared his throat. "Yes. Tell me what happened."

I told him about the incident at the marketplace.

❖

This time I was completely honest with him. I owed Kaseem nothing and I needed Rafi on my side if I was to stay alive and get back my passport.

"Are you sure it was a replica? You said the light was bad—"

"I could smell the paint. It would take scientific tests to distinguish it from the original, but I'm sure it was a reproduction."

He lowered his voice and leaned closer to me. "What you have admitted to me about working for Mounir Kaseem, you must never speak of it again while you are in Egypt."

"I didn't know what he was up to."

"It doesn't matter. He is a threat to the government. Your association with him is enough to get you imprisoned here. Maybe worse."

The threat gave me a prickly sensation down my back. I had read about police brutality in Egypt, especially when it came to political opposition.

"This is insane," I said. And that was an understatement.

He spread his hands on his knees and looked down at them. "This is life. But yours is not the only death sentence."

I knew he was talking about Dalila.

"I'll help you all I can," he said. "Do you have any idea where Kaseem is hiding?"

"He could be back in New York for all I know."

"No, he is here in Egypt. His time has come."

"His time for what?"

"As he would say, 'The time to answer the call of destiny has arrived.' But it's a call for blood that will be resisted by my government."

"Where does that leave me?"

"Collateral damage."

❖

55

❖

As the train neared Aswân in the morning, I left Rafi and Dalila eating breakfast in the club car and returned to my room to freshen up.

Opening my makeup bag, I froze as I saw a folded piece of paper. Unfolding it, I found a rough sketch of a scarab with an imperial cobra on its back. Nothing elaborate, just a simple freehand drawing, but done with a professional flair.

Rafi had said the heart scarab was the symbol of Kaseem's Golden Nile fascistic political group.

The message of the drawing wasn't lost on me—it was a warning, one that could have been left by anyone on the train.

Kaseem wanted me to know that I was being watched.

How he tracked me was beyond my grasp of spy apparatus.

I once knew an art dealer who lined the inside of his hat with aluminum foil whenever he went outside. He claimed "the government" was keeping track of him with satellites. It was his way of thwarting the government as to his whereabouts.

I could use some foil right now.

❖

I thought I had protection with Rafi. I was wrong. Kaseem indeed had a long reach. We were more than five hundred miles from Cairo.

The drawing presented another problem to me—an incriminating one. The last thing I needed was to be caught carrying the symbol of the outlawed group as if it were a membership card.

I was biting my lip and still mulling over the warning when Dalila entered the cabin.

"Are you all right, Maddy?"

"Yes, fine. I was just thinking that my feet are always carrying me into situations that make my head swirl."

I slipped into the bathroom, tore the drawing up, and flushed it down the toilet.

56

❖

Lana brought a long face with her when she came to pick us up at the train station.

I don't know what she did in her life—or had done—to make her such a bundle of doom and gloom, but I hoped it wasn't my presence that was bringing it on.

I didn't need another enemy in Egypt.

Whatever it was, I noticed that Lana was angry at Rafi for not paying attention to her and not responding the way she wanted him to.

Rafi was a good-looking, unmarried guy; Lana was unmarried and worked closely with him and no doubt was in love with him. If she caught him making a play for me, she would definitely cause trouble.

Since she worked for Rafi, I wondered if she was aware of my connection to Kaseem. I had to assume that she knew, which meant she could bring hell down on me with a phone call to the Egyptian political security police.

I was beginning to think that I would've been better off hiding in a room at a busy hotel in Cairo and never leaving it.

❖

Or better yet, I should never have left home.

The antiquity site of Abu Simbel was located nearly two hundred miles southwest of Aswân on the western bank of Lake Nasser.

Other than the Ramses colossi being among the world's most sensational remnants of the ancient world, the location had little else going for it, mostly desert sand and blazing sun, even though the Temple of Ramses II and neighboring Nefertari's Temple were a stone's throw from Lake Nasser, a body of water formed by the Aswân Dam.

More than three hundred miles long, the lake extends into the Sudan. Abu Simbel itself was at the extreme southern end of Egypt, only about twenty-five miles from the Sudanese border.

Something truly magnificent on the shores of a lake in the middle of nowhere and almost completely surrounded by trackless desert was the best way to describe Abu Simbel.

Visitors got there from Aswân by bus or plane because private cars weren't permitted to make the trip for security reasons. Usually a convoy of vans and buses left in the wee hours, between three and four in the morning.

Knowing that the trip was made in convoys for security like Old West wagon trains wasn't the most comforting thought after witnessing what a single burst of automatic weapon fire can do to a human being.

Hopefully the official emblem on the van that we were in, and the guns I assumed Rafi and Lana carried, provided enough protection for us to travel safely without a convoy.

We arrived at Abu Simbel after a long ride that Dalila and I both found uninteresting and tiring and that made us sleepy. She had leaned against me, her head resting on my shoulder for half of the trip. I was afraid to move for fear of waking her up.

I was bonding with the child and wondered what could be done about her condition. There had to be a donor candidate somewhere. I didn't know how that sort of thing worked, but I'd be willing to be a donor if I was a match.

Tour buses had left hours earlier than we did because the heat during the day becomes unbearable.

We arrived at midday under a baking sun and retreated quickly

❖

into a shady garden of a picturesque villa near the lake and walled all around.

The house belonged to Rafi's friends, Amir and Noor, both of whom were archaeologists. The couple also had a sailboat tied up at a pier on the lake.

The two of them were attractive, in their thirties, very urban professionals even though their careers stuck them in what must be utterly boring isolation.

No neighbors, no shops, no Starbucks within hundreds of miles, not even a bagel shop or a Thai restaurant. How did they survive? I didn't even see a satellite dish.

I wondered what people had done in rural areas at night before the arrival of cable and satellite TV and the Internet. I didn't watch much television myself and was criminally ignorant of things like texting and putting my picture on Internet social sites, but I at least turned on the TV when I woke up in the morning just to see if the world had ended while I slept.

Despite the abundance of water that flowed from deep in Africa to Lake Nasser, Aswân was considered one of the driest places on earth, often going years between rainfalls, while summer temperatures could reach more than 120 degrees. It was so hot and dry that many poor people lived in houses that didn't have complete roofs.

Lana joined us for lunch and cold drinks and left soon after. She told Rafi she was meeting a friend in the village. They arranged to meet in the morning to interview the villagers who had traded in antiquities.

Her coolness toward Noor hadn't gone unnoticed by me. Did she dislike women in general? Or was it just certain people who she saw as a threat when it came to her relationship with Rafi?

She certainly didn't like me.

With Dalila going on an overnight camel outing to an antiquity dig with Amir and his daughter and son who were about the same age as her, that left Rafi and me with Noor who invited us to watch the evening light show at the Ramses colossi from their sailboat, a felucca with a triangular, lateen sail.

"Rafi tells me you've visited Abu Simbel before," Noor said.

❖

"I did, many years ago and just for the day, but I've never seen the light show. Or the temples from the water."

"Then you're in for a treat. To watch the light show from a boat is enchanting, especially when you already know the history."

I found the body language between Noor and Rafi interesting. They were so formal with each other.

They completely ignored each other, as if the other didn't exist and seemed careful not to meet each other's eyes. Also, the slight hug they had exchanged when we first arrived seemed purely perfunctory.

I had to wonder what the arrangements would have been if I hadn't suddenly been thrown into the equation. Dalila had mentioned to me that her outing with Amir and the kids into the desert had been planned weeks ago. Noor and Rafi would've been left alone, tending the home fires.

Maybe my imagination was running wild, but I had the feeling the two of them had something going on.

Or maybe it was just my dirty mind. Or my own past transgressions of a carnal nature. I instinctively thought of men and women in sexual terms.

Same people might say there's nothing wrong with leaving a good-looking guy like Rafi and a sensuous woman like Noor alone together, literally on a deserted island of sand in the middle of nowhere, on a hot night with a full moon and . . .

Oh, hell, having a little experience in such things myself, I was sure the two of them had something going on.

Which, of course, made me wonder about the role of Noor's husband in the ménage à trois. Was he intentionally taking the kids out for a field trip to let the two have at it . . . or was he completely in the dark?

❖

57

❖

Noor handled the thirty-foot sailboat expertly, with Rafi managing the
lines and sails with equal skill. I just held on, letting my hand dangle
into the cool water when the boat heeled on its side.

Night was falling and a light breeze flowed over the water, bringing
a little relief from the stifling heat of the day.

Noor brought the boat around a bend and we came into sight of the
temples. The light show hadn't started yet.

While Rafi put out an anchor to create a drag so we wouldn't drift
too far, Noor brought out iced lemonade for all of us. After the first sip,
I realized the lemonade carried a punch—the alcoholic kind.

Obviously, Noor was a modern Egyptian who didn't adhere strictly
to the Muslim prohibition against alcohol.

The view of the temples from the lake was nothing less than spectacular.

I still wanted to visit the site very early in the morning to beat the
merciless sun and tourist buses.

Although the site was commonly referred to as Abu Simbel, there

❖

were actually two temple complexes: The Great Temple faced by the four statues of Ramses at Abu Simbel itself, with a doorway into the inner chambers in the middle, and the Small Temple a short distance away dedicated to Hathor, the goddess of love and joy, and Ramses' wife, Nefertari, with smaller statues walling the temple.

The four sitting Ramses statues, each about as tall as a six-story building, not counting the bases, were among the most impressive artifacts in Egypt—which meant they ranked high among the wonders of the world itself.

"We really don't know why these colossi were built here," Noor said, "so far from the heart of Egypt. The best explanation seems to be that Ramses built them to intimidate potential invaders coming from the south."

"How big is the Nile?" I asked.

"It's the longest river in the world," Rafi said, "about four thousand miles, and less than a quarter of it flowing in Egypt itself. That made it a natural pipeline for invading armies to follow into Egypt."

"A good reason to have built a monument to impress them that the pharaohs of Egypt were god-kings of awesome power," Noor added.

I knew a good deal more about Abu Simbel than they realized, but I listened politely as they described one of the great engineering feats in history: Salvaging the two temples from what would have been a watery grave.

Back in the 1960s, the Aswân Dam was built to control the annual flooding of the river that had caused havoc since time immortal. Lake Nasser was created as a result, with the temples doomed because the waterline would be above them.

An international relief to save the temples was organized and millions of dollars raised. It took about four years, but piece by piece the giant statues and all the other parts of the temples were cut into pieces, lifted, and put back together again above the waterline.

Pieces weighing twenty and thirty tons were lifted by cranes, with the most stunning sight being the giant head of Ramses, lifted three times before it finally was put on the statue's shoulders. There were actually four Ramses colossi, but one had lost its upper body during an earthquake two thousand years ago.

❖

"There's a legend about the toppling of Ramses' head," Noor said.

I already knew it but let her continue.

"It's said that a Sudanese king invaded Egypt with a vast army and that he stopped at Abu Simbel to slap the statues of Ramses with his whip to show his army that the Egyptians were not as mighty as they appeared.

"When he struck one of the statues, the earth shook, sending Ramses' head and torso down to crush him."

He got his just dues, I thought. The sheer size of the statues was truly amazing.

To give a foundation and backdrop for the cliffs that the temples were positioned against, a gigantic artificial mountain, looking very real, was constructed to place the outer statues and to provide inner chambers for the insides of the temples. Some of the interior of the mountain was occupied by the temples, but most of it was empty space.

The temples ended up facing the same general direction they had been before they were moved.

"We have something similar," I told them. "Mount Rushmore. About the same size, too, though the statues of our presidents only have heads."

I recalled another legend about the temple name.

"Abu Simbel" was Arabic, which meant it could not have been the ancient Egyptian name of the temple. The story claimed Abu Simbel was a shepherd boy who led an archaeologist to the site about two hundred years ago to show him a part of the temple that poked out from the sand covering it.

Still staring at the temples and imagining the years and the thousands of workers it took the ancients to create them, I caught a sudden flash of flesh out of the corner of my eye.

Rafi had dived into the lake, naked.

Noor was already down to her panties when I turned in her direction. And then, all skin, she dove in, too.

❖

58

❖

Oh, well, I thought, why not? Like the proverb says, "When in Rome, do as the Romans do" . . . a perfect way to destress and relax. Besides it was still hot; a swim would be cool and refreshing. Watching their naked bodies gliding in the water also got me excited. So I stripped and dove in.

The top foot of the lake had been warmed by the broiling sun but my dive took me deeper below to water that felt clean, cool, and refreshing.

Rafi and Noor had both swum away from the boat, burning off the grime of the dry desert day, I guess, but I just did a stroke that was a cross between floating and a dog paddle that kept me afloat, occasionally dipping my face in the water, enjoying the moisture soaking into my dry pores. If I lived in this climate, I'd probably be coated with cream all the time. Desert living accelerates the aging process of skin.

None of the Nile cruise ships that often waited off the shoreline after ferrying in guests to watch the light show were present tonight. Most of them reminded me of the old-time Mississippi riverboats.

I couldn't hear Rafi's or Noor's voice and we were too far offshore to hear any activities around the temples.

❖

Floating in the inky water, the limitless dark sky overhead, and no bottom beneath my feet made me feel as if I were floating in space.

I shut my eyes and enjoyed the sensation of being absolutely free of all worldly demands, money worries, fear for my life, and what the future held for me.

The water beckoned, luring me deeper into the black void underneath, and for a moment I wondered what it would be like to just let go, to slowly sink beneath the soft, cool water . . .

I opened my eyes when I heard Rafi and Noor nearby me, neither their look nor expression giving any indication that skinny-dipping was anything but natural.

A thought suddenly occurred to me. "I just remembered that I saw crocodiles up and down the Nile in the past when I visited Egypt. Are there any in the lake?"

"Of course," Rafi said, "the lake was formed by damming the Nile."

"Great. Do they sleep at night?"

"Only after their bellies are full."

I swam to the boat like a bat out of hell, their laughter floating in the warm night air.

❖

59

❖

I had already made myself comfortable on the long seat cushion with a small pillow behind my neck, the beach towel covering my nakedness, when the two of them leisurely hauled themselves back on deck.

The warm air, refreshing swim, and spiked lemonade put me in a relaxed mood.

"Hey, I didn't mean to scare you off like that," Rafi said as he climbed up the boat ladder after Noor.

Both of them seemed much more relaxed with each other.

"That's okay, I was done anyway."

"I'll get us some more 'lemonade,'" Noor said with a surreptitious glance at Rafi and disappeared to the cabin below.

The light show had just started at the temples as Rafi came and stood in front of me, wiping himself with his towel.

He stood there, unashamedly, knowing full well that I was looking at him.

I couldn't help but get aroused, the sexual excitement inside my body slowly starting to build. I stared at his muscular chest.

❖

Men always have an irrational compulsion about a woman's breasts. I could understand the feeling because a man's breasts have always appealed to me. I didn't care if they were hairy or waxed; it was the nipples that I loved to tease.

His dark eyes captured mine for a moment and my body stirred again in sexual anticipation of what I knew was about to happen.

He dropped his towel to the side, exposing an erection that grew in size as I stared at it.

I felt the heat in my body surge.

He bent forward and removed my towel, letting it linger a moment as it slipped off my breasts, down my navel, and from the mound between my legs.

I instinctively reached out and grabbed his cock, sliding my hand down his shaft, feeling its power and girth as it swelled in my hand.

His lips hungrily found mine, his tongue probing my mouth. I arched up, responding to his mouth on mine, the sexual urge getting stronger as he kissed me.

I closed my eyes, blocking out all of the world around me, desperately wanting him to enter me. I wanted to grab his cock and jam it inside me.

He pulled away, his mouth traveling down to suck my nipples, teasing the tip of each one with his tongue. The farther down he traveled, the more my body responded to his touch.

I felt a nibbling at my ear.

Opening my eyes, I saw Noor lean close to me; her lips were just a kiss away and I could feel her heat.

"This is how Bedouin wives pass their lonely nights when their husbands are with their other wives," she said before she passionately kissed me, giving me a taste of her sweetness. Pushing her breasts in my face, I caressed each of her nipples, and then she did the same to mine.

I was ready to climax at any moment.

Noor guided my hand down between her legs. I gently fondled her clit as she sucked on my nipples again.

❖

My blood fired as Rafi opened the garden between my legs and began to massage it with the tongue of a lizard.

I let out a gasp and then a scream as I vibrated from the passionate explosion inside my body.

❖

60

❖

After satisfying our sexual needs, the three of us filled our stomachs with more hard lemonade and stuffed ourselves with food from a large platter that contained several different types of hummus with pita bread for dipping, olives, and stuffed fried pastries filled with meats and cheeses. A dessert tray was filled with a variety of fruits, figs, and honey-drenched baklava.

I stared dreamily at the golden temples as I ate, imagining that they were lit by torches and awaiting the arrival of Ramses to inspect the colossi of himself.

I also learned a little more about the surprising relationship between Rafi and Noor. She was the twin sister of Rafi's ex, who had married a rich French man and moved to Paris. Amir had been Rafi's best friend at college.

I wondered what Freud's analysis would've been of Rafi fucking his ex-wife's double who was married to his best friend?

Rafi caught me staring at a big scar on his left side.

"Crocodile," he said.

❖

BACK AT THE HOUSE, I had just finished combing my hair when Noor came out of the shower.

"I need to tell you something," she said, "but don't say a word to Rafi. He would kill me if I told you."

"Sounds serious."

"It is—for him. That scar you saw on his side?"

I knew it wasn't from a crocodile.

"He had a kidney removed."

"Cancer?"

"Yes, but not his. He sold a kidney."

"No. *Why?*"

"Dalila's condition is terminal unless she gets treatment only available in Switzerland. It's very expensive. Rafi doesn't have the money and my bitch sister won't help and doesn't care because Dalila likes living with her father rather than her."

"My God—he had to sell one of his kidneys to get money for Dalila's treatment? That's . . . that's insane."

"That's life on this part of the planet," Noor said. "It's not uncommon for poor Egyptians to sell a kidney to an oil-rich Saudi or a Dubai real estate baron. The money can get someone out of debt and even into a better life, though most people end up so sick afterwards from the backroom operation that they end up dead . . . or wishing they were dead.

"You can live with one kidney, until it gives out, of course. Rafi recovered from the operation better than most people, probably because he was in superior physical shape to begin with."

I couldn't believe what I was hearing.

Like everyone else in America, I was frustrated and angry at the outrageous cost of medical insurance and the way the insurance companies provided benefits. But to sell body parts to get treatment for a child?

Thinking about little Dalila slowly dying and her father selling off body parts made me sick.

"I wish you hadn't told me," I said. "I liked the crocodile story much better."

❖

"I told you for a reason. Selling his kidney got Dalila a trip to a specialist in Zurich and started on a medical regimen, but Rafi can't keep up the costs of further treatment on his salary."

She paused and gave me a concerned look. "He's planning on selling a piece of his liver."

Jesus. I grabbed the edge of the dressing table to keep myself from running out of the room. This couldn't be true.

"What the hell could someone do with a piece of liver except feed it to their dog?" I asked her.

I wasn't trying to be facetious but I just couldn't believe anyone doing something like that.

"They can take part of the liver from a living donor and use it for a person dying with liver disease. But it's a much more serious operation, and the person giving up part of their liver often dies or is incapacitated."

Her voice quavered as she continued. "You have to understand that selling organs is illegal in Egypt, so the operations are not done in the best hospitals and under the most sterile conditions. People who give up part of their liver receive a great deal more money than kidney donors, but . . ."

She couldn't finish.

I waited a moment and then asked, "Why are you telling me this?"

"Because I'm worried. For Rafi, and for Dalila."

She suddenly grabbed ahold of my arm.

"Rafi has been acting strange lately. He's always been worried about Dalila . . . always desperate to save her. And he's more bitter than most people in my country about the lack of universal medical care because he has traveled to the rich countries and sees children like Dalila getting good care."

She took a peek out the door to make sure we weren't being overheard. "I'm afraid he might do something irrational . . . something out of pure desperation," she said.

"Does he realize what could happen to him?"

"Of course. Rafi knows he may die from the liver procedure or just as bad, he may be so weak he can't work."

❖

"What do you think he's planning to do?"

I really wanted to ask if the act of desperation had anything to do with the Heart of Egypt.

It seemed pretty obvious that whoever took the scarab from Fatima had inside information about the transfer. Rafi's position as the chief investigator of the scarab was perfect for getting that sort of information.

"I don't know," she said. She hesitated and then gave me a look of defiance. "And if I did, I wouldn't tell you. I don't know why I even shared this much with you."

I wondered that myself. "Why did you?" I asked.

She broke out in tears. "Because I love Rafi and don't want to see Dalila die." She ran by me and went to her room.

I left the house and went for a walk in the desert, not giving a damn if I stepped on an Egyptian cobra or a big scorpion or whatever other nasty things lurked in the desert.

Noor's sharing of Rafi's efforts to save Dalila had gotten under my skin.

What kind of world is it when you have to part yourself in order to save someone you love?

I hoped to hell Rafi hadn't done something stupid and gotten himself involved in the scarab theft. But I had a feeling that that was exactly what he had done.

Which meant that Kaseem might have guessed that also.

And was coming after both of us.

❖

61

❖

I slept hard and woke up the next morning before the break of dawn. After I made some strong coffee, I grabbed a piece of baklava and walked out into the tranquil garden barefooted, keeping an eye out for scorpions, cobras, and whatever else enjoyed the desert climate.

The rising sun stirred the desert, whipping up a little breeze that ruffled the palms in the garden. As I sat on the edge of the fountain with my feet in the cool water, I tried shaking off the horror of what Noor had revealed to me about Rafi selling a body part. It was on my mind when I hit the bed and my first thought when I woke up.

A price on life . . . that's what kept coming back around at me.

How do you feel when you know you can't afford the cure to save your life? Or the life of a loved one?

A parent selling parts of themselves for medical care for a child?

What the hell kind of world is that? That Rafi had to resort to that kind of horror was hard to stomach.

I had to do something to help Dalila.

I didn't know exactly what, but there had to be a philanthropic or-

❖

ganization in New York I could approach when I got home. I'd raise the money to help her somehow, starting with tossing a big chunk of what Kaseem paid me into the pot.

Knowing I would do something to help her relieved my mind and let me think about my present situation.

Isolated in the desert, I felt like a prisoner and wondered if that had been Rafi's intent, but dumped that idea. He couldn't have known that I would end up running wildly through the streets of Cairo with killers after me.

He had to be up to his neck in the scarab thing, that was a given as far as I was concerned. And not just in his role as an antiquities cop.

I mulled over my involvement with Rafi—a couple of brief sexual encounters that hadn't required any emotional connection—and my own state of mind concerning men.

I found myself becoming more and more of a hedonist, seeking the pleasure of the moment rather than a permanent connection with anyone. I wasn't a loner. I'd had a brief marriage that broke up when our careers split us geographically and our love wasn't strong enough to span a continent.

Having experienced what was supposed to have been a permanent relationship, I was ready for another, one that I hoped would last the rest of my life, but over the past decade that I'd been single, I had only met one man who felt like the right fit with me, and he had died in my arms.

In the back of my mind I still hoped to find my soul mate, the person who would make my life complete. I knew he had to be out there somewhere. Everyone needed a soul mate.

I liked Rafi, was definitely attracted to him sexually, and found pleasure in his arms. Maybe if he lived in New York I would have the sort of casual, sexual friendship I have with Michelangelo, that booty thing, but I didn't have that sense of everlasting affinity with either of them.

My rumination on men was cut short by the sound of a car pulling up outside the walled house.

I got up and opened the gate to see who had arrived so early in the morning.

❖

It was Lana, arriving on the heels of a wind shear that swept across the desert, raising a cloud of dust in its wake.

An ill wind had arrived.

"Where's Rafi?" she snapped.

"Use that tone of voice on someone who cares," I said.

She stormed by me, giving me the sort of stare that Medusa had used to turn people into stone.

Her glare at me was a reality slap reminding me that I wasn't just a prisoner in the desert . . . Egypt was going to be my personal supermax if I didn't get back my passport. And she could definitely sabotage it.

I followed her into the house to make sure I knew what was coming down.

In the living room, she confronted Rafi who was coming in from a hallway. He looked like he had just woken up.

"Your phone has been off!"

She made it an accusation.

"You could have turned it back on after *coming*," she said, speaking in English to make sure I knew what she was complaining about.

They reverted to angry bursts in Arabic and I caught that it had something to do with Dalila.

Rafi reacted as if she had slapped him in the face.

Noor came into the room behind him and started wailing at whatever was being said.

I had picked up a little Arabic over the years during my travels in the Middle East, little more than telling a taxi driver where I wanted to go, but caught nothing of the rapid-fire exchange.

Rafi suddenly bolted back down the hallway with Noor running behind him, yelling something.

The room was suddenly quiet as Lana turned to me. Her features were cold.

"What's going on?" I asked. "Is Dalila okay?"

Lana gave me a long, appraising look, as if deciding whether to answer me or squash me like a bug.

I guess sleeping with the boss who she had a thing for didn't endear me to her.

❖

"Kaseem has her."

"He has Dalila? How—"

"Amir handed her over to him while Rafi was fucking his wife—and you." She gave me a malicious grin. "That makes all of you responsible if anything happens to her."

I had a sick feeling deep in the pit of my stomach.

"What does he want from Rafi?" I asked, dreading what she was about to say.

"The scarab, of course." She gave me a smirk. "Not that piece of junk you saw at the Khan."

62

❖

The world around me disintegrated.

Rafi ran out of the house, checking his gun as he left and jumped into Lana's car.

He took off without her.

She gave him a grin full of spite and jealousy as he left and then turned her venom on Noor.

"It's your fault, you slut," she said. "Did you think your husband was completely stupid?"

Noor slumped down in a chair and burst into tears. She didn't say anything.

I stepped in between them.

"Leave her alone. She has enough to worry about without you kicking her when she's down."

For a moment I thought Lana was going to attack me, but her phone went off. She checked the number and gave me a sly look before she went off to answer the call in privacy.

❖

She identified herself as Sphinx as she left the room, shooting a glance back at me as if to taunt me.

Good work, I thought. With my usual ability to dig a deeper hole for myself, I had taken the side of a woman who could do absolutely nothing to help me and pissed off the one who could.

All part of my life plan to do what I think is right without giving a single rational thought about the consequences.

"It is my fault," Noor said, sobbing "I've always loved Rafi. How could I help it? My sister loved him. Everything she felt, I felt, too. I should never have married Amir. He's a good man and I'm a bad woman. I hurt him, I hurt our children, and now I've put Dalila in danger."

"You didn't do half the wrongs you think you did," I said. "You don't choose who you love; you just get victimized when it doesn't work out."

She collapsed in tears and I tried to comfort her, but she was too distraught.

I could understand her wrong turns and bad choices—I had a long list of mistakes in my own life that I wished I hadn't made.

Sitting down beside her, I stroked her hair as she cried while wondering what the hell was going to happen.

My mind swirled with questions.

Why did that bastard Kaseem take Dalila? To get Rafi off his back? Did Rafi really have the scarab as Lana intimated?

More important than Kaseem and Rafi, what was going to happen to Dalila? Had anyone called the police? Would that even do any good?

The more I thought about it, the angrier I got.

Amir turning a sick child over to Kaseem because he couldn't keep his wife in his own bed?

Kaseem laying claim to being a man of destiny but kidnapping a child to use as bait?

Rafi giving up an organ for his daughter, but letting her be pulled into this mess?

What kind of games were these people playing?

I'd call the damn police myself if I spoke the language and thought

❖

anyone would listen to me. Or believed that they weren't all in Kaseem's pocket.

I was getting ready to hike to Abu Simbel and get a taxi to the airport when Lana offered to drive me in Noor's car. She didn't bother asking Noor's permission to use the car.

If Lana was feeling sorry for Rafi and worried about Dalila, she hid her emotions well. She seemed to take pleasure knowing that the man who slighted her affections was suffering.

I still wanted to know Rafi's full involvement.

In the car, I probed her willingness to give me the lowdown on the extent of Rafi's machinations to get the money to save his daughter.

"Noor told me Rafi was desperate to get money for Dalila. That he needed a lot of it," I said.

"You want to know if that's why he took the scarab, don't you? And how he did it, too."

"Yes, I'd like to know."

Lana kept her eyes on the road as she talked.

"She probably told you about the kidney and the liver. The liver thing would have killed him or left him incapacitated, so he decided to steal the scarab when we got word that it was being returned."

That confirmed my suspicion as to why Kaseem grabbed Dalila. He wanted to swap the girl for the scarab.

"How did Rafi find out it was being returned? Kaseem told me it was being brought back in secret."

"Fatima Sari liked to talk. And she was all caught up with the thrill of being a great heroine of Egypt, of being the one who brought the heart back to us. She told a friend who had been a classmate of hers when she studied Egyptology. The friend knew Rafi was the head of the Supreme Council's recovery team and she told him."

"So Rafi decided to intercept the scarab? To steal it from Fatima before she got on the plane to Cairo?"

She shook her head. "Rafi knew she would never make it to the plane, that Kaseem had no intention of letting Fatima bring the scarab back."

"Because Kaseem wanted to return it himself and be a hero."

❖

"With a bang." She laughed harshly. "He wanted to return the scarab in a way that showed the greatness that Egypt would be able to achieve again."

"So Kaseem intended to take the scarab from Fatima all along. From the beginning he was never going to let Fatima bring it back."

"Exactly. He got that crazy British woman to agree to have it returned by bribing that ridiculous mentor of hers who calls himself Ramses, but once the scarab was out of the vault, Kaseem planned to grab it. He set Fatima up because she was easy to manipulate."

"What went wrong?"

She shrugged. "Both Rafi and Kaseem had the same idea of getting the scarab without causing a lot of noise."

"Drugging Fatima?" An overdose would explain why she had seemed so dazed to me.

"Yes, drugging her. Kaseem put a dose in the bottle of water she had by her hotel room bed without knowing that Rafi had bribed a hotel maid to deliver tea laced with sleeping medicine. She drank both."

It sounded like the Keystone Cops with a woman's thinking process at stake.

"It affected her mind, especially when she realized she had lost the great treasure she was supposed to deliver."

She gave me a narrow look. "I was not part of it, you understand? I stayed in Egypt. Rafi told me what happened."

That didn't ring true to me.

I suspected that Lana was something more than an innocent by-stander, but it didn't matter. If I started making accusations, I knew she would clam up.

"So while Fatima was under, Rafi took the scarab and was going to bring it back to Cairo?" I asked.

"Yes. He slipped into her room and got on the next flight to Cairo. It was easy for him to bring it back undetected. As an antiquities officer, he was not examined at customs."

"How does the scarab replica fit into all this?"

"He had a duplicate made to delude Kaseem. Fool that Rafi is, he didn't want Kaseem to get his hands on the scarab. Rafi thought he

❖

could get money from Kaseem for the fake and in the end, turn the scarab over to the museum in Cairo."

The counterfeiter told me a woman had approached him and his assistant to have a fake made. I was certain Rafi sent Lana to have it done, but again I kept my mouth shut.

Larceny, fraud, deception—and desperation for his daughter. Maybe even murder. An all-around bad combination, especially for a basically honest man like Rafi to handle.

She eyed me as she drove. "You realized it was a fake when you examined it in the Khan, didn't you? Rafi was sure that the reproduction was good enough to make you think that it was real, especially in the poor light. How did you know?"

"Experience? I don't know. Maybe just instinct. The reproduction for Isis was duplicated from the real scarab. The second one was done from pictures because the employee who made the fake got paid to do it on the side. Both looked exactly like the original . . . but no matter how much they look alike, there is a difference that's hard to quantify.

"It's like reproductions of the master painters. Modern painters copy them exactly, but most of the time an expert can tell which one is the imitation."

I waited a moment before I asked, "Why did Fatima try to kill me?"

She shrugged, but I could see the smirk on her face. She really enjoyed feeding me information . . . but just enough to whet my appetite. With Lana, there was always going to be another shoe that dropped. And it might just hit me on the head.

I was still puzzled by her role. She seemed to know what both Rafi and Kaseem were up to, yet stated that she wasn't involved.

"Who knows?" she said. "Her mind was mixed up by drugs and guilt. When Kaseem was angry with her after Rafi stole the scarab, she got it into her head that Kaseem had been the one who stole it. She got away from him but came back like a ghost, watching him."

Although she kept up the pretense that she wasn't a participant in what had happened, she sure had all the answers.

"So she started stalking him and he led her to me?" I asked.

"Your name had come up earlier with Kaseem, before the theft. He actually was going to have you examine the scarab taken from Fatima to make sure that he hadn't been given a reproduction by that fraud of a mentor who controls that Radcliff woman."

"No honor among thieves."

My phone went off with a message from Michelangelo that said *subway tape* with an attachment. What lousy timing Michelangelo had. Just like in bed.

I hit the link and waited for the connection.

"Rafi?" Lana asked.

I shook my head. "No. A cop friend in New York has sent me the security camera tape of Fatima running in front of the train."

"Why?"

"Because I have bad karma, I guess. Or shitty luck. Fatima tries to puncture me with a letter opener and jumps in front of a train and I suddenly find myself the chief suspect in her death."

I got a nod of agreement out of Lana—whatever that meant.

The picture was tiny and fuzzy on the smartphone screen. The camera view was wide-angle, taking in most of the small subway station. As I'd been told, the camera had been mounted behind Fatima, facing me, so my expression was visible and not hers. More importantly, her body blocked a view of my arm, making it impossible to see that my gesture was a defensive one, rather than striking out at her.

Watching the video, I remembered something had frightened Fatima, causing her to veer off toward the tracks like a startled doe. I didn't see anything obvious but the tape was only a few seconds long and I replayed it, looking at the people it captured in the crowded station as Lana pulled over to the side of the road.

I ran it three times before I recognized someone.

My blood froze and my heart jumped into my throat.

I turned to Lana, to that evil smirk she had plastered on her face.

"I guess you didn't stay in Egypt."

There she was, in a starring role in the subway video.

Lana was the one who Fatima had recognized—and the mere sight of the woman threw Fatima into a such a panic that she ran in front of the train.

❖

Lana pulled a slender rod up from the side of the seat. I stared at it, puzzled. For a moment I thought it was a long flashlight.

"Cattle prod," she said.

I grabbed for the door handle, jerking it down, and tried to open the door, but nothing happened.

"Locked," she said.

I opened the lock just as she touched me on the shoulder with the cattle prod and my head exploded.

63

❖

A road to nowhere. That's where Lana took me. A dirt path in the desert with fresh tire tracks, but even those would be covered by the next sandstorm. A landscape far away from the life-giving waters of the Nile—the far side of the moon, an endless wasteland where only the hardiest creatures on the planet survive—snakes, spiders, scorpions, and hard-shelled insects that devour each other in a never-ending cycle of life, death, and rebirth.

All my strength and coordination had been snapped by the electric shock so I sat helplessly while she handcuffed me.

My eyes were burning, my throat felt raw, and my bones had that achy feeling I remember having when I had the flu. The worse part was my head—it felt as if she had jumped up and down on it wearing spiked heels.

I was drained and exhausted without having done anything strenuous. I could sit upright now and stretch my limbs but I knew physically I couldn't have gotten out if she had stopped the car and let me escape.

❖

Not that I would have gone very far—the only reason Lana would let me out would be to run me over.

The cattle prod she used to stun me was tucked into the side of her seat. I could reach for it, but knew that I'd only get another jolt, maybe a lethal one that would kill me.

Lana had not spoken since giving me a whap that would have knocked a bull on its butt.

A CD played at loud volume and she hummed and sang along with the music, a song with that jangling wail and tinny rhythm of the Middle East. I admired many things about Arabic culture, but its music wasn't one of them. Neither was Lana's singing voice.

I wanted to scream at her to shut up, but it would only make her laugh and turn up the music even louder.

I don't know how Rafi could have missed the signals of hate, spite, and jealous rage that Lana radiated. But I also didn't know her total involvement or who she was connected with, though Kaseem was my candidate. That meant she had sent Rafi into an ambush that would no doubt get him killed as soon as he turned over the scarab to Kaseem.

At the moment I was worried about my survival.

If I had a choice between the two men, I would pick Rafi as the one giving me a slightly better chance of staying alive than Kaseem.

At least Rafi's motives for getting involved appeared to stem from his concern for Dalila. And even at that, he had what sounded like a plan rooted in hope and madness to make sure that the scarab found its way back to King Tut at the museum.

I could cut a deal with Rafi to keep my mouth shut if he came out on top. But Kaseem again struck me as the type who wouldn't want to leave any dangling ends.

"It's not about the scarab," I said out loud.

I don't think Lana heard me over the noise she thought was music. She probably wouldn't have answered me if she had heard me.

Rafi's only motive to get the money was to save Dalila.

What was Kaseem's game? Political, for sure. I didn't think he planned to come back to Egypt riding a white horse and waving the scarab. No,

❖

he had something bigger planned, something that the scarab was only a part of.

Giving Lana a sideways glance, I wondered what she had in mind.

She hit the radio power button. The sudden silence was like a breath of fresh air. But heavy with anticipation—she was waiting for me to say something.

"I have money," I lied. "If you help me and let me go, you could be a rich woman."

She laughed. Not a ha-ha laughter full of humor, but a screech that got under my skin like fingernails on a chalkboard.

"I help you and I will be a dead woman." She smirked, full of arrogance and contempt. "Besides, you made a mistake when you fucked my man."

That got a sigh of defeat from me. I had to admit that my attitude about sex had gotten me into trouble on more than one occasion.

She hit the radio power button again and started that mournful wailing that passed for music with her.

If I could have gotten my hands on the cattle prod, I would have stuck it in a place I knew would really make her wail.

64

❖

Lana turned off the radio and slowed the car as we came around a bend in the road.

Parked on the roadway was the car Rafi had driven, coated with dirt. It had an abandoned look and that's what I would have assumed it was had I not seen him ride off in it earlier.

She drove slowly up beside the parked car and inched around it, pulling a small pistol out of her purse as she steered.

I didn't know if she wanted to see if it was occupied by anyone—or looking for Rafi's dead body.

"You'd kill him, wouldn't you?" I said. "And let Dalila suffer and die. Just because he didn't give you the attention you wanted?"

She raised the pistol and put the muzzle against my temple.

My blood froze. I didn't move, didn't breathe, out of fear she would actually pull the trigger.

"Bang," she said. And giggled like a crazed banshee.

She suddenly tensed and gave me an evil look. "I would kill you if Kaseem didn't have plans for you."

❖

The hatred in her eyes meant she was serious.

"You are a—"

She didn't let me finish, but hit me on the side of the head with the butt of the gun.

I saw stars but got out "crazy bitch" before she hit me again.

"When he's finished with you, you're mine," she said.

❖

65

❖

Lana continued driving down into a wadi, following tracks in the dry riverbed, and back up again. She drove very slowly, the car engine making little sound and raising no dust.

Finally I saw a house, a mud hut with a flag near the front door that appeared to be a small, remote military outpost; a sand-colored van with an Egyptian Army insignia on its doors stood parked in front.

A body lay on the ground near the van. Another body was sprawled nearby. Both bodies wore military uniforms.

Lana stopped the car and slipped out, leaving her door open as she did, gun in hand.

The door to the hut opened and Kaseem came out.

Someone stood behind him. It was Rafi, with Dalila next to him. Rafi had a gun pointed at Kaseem.

Lana slowly approached the two men, holding her gun casually pointed downward. She acted as if she was approaching a situation that Rafi had well in hand.

What Rafi didn't know was that she had sold him out to Kaseem.

❖

I heard Rafi say something in Arabic to his daughter who started to run back in the house, then he suddenly gave Kaseem a shove as Lana approached them.

I unlocked my door and got one foot out and my head above the door frame and yelled, "It's a trap. She's on Kaseem's side!"

Rafi turned toward Lana as she fired her gun. He staggered backwards and went down. As he lay on the ground, Kaseem stepped on Rafi's wrist and took the gun out of his hand.

Lana spun back around to me.

I gawked as she raised the gun and fired.

I was already falling backward as my door window shattered and sprayed me with flying glass.

66

❖

I was still lying on the ground when Kaseem came to the car and stood over me. I figured it was the safest place to be.

"You have antagonized Lana to the point that she has a bloodlust to kill you. She's like a jackal that's tasted blood."

I didn't say anything.

"Just stay where you are until I am ready for you. There's nowhere for you to run. Besides, you would just give Lana an excuse to put a bullet in the back of your head."

While I sat by the car and watched as events I knew little about unfolded, Dalila sat beside her father as he lay on the ground, pressing a handkerchief against the wound to his left shoulder.

Kaseem snapped an order to Lana. She disappeared into the hut with him and came out with a first-aid kit and knelt beside Rafi to tend to his wound.

I had no idea how badly he was hurt or why they were bothering to give him first aid rather than kill him, but I figured it had to do with

❖

something Lana had said to me—I was being kept alive because Kaseem had plans for me.

Apparently, Rafi was also in the category of necessity for whatever was about to come down.

Two more Egyptian army vans arrived and Kaseem now came out of the hut wearing an officer's uniform.

Sitting in the dirt, handcuffed and clueless, I wondered if Kaseem planned a revolt or a coup. But it struck me that half a dozen soldiers in a couple of vans were hardly the stuff of revolution.

When everyone was busy doing something or busy with each other, I leaned up inside the car and reached across the seat and grabbed the cattle prod Lana had left behind. Sitting back down in the dirt, I kept the weapon hidden against the side of my body.

The cattle prod was about the length of my leg from ankle to knee. I slipped it up my pants figuring that would be a good hiding place, but I needed something to hold it there. Tape or a shoelace would have worked nicely, but my shoes were laceless and no roll of duct tape jumped out at me.

In the side storage pocket of the car door I found a long, thick rubber band that looked like something Lana would use to hold back her hair. Trying to look like I wasn't hiding a stun weapon, I stealthily slipped the cattle prod inside the bottom of my pants and pulled the hair band over my ankle and the prod, doubled.

I just hoped the prod wasn't going to embarrass me by slipping down from where I had it secured to my leg. And that Lana wouldn't notice that her favorite toy was missing.

What good the weapon would be against people with guns wasn't something I wanted to think about as I sat in the dirt and wondered when the next shoe would drop, but at least I had some sort of self-defense.

After the soldiers loaded Rafi into a van, with Dalila in tow behind him, Kaseem walked toward me carrying a small, black box.

He carried the object as if he had been entrusted with a sacred duty and in his mind he no doubt had been.

"Get up," he told me.

❖

Easier said than done when you're handcuffed and hiding a cattle prod in your pants, but I managed it, though with little grace.

Kaseem set the box on the hood of Lana's car and carefully opened it, revealing a red velvet pouch. He uncuffed me.

With the deliberation of a surgeon cutting flesh, he opened the velvet sack and drew out a scarab. He spread the pouch on the car's hood and delicately put the artifact on it.

"Where's your loupe?" he asked.

"I don't need it. It's the Heart of Egypt."

"Don't play games with me—you haven't examined it."

"I don't need to examine it."

I took the heart-sized scarab in my hands, feeling the object against the skin of my palms, then brought it up to my face to sniff it.

Resting beneath a mummy's wrappings and against the chest of a boy king for three thousand years, I could smell the musty dust of antiquity on the scarab, sense the long-dead hands that lovingly shaped it.

"Don't try to appease me. I have to know."

He drew his gun, although pointing it away from me.

"It's the heart," I said. "I've examined two incredibly good fakes and I know what I have in my hands is real because of the way it looks and feels, smells, and most of all . . . because it speaks to me."

I didn't know what was going on in his head, but I was pretty well convinced that Kaseem believed the scarab had magical powers. And now he had it in his hands.

Fear rose in me, grabbing my breath and jerking it away as I realized that I had fulfilled the task that Kaseem had laid out for me.

I carefully set the scarab back down on its velvet bed and met Kaseem's eye.

"I did what you asked me to do. Now I suppose my reward is a bullet in the head."

He said nothing for a moment, his mind still locked in whatever thoughts and passions about the Heart of Egypt dominated him.

The gun in his hand came up at me and wavered for a moment, then he slipped it back in its holster.

"You still have a role to play," he said. "Cuff her."

❖

67

❖

Lana pulled me with a grip on my hair to the van that Rafi had been loaded into. The cattle prod banged and slipped on my ankle but wasn't exposed.

Rafi lay lengthwise on one side of the van, his left shoulder and chest area bandaged enough to stop the bleeding. When they had put him in the van, his left arm hung limp from the wound in his shoulder and now it lay at an odd angle.

His face had lost color and his eyes were closed, but his chest rose and fell in a normal breathing pattern.

Dalila knelt beside him, holding on as if he was a life raft.

I smiled at her. I wanted to give her a hug and comfort her, but I was warned not to speak or move.

"It'll be okay, Dalila," I whispered.

I didn't honestly believe that and I don't think she did, either. She gave me a look full of fright.

When we hit a big bump, Rafi let out an exclamation of pain.

Lana snapped an order to a soldier in back with us and he scooted

❖

over to Rafi. Dalila tried to push him away and Lana lashed out at her in rapid Arabic that caused the little girl to back off in fear.

"More painkillers to keep him quiet when we go through checkpoints," Lana told me. "When I shoot you, you won't get any drugs. I want you to feel the pain." She gave me an evil grin.

"You know why you can't keep a man?" I said. "The ugliness inside of you oozes out all over so everyone can see it."

She started for me and stopped as Kaseem snapped something at her from the front passenger seat.

"Keep your mouth shut," he said to me, "or next time I'll let her cut out your tongue."

Lana looked about the van as if she was searching for something.

I turned away, sure she was trying to remember what happened to the cattle prod. Hopefully she would think she had left it in the car, which was still back at the outpost.

The rough road and lack of a seat or restraints in the back of the van kept me in a constant state of swaying back and forth and being slammed over and over against the wall behind me.

The cuffs hurt my wrists, the cattle prod rubbed raw against my leg and felt as if it would slip off at any moment and roll down the van floor to Lana. My throat felt like a hot, dry road to hell, and I had a bad headache. I wished I could take off my head and shake out all the hurt.

At least the pain and discomfort reminded me that I was still alive.

From what I could make out through the dirty windows, we were on our way back to Abu Simbel, following the same route that Lana had taken us on the way over.

Why we were going back to the monuments was a mystery to me and a question I was dying to ask, but didn't.

"Two days," Lana said.

The remark came out of the blue.

When she spoke, I had been dozing as best I could, my head bobbing back and forth, occasionally hitting the van wall I was leaning against.

I opened my eyes.

She was looking at me. Rafi and Dalila both appeared to be sleep-

❖

ing, though in his case, he was in a state of agitated unconsciousness and groaned from pain every so often.

"What did you say?"

She appeared surprised by my question.

Maybe the remark had dribbled out of her mind rather than having been directed at me. She had a weird look to her, a quiet madness, like a serial killer whose mind was controlled by a demon living in her head.

Maybe she was waiting for instructions from the thing in her head.

I wondered what she smoked, sniffed, or shot up that made her look like one of Charles Manson's flower child followers who had stabbed innocent people in a frenzy of drugs and bloodlust.

"Tomorrow," she whispered so Kaseem wouldn't hear her.

"For what?" I asked. "Until you put an ad in a personal column? Something like 'Crazy Bitch Seeking Nice People to Hurt'?"

There I went again, giving her a reason to cut out my velvet tongue.

"What about tomorrow?" I asked, hoping to divert her from my insult.

"The end of your world. The beginning of ours."

"How's that going to happen? Are you planning to rub the scarab until a genie pops out?"

She leaned back, closing her eyes, rocking back and forth as the van sped over the rough road.

She had shut down, tuned me off, after dropping the cryptic remark. Maybe the thing in her head told her to close her trap.

Other than giving me some hope that I had another day to live— maybe—her answer told me little.

What was going to happen tomorrow?

I shut my own eyes, trying to keep the back of my head from banging against the van wall too much.

It took only a moment for me to make a connection with "tomorrow" and what I'd heard standing in the customs line at the Cairo airport after I'd arrived.

The president of the United States would be in Egypt, more precisely at Abu Simbel, to present his Egyptian counterpart with an antiquity being returned from the Smithsonian.

❖

What did Rafi, me, and the Heart of Egypt have to do with two presidents and the end of the world?

The van finally came to a halt.

I leaned up to get a look out the front window and saw something strange.

Up ahead stood a door in what looked to be the side of a mountain that I at first thought was made of sand, but appeared to be hard-packed dirt. Recessed back a few feet, the door had a framework of concrete to keep it from being covered by sand.

Military guards wearing the same uniforms as the men in the convoy had established a guard post tent by the door.

My first impression was that the door led into a mine shaft, but I couldn't see enough of the mountain, mound, dune, or whatever it was to get a good context about the door, but something about that door definitely stirred a memory.

Then it struck me.

Abu Simbel was an artificial mountain. The site was a massive steel-framed, concrete structure that was covered with the same dirt and rock as the surrounding area to make it look like a real mountain, but it was mostly hollow inside.

The dome over the Great Temple measured about two hundred feet in diameter and was about seven stories high, making it at the time the largest man-made dome in the world.

It seemed like an eon ago, but it was just last night from a boat on the lake that I admired the colossal statues and temples that had been broken into over a thousand pieces and put back together on the face of the new mountain.

Now I was looking at the back door to the mountain, put there for maintenance reasons.

After our vans had pulled up to the tented outpost and the soldiers exited the vehicles, I heard a muted sound, almost like champagne corks popping. But the sound came from automatic weapons with silencers—the soldiers coming out of the outpost tent were being shot by Kaseem's men.

❖

The massacre was over in seconds.

The bodies of the men who had jerked like punched dolls disappeared into one of the vans. Blood on the ground was covered with sand and Kaseem's uniformed soldiers took up the positions that the shot guards had held.

Images of the priest's body at Luxor made me gag and I fought throwing up.

The back door to our van opened and soldiers took Dalila out first, then Rafi was taken out and put on a stretcher. He woke up from the pain caused by the movement and let out a yelp.

Dalila tried to break loose to get to her father, but the soldier restrained her while a medic put a cloth over Rafi's face that was soaked in something that put him under again.

"Get out," Lana snapped at me.

I scooted on my tush toward the back door, getting a kick from her to help me along.

Slipping off the edge of the van with my wrists still cuffed behind me, I felt the cattle prod coming loose.

There was nothing I could do to keep the prod in place. I sweated blood as I felt it slip down against the top of my shoe. I didn't dare look down to see if it was visible at the bottom of my pant leg.

"*Bitch!*" Lana screamed.

That answered my question about whether the prod was visible.

She grabbed me by the hair and tripped me, throwing me to the ground, yanking the cattle prod out from where it had been hiding in my pant leg.

As she fumbled with getting ready to use it—in her excitement, she was all thumbs—I looked up at the top of the mountain.

The president of the United States and the president of Egypt were going to be meeting on the other side. It didn't take much imagination to figure out where the two of them would be standing during the ceremony for the return of the ancient falcon.

The bird would be returned to where it once stood in front of the Ramses colossus on the far left.

❖

That meant the two presidents would be standing in front of a statue that was nearly as tall as a seven-story building, not to mention that the front façade of the temple the colossus stood against was even higher.

A ridiculous thought occurred to me as I waited to get zapped from Lana.

Abu Simbel had been featured in many movies, including a James Bond film where one of the caverns in the partially hollow dome was the field office and secret laboratory of the British secret service.

But it was an Agatha Christie movie whose title insanely titillated me as Lana bent down to give me my comeuppance.

Death on the Nile.

68

❖

With my right hand cuffed to a steel post, I couldn't lie completely down or sit up straight. I leaned sideways against the pole, my back to the wall, sick to my stomach, and so dehydrated that my bones ached and my eyeballs felt as if they had been brushed with sandpaper and were ready to pop out of their sockets.

When I got my senses back, I learned from Dalila that I was inside a chamber somewhere in the guts of the man-made mountain.

The area had rough concrete floors and walls and steel beams that had been sprayed with a stucco-looking insulation material to keep them from rusting. With my luck, the insulation was asbestos.

Canvas had been draped overhead for a ceiling and to partition off the area being used. My guess was that the tent material was used to keep noise and light from being detected if anyone ventured into the unfinished portions of the artificial mountain.

Low lit with battery-operated lights that left shadowy areas, had it not been for the symmetrical lines of walls, ceiling, and beams, I would have thought that I was in a cave.

❖

Rafi, with Dalila by his side, sat against the wall opposite from me. His wrist was also cuffed to a post, but it struck me as a waste of handcuffs because I doubted he'd be able to run very far, less more put up a fight, because of his injury.

Dalila wasn't restrained but she obviously wasn't about to go anywhere but by her father's side.

"How long was I out?" I asked.

"All night," Rafi said when I struggled awake and had enough aches to confirm that I was still alive.

"Lana gave you an extra dose," he said. "She hates you almost as much as she does me."

I was lucky she hadn't fried my brains permanently, but wasn't certain she hadn't tried. Or succeeded.

"What level are we on in the mountain?"

"High up," Rafi told me. "Dalila said we were brought up many flights of steps."

He had looked as bad as I felt when he was taken out of the van on a stretcher, but could sit up now and had a little color to his face.

While I was under, his field first-aid bandages had been removed and replaced with ones that looked like they had been put on by a doctor. That assumption proved correct when a man wearing an army officer's uniform appeared to treat him.

For reasons I couldn't fathom, Rafi was getting professional medical treatment. *Fattening the calf,* I thought. Kaseem has a reason to want him back on his feet.

And plans for me, too.

I wasn't being kept alive out of Kaseem's gratitude for me chasing the scarab halfway around the world. He wasn't finished with me, but that meant I wasn't finished, either, not yet, not until Lana got the okay to put a bullet between my eyes or killed me slowly and painfully by frying my brains with that cattle prod she used as lovingly as if it were her vibrator.

Keeping my fear and fright from turning into pure panic was tough. I was scared, but I had no outlet for panic except a good scream and that would only bring more pain from evil Lana.

❖

I wanted to ask Rafi if he knew what Kaseem's plans were for him— and me—but hadn't gotten the opportunity yet because Lana told us to shut up when she caught us whispering.

Lana, Kaseem, and the military personnel stayed mostly in the adjoining section where tables were laid out with communication equipment and TV monitors on them.

From what I could see, the monitors showed the back of the mountain, including the door leading into the mountain, along with the front of the great Abu Simbel colossi complex and the smaller temple complex of Hathor and Nefertari.

I had a good view on the big television monitor of the tented pavilion set up for the presidential meeting in front of the Ramses colossi center stage.

No wall separated us prisoners from Kaseem's command center, but other than an occasional look shot our way, they tended to their monitors and communications equipment and ignored us.

The only thing I got out of watching the interplay was that Kaseem was in charge. I couldn't understand what was being said, but it was obvious he was the one cracking the orders.

The fact that a large area was being monitored by cameras his conspiracy had set up made it evident that the soldiers I saw were probably just part of his contingent, maybe even just a small part.

I felt as if I had been beat up—punched and kicked until I had a generalized feeling of burning raw agony all over my body rather than a particular point of pain.

"Besides being high up, where exactly are we at in the mountain?" I whispered when Lana was busy listening to Kaseem.

Rafi nodded his head toward a large schematic map on the wall across from me.

"That's an engineering plan drawn up when the mountain was being built forty years ago. We're near the top of the Ramses statue that is farthest to the left of the temple entrance."

That was the Ramses statue where the stone falcon would be returned.

I asked what Kaseem's plans were for us.

❖

Instead of answering me, Rafi turned his head away.

Dalila asked him to answer my question and he told her to be quiet and hugged her with his free arm.

It gave me another rush of panic.

That bad, huh.

I looked at the television set on the table where Kaseem had created his headquarters.

I couldn't understand the words, but the pictures were easy to decipher—the U.S. president was coming to Abu Simbel. Scenes of soldiers in armored personnel carriers at the airport and in positions in front of the temples told me that security was tight.

But obviously not tight enough since Kaseem's cohorts were able to sneak a clandestine group in under the very nose of Egyptian security. To kill Anwar Sadat, Egypt's Nobel Peace Prize–winning president, the assassins simply stopped their military truck in front of the grandstand, stepped out, and opened fire.

Kaseem had literally created a command center in close proximity to where the presidents would meet. It was obvious that he had something more complex in mind than a hit-and-run assassination.

How he managed to create his headquarters in the middle of the security perimeter the Egyptians would have established to protect the meeting of the heads of state was incredible. He could not have pulled it off without the support of high-ranking Egyptian military officers.

What Kaseem was planning to do suddenly hit me—launch a full-scale coup, killing the head of state, and seizing the reins of power.

And I was sure I had figured out how he was going to do it—he was going to blow the giant head off of Ramses, all forty or fifty thousand pounds of it, with the debris killing everyone within a football field of the explosion.

He'd need a powerful blast, but modern explosives came in small packages that caused major damage.

A wonderful symbolic gesture, I thought—Ramses toppling another "foreign enemy" as he did a couple of thousand years ago when Egypt had been invaded. Throw the heart of King Tut into the scenario and it would appear that the ancient gods of Egypt had come back to strike down the enemies of the people on the Nile.

I wasn't sure how Kaseem would pull it off, but after the presidents were buried in rubble, I imagined him holding a press conference announcing that the curse of the pharaohs had destroyed the nation's enemies because he had brought home the Heart of Egypt.

Dying with curiosity as to whether I was right, unfortunately in an almost literal sense, I couldn't keep my mouth shut when Lana came by to check on us.

"It will never work," I said.

She gave me a look that implied I was a dog that needed a good kicking.

"What are you talking about?"

I gestured at a large black box against the wall that I assumed was where the left Ramses statue sat on the other side. I had pinpointed the box as holding the bomb that would bring down the statue.

"They have bomb-sniffing dogs, rock-penetrating sound waves, and X-rays; you'll never bring down Ramses on the presidents. Even if you did, consider that you will have destroyed one of the most incredible pieces of Egyptian antiquity."

Lana gave me a kick and walked away, muttering something in Arabic that I took to be "stupid woman."

I caught Rafi's eye and he shook his head again and looked away.

Was I wrong?

Then what the hell was coming down?

"Tell me," I said. "I have to know why I'm going to die."

He turned his head away.

Dalila cried, "I don't want to die," and hugged her father.

I shook my head, defeated and disgusted.

"Don't tell me. I'd rather die surprised."

❖

69

❖

I dozed off and woke up when the doctor arrived to treat Rafi. He was changing the bandages when Lana came in with some soldiers.

The men went to the black box against the wall that I thought contained a bomb and opened the lid. They removed AK-47 assault rifles and began checking them and filling magazines with bullets.

One look at Lana and I could see she had taken something. She stared at me in that happy-crazy way and looked like she could float across the room. And maybe she could.

"You thought it was a big bomb, but it's much simpler," she said. She gestured at Rafi being treated. "Let us say that General Kaseem designed his plans with surgical precision."

"What will happen?" I asked.

"The two presidents will be killed, the general's shock troops will take command here and all over the country, television, radio, government buildings. He will proclaim himself president of Egypt . . . just as political coups have been done for thousands of years."

❖

"And then he won't need you," I said. "You'll just become another one of his victims."

Kaseem came in behind Lana. I didn't need an interpreter to tell me he was chewing her out, probably for talking to me. But she was high enough to shout back at the commander in chief.

While the squabbling was going on, Dalila left Rafi's side and brought me a plastic bottle of water. When she gave it to me, she slipped something into my free hand.

I squeezed it in my palm. It felt like an old-fashioned key, the ones that look like skeleton keys used to lock cabinets.

I realized what it was and got a sudden bolt of adrenaline.

A handcuff key.

70

❖

I had used a handcuff key before. I had once cuffed Michelangelo to the bedposts when things got kinky.

If I was clever, I could get my wrist free from the pillar. But what was I supposed to do then? Grab an assault rifle and begin spraying bullets?

I hardly knew which end of a rifle to point, less how to figure out how to get it going if it took anything more than pressing the trigger.

Rafi spoke to Kaseem in Arabic, but Kaseem shot a glance at his soldiers and said to him, "Use English. I don't want them to hear."

"Dalila is not supposed to be here. That was part of the bargain."

"The bargain was for you to accept the implant. You violated that by interfering in my efforts to obtain the scarab."

"Send her away with Maddy." Rafi nodded at me. "She's no fool. Let her go with Dalila and she will promise not to go to the authorities."

"I can't do that. I need your daughter to guarantee you will go through with the mission. As for the American—she will shoulder the blame if anything goes wrong."

Kaseem walked away, talking to an aide who had a question.

❖

Implant? That was something put into a body. Noor said Rafi had given up a kidney and was about to give up a piece of his liver. That made him the donor for an implant, not the receiver.

And Lana had said Kaseem's plans were designed with surgical precision. Was that a play on words from the sarcastic bitch?

Kaseem and the others gathered at a TV screen in the next area. Through the opening between the two cavernlike rooms I could see enough of the TV to realize that the historic meeting between the two presidents had already started here at Abu Simbel.

I fumbled with the handcuff key as I pretended to be engrossed with the television story.

Lana floated away from the group around the TV and came toward me. She had her cattle prod in her hand, tapping it against her leg like a military officer tapping a commander's baton.

At first I thought she had come over to give me a jolt, but instead she pointed the prod across the room at Rafi's bare chest.

"Boom!" she said.

I didn't have the faintest idea what she was trying to get across and my face must have shown it because she ran to a table to my left. She set down her weapon and picked up what looked like a remote control to a television.

She danced around a little and pointed the remote at Rafi and said, "Boom! Boom! Boom!"

"Lana!"

Kaseem shouted her name loud enough to give the Ramses colossi a start.

She tossed the remote on the table and hurried to Kaseem.

For a moment I thought he was going to strike her. He was in a rage. I wished the hell I could understand what he was saying, but thought I had heard and seen enough from Lana to understand.

I caught Rafi's eye and mouthed the word "bomb" and patted my chest.

He nodded. Grimly.

Rafi was the bomb!

Rather than risk dying from giving up part of his liver after parting

❖

out a kidney, he had made a deal with the devil. God only knows how much Kaseem paid him to have a bomb implanted. Certainly enough for Dalila to have the best medical treatment available in the world and to have someone, probably Noor, raise her without financial worry.

But Kaseem had probably dropped funny money on him, too.

I had the cuff unlocked but no place to go.

It struck me that despite the pure insanity of the scheme, the killing of two presidents, Rafi had only one objective—to save his daughter from suffering a horrible death because she was born in a country where medical services for her condition weren't provided.

He was willing to do whatever it took to get his daughter the treatment she needed. He attempted to be honorable and get the money with the scarab, even to the point of trying to palm off the reproduction rather than letting Kaseem get his hands on the real antiquity.

I now realized what Kaseem's plan was for me.

He would frame me as part of the assassination plot. I was an American. That made me an easy target for the Egyptians to hate for killing their president and to throw the blame on when the next U. S. president wanted an explanation or blood.

Things started moving fast, with more communications coming in and more orders being issued by Kaseem.

A uniform was brought to Rafi and he was helped to his feet. He stood up a little hesitantly, but appeared to get his feet under him. I could see from the name tag on the uniform it was Rafi's own and more of Kaseem's scheme fell into place.

I tried to imagine how it would play out.

There would be a tight security wrap around the presidential event that would be impossible to breach. But the security people and government officials already in the cocoon would not be able to move around. And Rafi was inside the security perimeter—the interior of the dome contained the Ramses temple, with a complex set of corridors and chambers. It had the triangular layout of most Egyptian temples, but had an unusual number of chambers, literally a maze of them.

Rafi would enter from the unfinished area into the temple through one of the doors used to access the dome for maintenance. Once he was standing in a temple chamber, he became part of the security force.

All he had to do was stroll outside and get close enough to the presidents to blow them to hell when Kaseem pressed the wireless remote.

I had no idea what sort of bomb he was carrying, but I knew even a small ounce of explosive could cover a wide area, so he wouldn't have to be in spitting distance to bring down the two men.

Dressed in his officer's uniform, Rafi walked around a bit, getting his feet under him. And then he looked over at me.

Showtime.

❖

71

❖

Rafi met my eye and then stared at the table near me. I thought he was telling me to grab the cattle prod and wondered what he expected me to do with it against assault rifles, but as I watched him, he held up his hand in a fist and pressed his thumb against his index finger and then a sweeping motion over the scar on his abdomen.

Jesus—*he was telling me to get the remote and blow him up.*

Bile surged in my throat and I gagged.

From the outer edge of the group of soldiers crowded around watching the monitors Lana turned and grinned when she saw the fright and repulsion on my face.

When I turned my attention back to Rafi, he was whispering to Dalila.

He looked up and caught my eye again.

As the noise level in the command center increased when the video monitors showed the two presidents coming to the pavilion, Rafi leaned toward me and spoke loud enough for me to hear.

"Run and get away before you press the button."

❖

I sat frozen, staring at him and Dalila, too petrified by fear and indecision to move.

Dalila suddenly stood up and came toward me. Rafi desperately wanted me to save her.

I jerked out of my stupor and rose, dropping the unlocked cuff behind me as cheers from the monitor screen erupted when the two presidents came face-to-face with each other in the pavilion.

Lana turned and saw me as I started for the table.

We made a race for it.

The cattle prod was closest to me and I grabbed it as she slammed into me, sending me spinning around, knocking over the table and sending everything on it flying.

She pointed her pistol point-blank at my face. Dalila reached up and grabbed Lana's gun arm, bringing it down. The pistol went off, the bullet striking the floor at my feet as I leaned forward and smacked Lana on the side of the head with the cattle prod, but I wasn't able to pull the prod's trigger to give her a shock. But I connected good, sending her stumbling backward.

A soldier was suddenly in front of me, his assault rifle pointed at my gut when I heard Kaseem shouting, literally screeching something in Arabic.

Everybody froze.

I don't know what he said, but the reaction of the soldiers in the cavern was instantaneous, as if he had pressed a button that stopped robots from moving.

My feet were planted, too.

Rafi was pointing something at Kaseem. At first I thought it was a gun, but then I realized Rafi had the remote that had been on the table with the prod.

He kept it pointed at Kaseem as the general spoke to him in a quiet, soothing tone of Arabic.

"Father!" Dalila cried out and started to bolt toward Rafi, but I grabbed her and held her back.

Rafi stared at his daughter with eyes full of love and pain, and then

❖

his eyes met mine. The message was to run because he was going to blow himself to hell to save us.

I pulled Dalila with me and quickly moved as Kaseem started toward Rafi and Rafi again pointed the remote at him as if it were a gun.

I didn't look back but ran with Dalila as if the hounds of hell were snapping at my heels and I was sure that they were.

Suddenly I wasn't running but blown forward, flying off my feet, as a powerful explosion erupted behind me.

❖

72

❖

Dust filled the air, choking me as I got onto hands and knees and finally wobbly feet under me.

I heard Dalila coughing before I saw her in the fog of tiny particles.

A few dozen feet beyond us was a dim light—not artificial light, but daylight.

Rafi said we were high up on the mountain, near the top of a seven-story-high statue of Ramses. The light made sense if the explosion had created an opening.

I helped the girl along, keeping her on her feet as we trudged for the light.

She was weak and coughing and I had to get both of us to the fresh air and the help I hoped was in shouting distance from what I assumed was a crack in the artificial mountain.

As we got closer to the opening, I realized that some sort of hatch had been blown partially open. The hatch would have been created during construction and perhaps used in maintenance over the decades since. The small door was about four feet high by four feet wide.

❖

I pushed the hatch door open farther and could see blue sky, a short, flat platform, and a sand-colored, round, conical shape.

"Ramses' crown," I said aloud.

Rafi had been right. We were high up near the top of a Ramses colossus. The tallest of the statues had a small platform between the mountain and the cone-shaped top of the crown, so it was the one I could almost reach out and touch.

I could see people milling about in the distance.

I cautiously leaned forward to get my head and shoulders out to shout for help when something smacked me in the middle of my back and my breath exploded out of me.

I was being pulled by my legs back inside. I twisted and stared into the crazed eyes of Lana.

Her face was bloodied, her clothes ripped, with fresh bloodstains on the clothing, but the crazy bitch was still moving like a snake whose head had been chopped off but had enough nervous energy left to sink its fangs into someone.

She screeched, a howling animal rage, and punched me in the face, hitting me so hard that I saw stars. Then she grabbed me, using the strength of a wild animal to pull me up until I was almost erect and then shoved me backward into the open hatch.

For a second all I felt was the terrifying feeling of falling through empty space, until my back hit something solid.

I was halfway out the hatch, with my back on the platform and the top of the pharaoh's crown behind me. On both sides of me was a seven-story drop.

Lana grabbed both of my feet to push them out, leaving me entirely on the short, flat deck.

She suddenly let go of my feet and reared up with Dalila holding on tight to her, her arms around Lana's neck, both of them staggering back from the hatch as they struggled.

As I pulled myself up and stared down at soldiers with rifles pointed at me from the ground below, a wave of vertigo suddenly hit me.

"Don't shoot! Help!" I yelled.

❖

The world started spinning and I staggered back, falling against the cone, and nearly stumbled off the platform.

A cry of help from Dalila got my head straight and I crawled back into the mountain.

When Lana saw me, she threw Dalila off her and let out an animal scream and charged at me like a preternatural beast. I dropped down on my knees and to the side as she flew at me, her momentum carrying her past me and to the hatch.

She saved herself from flying out of the hatch by grabbing onto the side of the opening.

I found a piece of rocky debris on the ground, and as I started up to meet her, I brought the rock with me. When she turned to attack me, I hit her with the rock, the jagged end catching her in the eye. She fell backward through the opening, onto the platform behind the crown.

She twisted wildly and rolled.

I instinctively reached out to grab her, but my hands didn't move fast enough. She turned over and went off the ledge.

❖

73

❖

Mr. Flem, the passport Nazi at the American Embassy, smiled brightly like the groveling toad he was as he handed me my passport.

"How's your solitaire game?" I asked.

His smile thinned and he visibly shook as my question gave the ambassador a puzzled expression.

I was a heroine, but alive only because of a bigger one, and she was waiting outside to take me to the airport with her aunt Noor.

Dalila had lost her father, but hopefully would not lose her life.

I had thrown everything Kaseem had given me—the real McCoy money—into the pot and was told that other gifts celebrating Rafi's heroic self-sacrifice would be enough to get her the needed treatment in Switzerland. If there had been any doubt left, I was ready to pull a museum caper to get her whatever she needed.

Dalila deserved it.

No one actually knew Rafi's full involvement but me and I wasn't going to tell. The scarab was gone, blown to pieces by the explosion or maybe buried under the rubble.

❖

As far as I was concerned, it was tainted by the pharaoh's curse and could stay hidden for another few thousand years until some unwitting archaeologist uncovered it and unleashed the curse again.

I wasn't really certain that De Santis, the monk, hadn't been correct in his theory that the boy king never had a heart scarab.

It occurred to me what the "clue" was on King Tut's body: Tut had no actual heart; the implication being that his heart was destroyed in the accident or animal attack that ripped open his chest and killed him. If Tut didn't have a heart, he didn't need a heart scarab to tell lies to the eater of hearts in the afterlife.

That meant Sir Jacob Radcliff had lied when he intimated that he had Tut's heart scarab. Why? Because he was a vain, arrogant bastard who was angry that he had helped finance the greatest treasure find in history and wasn't going to get any of it. The scarab I said was an artifact was definitely ancient, but he could have purchased one in those days for a few hundred dollars.

I really didn't care.

If Tut having a heart scarab was important to the common people, it wasn't in me to rain on their parade. So I kept my mouth shut and left the mystery of the scarab, now lost, intact.

"We're all very proud of you here at the embassy," Mr. Flem said, as the ambassador wandered off to get his picture taken.

The attempt at a peace offering was too little, too late for me.

"When I was hanging from a cliff, you stomped on my fingers," I told the weasel. "When I get back, I'm going to let my friend the president know how American citizens are treated at their Cairo embassy by the passport guy."

I walked out, full of bravado.

Things were good. I was going home broke, but waiting in my toilet tank was the money Kaseem originally had given me.

❖

74

❖

"Do I look like a terrorist?"

It was all I could say when I was pulled out of passport control at JFK and taken into a customs investigators office where two Secret Service agents were waiting.

"It's about the counterfeit money," the female agent said.

"What counterfeit money?" I asked, knowing damn well what she was talking about.

How did they find out about the money in my toilet tank?

"We were advised by the passport clerk at our Cairo embassy that you came into possession of contraband money made in Iran."

"The passport clerk in Cairo," I repeated in a daze.

That bastard Mr. Flem.

May he rot in hell.

May he be pinned to a mountain and have vultures pick at his liver for eternity.

If I ever got my hands on him, I'd punish him the way Bedouins did with men who trespassed against their women: I would cut off his tes-

❖

ticles, stuff them in his mouth, sew his mouth closed, bury him in sand up to his neck in an anthill, and pour honey on his head.

"Our White House security detail has cleared you from a counter-feiting charge. But we had to seize the money we found in your toilet tank."

"My toilet tank," I repeated stupidly.

I wished I could've given it to Michelangelo to hide for me. But he was a cop.

"A favorite hiding place for people who think they can fool thieves. And the police," she said.

"I'm innocent."

"You're free to go. Your landlord will also be released."

"My landlord?"

"Yes. Unfortunately, he was arrested a few days ago for passing funny money. Apparently you had paid your rent with it. But let me assure you, we will explain the situation to him and everything will be all right."

"Everything will be all right?" I started laughing and it turned into a howl as my eyes flooded with tears.

I was doomed.

My only chance at keeping a roof over my head was to out do Arnie's ten-thousand-dollar erotic robot at arousing his lust.

"Don't you understand? I've been cursed."

The two agents exchanged looks.

"I've been damned by the mummy's revenge, tormented by the curse of Allah, doomed by something I did in a past life, and I've pissed off the Fates—all three of those bitches who decide our destinies."

I pointed a shaking finger at the calendar on the wall behind the Secret Service agents.

"Look!"

Friday the thirteenth.

❖